Cover Credit: A Winter Day—Apsaroke, Edward S.
Curtis. Published 1908: July 6

Western Novels by G. R. Howe

No Time to Trust

Dragons of Fire

Short Stories Out of Kane

Crow Woman
On Deadman

G. R. Howe

Acknowledgments

I would like to thank the following people who took their valuable time to read and edit the manuscript. Their comments and suggestions were invaluable. Thanks especially to my chief critic and grammarian, Joy Howe, who has lived with every word. Special thanks as well to Rachel Montgomery, Martha Howe, Diane Halsey, and Glenn Halsey.

For Joy

CHAPTER ONE

For more than two hundred years the cottonwood trees, their alligatored trunks supporting a morass of thick branches, stood majestically on the banks of Cherry Creek. They provided shade for squirrels, chipmunks, an occasional raven, and the Deadman substation of the Hardin Stage and Transportation Company. It was July 1881. A hot breeze drifted down the draw from above the substation, gusting at times, furiously rattling the cottonwoods' leaves until they sounded like ten thousand rattlesnakes.

Across the wooden plank bridge, up under the edge of the red ridge and protected from the north wind, the substation sat squat and low in the morning sun. Years ago its logs had been snaked off the east Pryor mountain, notched, and laid one atop another. Each log had been planed smooth on two sides with a double bladed axe. They were shaped to fit tight, then chinked heavily with mud, straw, and split pine. Now it sat weathered, its logs bleached grey in the sun. Situated on the lee side of the ridge, it suffered no snowdrifts in winter and was blessed with cool shade in the heat of the summer sun.

The manager of the substation was a man called Pistol. No one knew why. It was an odd name for him. He did not favor a short gun, nor even a rifle, for that matter, but he did keep a double-barreled shotgun. He kept it under the counter mostly, though sometimes he placed it behind the back door. The back door led to the rooms where Pistol kept house with the Crow woman. As far as folks knew he'd never shot anyone with it. No one had ever seen him practice shooting tin cans laid side by side on a rotting log, or blast an empty beer bottle or a peach tin. But he had it. Folks knew that he had it because they had seen it. Several had admired the scroll work etched intricately down the long barrel. They knew it was a ten gauge and they knew that it wasn't for hunting a fool's hen, jack rabbit, or a sage grouse. Hunting wasn't what he had in mind.

Pistol drifted into the Montana Territory five or six years before and, as far as folks knew, lived in the cabin on Cherry Creek because he needed some place to set up house. It was as convenient a choice as any because, with the exception of a litter of pack rats, the cabin was empty. Ownership and rent were of no concern nor even a thought to him, or his neighbors, miles away as they were. They cared little about deeds or papers of entitlement. Neither he nor they could read or write. Ownership was simply a matter of stopping and staying.

He rode in atop a dun horse and kept that horse picketed and ready to ride. When it came to prime horse flesh, it wasn't much to talk about. Folks said that he would have been better off to make bait of it, to use strips of its hide to poison coyotes and wolves; or even to jerk it and use the sun-dried meat to feed the mangy yellow dog that came to live in his barn.

Folks said that before Pistol moved into the house on Deadman a man named Robert John Kern lived there. He'd built the cabin, notched and laid the logs himself on flat red rocks, and laid it solid. He was dead now. A trapper or a traveler had found him sitting at his kitchen table, a round hole in his head. The bullet hadn't gone clear through. There was only an entry wound and not much blood. No one knew who caused that hole to be there. No one knew of any enemies Kern had. Someone had found him two weeks dead and they buried him up the creek a hundred yards from the house he'd built. The fellow who buried him was the same who found him. When asked he said that Kern wasn't much to look at when he found him; couldn't tell who he was, not really; wouldn't know unless, of course, you knew the man. He did.

It was a year or so later that Pistol moved into the cabin and carved Kern a headstone out of the red shale rock he hauled off the north rim. The stone was erected approximately where the grave was thought to be. The man folks believed to have buried Kern said it was reasonably close, not that it mattered. No one intended to dig him up.

No one was hung for shooting Kern because no one knew who to hang. If they had known, and they had found the bastard, they would have hung him straight away. They would have used a cottonwood tree limb right there on Cherry Creek or wherever they happened to find him. That's what folks said when they talked about Robert John Kern being shot dead at his kitchen table. A man just shouldn't die that way. That's what folks said.

Folks thought the Crow woman came later, after Pistol had been there a couple of years, and after the Hardin Stage and Transportation Company had contracted with him to maintain the substation. He had agreed to keep three teams of six horses and to have one standing team ready to be hitched to the coach when it rolled in on Mondays, Thursdays, and Saturdays. If the stage was coming from the Big Horn Basin that would be at twelve noon. If the stage was going to Basin City that would be at two in the afternoon. It was a hell of a long ways to Hardin from Deadman. Or so folks said.

Those were the regular stage times and days. There were exceptions. In the winter when it was just too cold for the stage to run out of Hardin the hours varied. Additionally, Pistol agreed to care for the horses and to feed the passengers if they were hungry. That's what the paper said, the one that Pistol put his mark on, the one that made him the manager, the hostler, and the chef at the Deadman substation.

Some folks said that Pistol traded a blind horse for the Crow Woman. Nobody really believed it, considering who she was and who ended up with the horse. They said it, yes, but knew better. If that horse was blind, the Crow Woman's people would have lifted Pistol's hair. That was a given, a foregone conclusion. But that didn't happen and it would have, or so folks say.

The fact was Pistol did have a blind horse. It disappeared from the stage's holding corrals at about the same time the Crow Woman appeared. That small coincidence was the basis of the rumor. Truth be told, folks didn't know how Pistol got that woman. All they knew was that her name was Cherry Blossom. She was named after the chokecherry flowers from the trees that grew wild thereabouts. Chokecherries filled the packs of her people in the late summer; stored after they ripened on the limb, and were picked and dried in the September sun.

Pistol taught her, or maybe she taught him, how to make a pot of beans, how to flavor it with red peppers, sage, venison, and rabbit. Sometimes she used snake when they found a big one or dog when the puppies were young, fat, and so tender that the meat fell off their bones.

4

At the substation there was always plenty to eat, as much as anyone wanted. And that's what was important. With the beans she served hot bread pulled from the adobe oven that Robert John Kern had built. Occasionally in the fall when there was a sack of sugar and winter apples available all at the same time, they had apple cobbler or apple pie. Folks didn't know for sure just who made the pie but what did they care? When it came to eating, there was as much as a man would want.

The churchgoers from down in the south Big Horn basin said that Pistol didn't sleep with the Crow woman. They thought Pistol was a Christian and they firmly held to the belief that mixing blood was strictly forbidden. The drunks and other assorted fools that frequented the bars on the south bench and up toward Meeteetsee thought little of the Crow people and that was reason enough for Pistol not to sleep with her.

Others said that he slept with her because he was a man and the Crow woman was a woman. After all, what was the point in debating it? There were no children to prove it true or not. And the truth wasn't going to be learned short of asking. No one asked. It was none of their damn business, or so folk said.

Those who stopped at the way station said she was a looker, Indian or not. And Indian or not, they said she decorated the substation just by being there to serve beans, bread, and the occasional apple cobbler. The cowhands from the ML and the Brimbridge all damn well knew that he slept with her. *He'd be crazy not to. On a cold night in December what else would he do? Play poker or spin the top? Not with that woman living there.* They'd laugh when they said that. To listen to the Brimbridge hands Pistol slept with her twenty four hours a day, seven days a week. That's what they wanted to do. *Who wouldn't?* they said.

5

That's just what folk said. No one knew. It was something to talk about when the north wind blew the snow down off the east Pryor and filled the canyons along the Big Horn with the cold of winter.

Ted Steeple came to the Deadman substation on the Hardin Stage the first Thursday in July of 1881. He packed a reputation heavy to carry and not just because he stood six foot three inches tall and weighed two hundred thirty-two pounds. When he rode, he rode a good sized horse, stud horses mostly. The story was that he'd been raised on the plains of Southwest Texas. Later, while still a stringy lad, he'd come up the trail with the trail herds to Abilene and Dodge City, then up through Wyoming into Montana Territory.

It was rumored that he killed a couple of men with his fists and several others with a rifle or a short gun. That was a Kansas story. There was an Idaho story that Steeple, or someone who looked a lot like him, beat an Ohio pilgrim near to death, broke his leg on account he didn't like sod busters. The story went that he wouldn't let the man's wife set the leg bone or give him water to drink for nearly a week. The poor man died, folks say. There was another tale that he'd been caught stealing horses in the Judith Basin and nearly had his neck stretched. Through some tomfoolery, justice had not been served that day. It was just another story. Whether it was true or not, folks couldn't say.

According to the Hardin Stage records, in July 1881 Steeple was headed first to Fort Casper and then on to Cheyenne. According to the Territory Sheriff's report, when the stagecoach stopped at Deadman to switch teams, Steeple got off with the other passengers: one woman and two men. The latter, George and Gene

Gattlin, were cattle buyers; the woman, Alice Moltin, was a school teacher from Appleton, New Jersey.

CHAPTER TWO

Hank Stumble, running six horses, pulled the coach into the Deadman substation on a Thursday afternoon. The horses were dead tired, sweating, and breathing hard from a run across the north flat. They stood weary in their harnesses. William S. Caldwell rode shotgun, sitting up on the box next to Hank, watching over the U.S. Mail. The mail pouch resting in the jockey box at his feet included a letter of introduction, a marriage proposal, and a fifty dollar check payable to the order of the Basin City State Bank of Commerce, Basin City, Territory of Wyoming.

Theodore Steeple stepped down from the coach. He wasn't wearing a gun belt or packing a side arm tied to his thigh though he did so when he thought it necessary. Instead, he carried a Colt 1873 SAA revolver with a hickory grip stuck in his waistbelt. It was tucked out of the way and hidden by the flaps of his waist coat.

Inside, the substation was a refuge from the summer heat and the red dust of the road. It was cool and clean. While Miss Alice Moltin refreshed herself at the wash basin, the three gentlemen passengers waited. As she stood in line for her beans and bread, they waited as well. It surprised her that she was served these vittles by a Crow woman. After all, the Crow woman was an Indian and according to the Casper newspapers it had only been five years since George Armstrong Custer had met his fate on the Greasy Grass ridge.

Last in the grub line, Steeple watched the Crow woman, a phenomenon to which she had become accustomed. Her man, Pistol, enjoyed watching her as much as anyone. With people watching and waiting, she dipped the ladle into the beans and filled the wooden bowls one after another. Next, she sliced pieces of hot bread. No one minded waiting for that.

Steeple was the last to the counter. She poured him one ladle full of beans and looked up at him to see if he wanted more.

"You make this bean stew?" he asked.

She smiled, holding the ladle and looking at him.

"You make the bread?"

The Crow Woman smiled again still holding the ladle dripping with bean juices. She said nothing. She spoke the Crow language, as did her mother and her mother before her. English wasn't spoken in the lodge of her mother. She did not understand what Steeple asked her. In this crowd only Pistol spoke her language. That was enough for her.

The communication being one-sided, Steeple accepted a single scoop of beans in his wooden bowl and a two-inch slice of hot bread. He sat down next to the cattle buyers, George and Gene Gatlin, and listened to them banter back and forth. He picked up his bread, broke it in half, and examined each piece. Afterwards he dipped it in the bean broth and chewed the bread slowly. It was a methodical, wordless exercise. No one paid him any attention. He said nothing and called no attention to himself. Once the bean juices in his bowl were reduced, he used the pewter spoon to eat the beans and meat.

Abruptly he stopped, spitting a piece of broken bone onto the table. It was either the bone of a rabbit or a sage chicken since both meats were mixed together with the beans. The bone bore a scoring where it had been cut at the time the animal was dressed and butchered.

"I'll be damned!" he exclaimed.

Both George and Gene turned and looked at him and at the small sliver of white bone, remarking on how bones always get in bean porridge, especially porridge supplemented with chicken or rabbit meat.

"Happens every time," George said, Gene nodding in agreement.

Steeple turned and stared at the Crow woman standing behind the counter. As casually as if he'd been eating mince meat pie at a church bazaar, he pulled his pistol from his waistbelt and shot her through the heart.

Propelled by the blast, she fell backwards, hitting the floor hard, clutching at her chest, fighting for breath, breath that wouldn't come. Within milliseconds her smile had vanished, the light in her eyes dimmed; she was gone.

A minute later Pistol rushed inside. He had been switching the tired and worn-thin team for one well rested. He'd heard the shot and came inside not knowing what to expect, thinking that maybe someone had finally shot the old pack rat. To his surprise he found the two cattle buyers bent over his woman trying to administer assistance to her. There was nothing they could do for her; she'd been shot dead while standing at the counter wiping the bread knife with an old towel. Without warning.

The woman passenger sat at the table weeping quietly, her face buried in her hands. Steeple had gone back to dabbing the Indian woman's bread into his beans as if nothing had happened. Pistol, for the first time in his life, was so surprised at what he found that he didn't immediately react. He examined the lifeless body of his wife then asked the cattle buyers what happened.

Gene Gattlin pointed at Steeple. "He shot her," he said. "Ask him."

Pistol turned his gaze on Steeple. "Well?"

"She tried to kill me," Steeple said in a slow biting southern drawl. "Bone in the beans."

"Bone in the beans?" Pistol said in disbelief. "What the hell does that mean?"

"She put a bone in my beans," Steeple said. "She put a bone in my beans." He paused, having repeated himself, staring at Pistol. "She's a damn Indian," he added. "What more do you need to know?"

Pistol nodded slowly not fully comprehending what he was hearing, certainly not understanding it. His insides began to burn; a shiver ran through him as he turned and looked at the body of the woman on the floor. Outwardly he registered no emotion.

Finally he turned to the other passengers and said, "Another six or eight minutes and the stage will be ready." It was something he'd said a hundred times before so he said it again. He said it because he could think of nothing else to say, then he walked out the front door, closing it behind him.

Six minutes later he returned and pronounced the stage ready. "Take your time," he said. "Billy and Hank haven't eaten yet."

Having said that, he turned to the body lying on the floor behind the counter. It was then that he did a very strange thing. Pistol picked up a chair and set it in the corner where the counter met the east wall. While all four passengers watched, Pistol gathered the limp body of the Crow woman from the floor and placed her in the chair. Her right arm he laid on the counter and her left in her lap. Her short braids he drooped, one over each shoulder and across her small breasts. Blood leaked from her chest wound, running down her leather blouse onto her skirt.

He positioned her head so as not to roll to one side or the other. She sat thus, her eyes open. To the not so casual observer she was staring straight ahead.

It was god-awful. The cattle buyers looked away from the scene, as did the woman. Steeple swore softly and chuckled to himself. Finished, Pistol stepped back to study the woman who was once his wife. After a minute he went to the counter, pulled the ladle from the bean pot, cleaned it the best he could on the used dish towel, and fixed it in her left hand. It looked as if she were holding it, preparing to dip beans for a hungry traveler just getting off the stage.

She looked almost natural, though her eyes didn't blink. They stared across the room past the tables and chairs at a dark swirl of a knot embedded in the far wall. Blood covered her chest where it had pooled and run on her doeskin blouse. Her legs, hidden under a long, doeskin skirt, didn't bend like a live person's. Blood oozed from her lips. Pistol, in his fevered mind, thought she looked quite natural for a dead woman shot through the heart.

In the quiet of his mind Pistol studied her, his face impassive, his gaze moving back and forth across her body, committing it to memory. Abruptly he turned to look at the passengers: George and Gene, from Chicago by way of Abilene, Dodge City, and Cheyenne: Alice, the woman in the dark blue skirts and white blouse: and, lastly, at the big man, Steeple who'd just killed his woman over a rabbit bone.

Turning back to the woman passenger, he tipped his hat and said, "I'll be just a moment, Ma'am."

Pistol, having excused himself, disappeared out the front door. He could be heard speaking to the driver. There some small talk about this and that and nothing at all. Eventually the driver, Hank Stumble, a skinny man with a large Stetson hat and long leather gloves that reached mid-forearm, stepped inside the substation. He took a long look at the Crow woman sitting in the corner, his face emotionless, before turning to the passengers.

"Ma'am," he said, nodding to the school teacher, "Gents, we are ready to roll."

They followed him outside, the woman looking away from the Crow woman as she left. George and Gene walked out on either side of her. Last came Steeple with a handmade toothpick, cleaning his teeth. He didn't look at the Crow woman either.

A moment later, with the woman seated inside the coach and the three men standing waiting to board, Pistol appeared in the doorway holding his ten gauge shotgun. It was not just any shotgun; it was the shotgun with the hand tooled etching inscribed the length of the double barrels, double hammers pulled back and locked. The business end was pointed at the ground a few feet in front of Pistol's worn leather boots. The dull wood stock was pressed lightly against his right shoulder.

Hank, his hand extended to pull himself up onto the stage box, turned and saw Pistol standing in the quiet of the morning sun. Seeing the shotgun, he changed his mind, turned and said, "What the hell you doin', Pistol?" It was fairly obvious that Pistol wasn't out for a morning stroll hunting partridge on the Lodge Grass.

"Going to detain one of your people, Hank," Pistol said. "You might want to refund part of his fare seeing how he's not going to be using it."

"Pistol, you know---"

"Shut up, Hank," Pistol said, cutting him off. "This isn't company business. This is personal." Pistol moved slowly to his left as he spoke, his eyes fixed on Steeple. "Now, Hank, you dealing yourself in or not?"

13

Hank raised his hands slowly, "Not my woman, Pistol." He started moving slowly up the trace, keeping himself deliberately out of the way, his hands clearly in sight. "I reckon you got a right," he said, "to kill the man if you are of a notion."

The school teacher stared at Pistol from the stage window.

"You, Lady," he said to her, "get out the other side of the coach and start running. I expect there's going to be some shooting. Better move yourself out of harm's way."

Her pallid face disappeared from the coach's window. The far door squeaked as she opened it.

"You, two," Pistol said, talking to the cattle buyers. "You boys in or out?"

George had his hands in the air. Gene stared at Pistol. "Out. We're out," he said, backing away.

"Back yourselves up then. Clear to the creek. Stay where I can see you."

Both men did as they were told with purpose, moving quickly toward the creek and the shade of the cottonwood trees. Their quick removal might have been directly related to the icy, "I mean business" quality of Pistol's voice, or perhaps because neither had seen a shotgun of those dimensions before. It also might have been because that shotgun was in the hands of a very angry man who clearly didn't care whether or not they were involved.

Pistol turned his attention to William Caldwell, the shotgun rider for the stage company.

"That leaves you, Caldwell," he said. "You in or out? Mind you, I have no interest in stage business. I'm not holding you up. My only interest is Toughie, here. And he isn't leaving here alive."

14

William Caldwell stood to the left of Steeple. He was a smaller man but no less able. He had a carbine in his right hand and a right-handed pistol tied down on his thigh. He had no chance against a shotgun. Pistol knew this. Caldwell hesitated. Obviously he knew it, too.

"Now, Pistol, he's a passenger," Caldwell managed to say. His feeble statement, though true, was not all that convincing.

"Billy, from where I'm standing, you're a dead man. You deal yourself in and there will be no kissing your woman tonight. No hugging that youngin of yours. On the other hand, if you were to drop that rifle and that pistol, then maybe."

The rifle hit the ground, clattering on the hard earth like a child's toy.

Steeple reacted instantly. "You gutless sonofabitch," he said in a low voice, reaching for his pistol.

Caldwell threw himself to his left as Steeple's pistol cleared his waistbelt, and on that warm Thursday morning Pistol calmly shot Ted Steeple in the lower abdomen. He stood at a distance of thirty-six feet; he used one chamber loaded with double ought buck shot.

Steeple went flying backwards, his gun hand mangled, his lower intestines ripped and shredded. Clearly he wasn't leaving the substation alive.

No longer concerned with Steeple, Pistol shifted his gaze to Billy Caldwell rolling in the dust. He was sitting up.

"Billy? What are you going to do with that short gun of yours?"

"Nothing, Pistol."

"Then be getting up slow and toss it into the coach."

Caldwell did as he was told, pausing to look at Steeple writhing on the ground, groaning. Pistol's eyes followed his gaze.

15

"Hank? Billy? I'm going to need your help," Pistol said.

"What for?" Caldwell asked.

Hank stared in disbelief at Pistol. He held the horses' reins. They'd jumped at the sound of the shotgun blast. When they surged forward, he'd grabbed the ribbons and calmed the team down, talking to them as he would frightened children.

"Need you to grab this gent by the shoulders and drag him inside."

Hank looked from Pistol to Steeple. "He's gutshot, Pistol. You've done killed him."

"He's not dead yet. Get him inside." Pistol broke down the shotgun, removed the spent shell, and replaced it.

Hank Stumble climbed down and with Billy Caldwell's assistance took hold of Steeple, whose arms were wrapped around the ball of pain that was his abdomen. They grabbed him by the shoulders, trying to be merciful, trying to consider the pain which had to be enormous. Between them they pulled him across the hard packed red earth through the open door, bouncing his feet across the threshold. Dragging was about all they could do. He was too heavy and awkward to lift. Once inside, Hank looked about for a place to lay him but Pistol stopped him.

"No, Hank. Over there. I want him in that chair."

"Good Lord, Pistol. He's wounded bad. Don't you—?"

"No, Hank. In that chair. Tie him in it. I don't want him falling out. Tie him good and tight. Use the rope there."

"Good merciful God, Pistol—," Hank said.

"No," Pistol said, "I want him looking at my woman 'til he sucks his last breath. I want him seeing her. Seeing her clear."

"Geez, Pistol," Caldwell said. "Why don't you point that shotgun somewhere else?"

"I'm not pointing it at you, Billy. Now drag that bastard over to that chair and tie him hard. Fix him like I told you. I want him seeing my woman. Knowing what he did."

Tie him they did. Using cord that Pistol laid on the seat of the chair, they tied him so his shoulders were held straight by the chair's back. His legs were bound to the chair legs. Steeple wasn't going anywhere and there would be no slumping, no stretching his limbs.

Only after they were done and Steeple was tied in place did Pistol relax. It was then that Hank and Billy looked at him as if to say "What now?" except they didn't dare say it. They didn't say anything at all.

"Thanks," Pistol mumbled, laying the shotgun on the counter, softly letting the hammers seat themselves. It was then that Pistol slumped into a chair, barely breathing, no longer speaking, his insides aching.

"What you gonna do, Pistol? Lord . . . " Hank asked.

Pistol stared at Hank. "I'm going to watch him die. That's what I'm going to do. I'm going to sit here and watch him die."

After a pause he looked again at Hank, then Billy. "Thanks," he said, dismissing them. "Thanks to you both. Now get. You got work to do."

Caldwell nodded, reticent to leave. "Pistol, you know the Sheriff, he'll be coming. You done stirred up a hornet's nest here. Damn, I don't know what to tell you, Pistol."

"I'll handle the Sheriff, Billy, if he ever leaves Red Lodge. Now you both take care of yourselves. I'll be seeing you Saturday."

But Caldwell was insistent. "I don't know, Pistol. We hate to leave you like this. You having this trouble and all. It ain't right for us to do that."

"Billy, just get going. Please. I'm asking please."

"All right," Hank said. "All right." They went out the door, Caldwell glancing back at Pistol.

Minutes later Pistol heard the stage pull out, heard Hank yelling at the leads, slapping them on the butt with the ribbons as they pulled the grade south of the substation. He could hear them for ten minutes before they reached the south flat. He imagined that Hank was walking them then, giving them a breather once he got on top. It would be twenty miles before he reached Crooked Creek. Kane was another ten miles beyond that.

As hard as it was, Pistol looked at the man he'd gutshot, feeling a need boiling up inside to beat the hell out of him. He wanted to beat him unconscious until there was no movement left, no groaning; beat him until he was dead. *No. No*, he told himself. *This one needs to take a long time to die.* Pistol got up, found a pail, filled it full of water from the spring box, carried it to the man and threw it in his face.

The response was immediate. Steeple gasped and groaned. Bloody water ran in rivulets onto the floor, dropping through the cracks in the planking. Pistol chuckled. Steeple glared at him, his gut on fire, burning, sucking the life out of him.

A smile hung on Pistol's lips. "Good, good," he said. "Suffer, you sonofabitch."

Steeple continued to glare, pain stretching his face, his teeth gritting against the agony. Pistol smiled again, then went to the counter to dish himself up some warm beans. He cut himself a slice of sourdough bread to use to dip and soak up the bean juices. In the quiet of the substation he sat at the table and chewed slowly, watching the man, listening to his heavy breathing and the groans that escaped through his parched, straining lips.

An hour later Steeple asked for water. Pistol threw a bucket of water on him and watched him try to lick the drops of moisture from his mustache. The struggle amused Pistol so he did it again, then went outside to feed the horses and rub down the team that he'd just switched. He started the task by giving each a bait of oats. He took his time removing the harnesses from each, hanging the collars, the leather straps, traces and chains from the pegs on the log walls of the barn. It was a mindless task. After he finished with four and had two horses to go, he was so overcome with grief he felt compelled to go inside to look at Cherry Blossom.

CHAPTER THREE

Pistol had a visitor that evening. Weeks after his birth the visitor's mother had named him Little Duck, but that wasn't his "man" name. It wasn't the name given him by his Grandfather when he was fifteen winters. That name was Grey Elk. It was a name carried by his father's father's father. It was an old name, a worthy name. It was a name honored in the lodges of his people. His people did not go hungry in the deep snows of winter. His people's stomachs were full not only in the fall but in the spring when the snows began to melt and the new calves were dropped by the buffalo cows.

What his daughter saw in the crazy white man he did not know. At first he thought Pistol did not hunt. He did not count the occasional fool's hen that you could hit over the head with a stick. In those bygone days, if Grey Elk had been asked he would have said his first reaction was to kill him. But that would not do. Cherry Blossom would not have spoken to him if he'd done that, even if she would have been better off. She had not seen it that way.

Grey Elk sat his horse on the north ridge above the substation as he had many times before. Something was different. He noted the absence of smoke from the chimney. The windows were dark. The coach horses were standing in the corral, two still in harness. Maybe he'd steal them next week when he could think of nothing better to do. After all, they did not belong to his son-in-law, so what did he care? This evening he was thinking he'd eat his daughter's beans and venison, and maybe some hot sourdough bread with the yellow grease called butter.

Sometimes . . . most times . . . he came alone, especially when his lodge was on Dry Head Creek above the buffalo run where he was encamped this month. Today, however, he was not alone. He'd brought Long Nose with him for company, to eat the white man's beans and bread, to share the warmth of his daughter's smile in the lodge of his son-in-law, Pistol.

In the evening twilight, watching the swallows flit about the darkening sky, he felt uneasy, edgy. But there was no sign of danger, just something out of kilter. Maybe it was nothing. Still he checked the load in his rifle, then nudged the gelding forward. Soon he'd know.

In front of the substation he dismounted and briefly looked around. Then, followed by Long Nose, he walked inside. Both men held their rifles cocked and ready. In the interior darkness he could make out a man sitting in front of the counter that always held the bean pot. The man made no attempt to move. From his left came the labored breathing of someone not long for this world. Close to death, he thought. For a moment he stood in the middle of the room listening, watching his son-in-law. He motioned to Long Nose, told him to find the matches in the cupboard next to the oven and light the lamp behind the counter. He did so.

Soon yellow lamplight bathed the substation dining room. In it Grey Elk saw the wounded man bound to his chair, his head down, his breathing labored. He thought that odd. Then he studied his son-in-law, slumped in a high-backed kitchen chair, the long shotgun lying on the counter top. Pistol sat staring at him through sunken, dark, grief stricken eyes. Instantly Grey Elk knew the big white man tied to the chair was fighting for his life and would surely die.

It was Long Nose who saw Grey Elk's lifeless daughter sitting in her chair in the corner, staring straight ahead. He pointed. Grey Elk looked. His heart stopped beating. His breath caught and he struggled to take another. With trembling hands he crossed the room to where she sat in her chair, studied her in disbelief, touched the cold skin of her face with his fingers. He saw the ladle in her right hand, the single bullet wound to her chest, the dark red blood on the doeskin blouse. All of this he considered. It was not the shotgun of his son-in-law that had done this bad thing. Turning, he pulled back the hammer on his Winchester rifle and stared down the barrel at the crippled body of the white man, intent upon extracting a modicum of justice, of revenge. Its click echoed in the large room.

"No! No," Pistol shouted, coming off his chair, placing himself between them.

"I must have his heart," said Grey Elk. "I must have it."

"Then cut it from his chest when he's dead."

Grey Elk hesitated. "Why?" he asked. "Why not now?"

"He's a coward," Pistol said. "He makes a war on my woman. He kills the defenseless for a rabbit bone."

"A rabbit bone?"

"Yes. A small rabbit bone in his beans."

Grey Elk lowered his rifle. "He die soon?"

"I hope not," Pistol answered. "I hope he takes forever."

Grey Elk nodded, gently seating the hammer on the chambered cartridge. Motioning to Long Nose, he said a

22

few words and sent him running out the door, riding into the night. This was a matter for the People. This was a time for much grief. This was the time for hot anger.

By morning sixteen horses and their riders stood on the north ridge above Cherry Creek. Ten more stood on the hard packed yard in front of the substation, waiting, milling about, talking quietly among themselves. An additional eleven sat on the hill south of the bridge above the substation overlooking the tops of the cottonwoods. By noon the women and children from the Dry Head Creek encampment began arriving. Lodges were pitched above and below the station: the family closest, friends and acquaintances farther away. Thus, the mourning for Cherry Blossom began.

CHAPTER FOUR

Grey Elk watched the steady arrival of the people, watched the big white man suffering, saw the anger of his son-in-law and thought better of him for it. Pistol waited, taking his time like he had plenty of it, for his grief was large.

Finally, as the afternoon wore on into evening, Grey Elk said to his son-in-law, "We must care for Cherry Blossom. It's been two days. It is warm. Soon she stinks."

From his chair by the counter, Pistol looked at his father-in-law then turned to look at the decaying body of his wife.

"Yes," he said, speaking in the language of Grey Elk. "It is just that I wanted . . . I wanted this man to see her until his very last breath. I wanted him to know what he did was wrong. I wanted him to suffer long for what he did. I wanted him to suffer for stealing this woman from me, for stealing my unborn sons, and the daughters I will never know."

Grey Elk stared at the man tied to the chair, then turned to Pistol. "For this one to suffer is good for the heart," he said. "Soon Scolds the Bear, Gazes at Stars, Chaser of Rabbits will be here. They should not see their mother this way. It is a memory they should not have."

"You are right," Pistol said. "It is time to honor the dead."

Grey Elk thought about Pistol and his daughter; then he called for his wife. When she arrived, he spoke to her, being gentle, being careful with his words, for it was a time of great sorrow.

"Woman," he said, "please prepare your daughter."

Grey Elk's wife glanced at Pistol who sat in his chair rubbing three days' growth of beard.

"Yes," Pistol said to her, rising to his feet. "It is time. It is appropriate. We must respect the dead."

Soon women filled the room. "Where did she last breathe?" an old woman asked Grey Elk.

Grey Elk looked at Pistol who pointed to the floor behind the counter.

The body of Cherry Blossom was removed from her chair to that very spot on the floor. She was arrayed in her best clothes, her face painted. Her body was wrapped in the yellow leather of the tipi cover and tied together using buffalo sinew.

The old woman spoke to the dead Crow woman.

"You are gone lovely one," she said. "Do not turn your face to us who remain. We wish you well."

Having said that, the Crow woman's body was passed through an open window, not a door regularly used lest someone else die. Once outside she was taken to the north ridge behind the substation. A scaffold was constructed using four forked juniper poles. Her body was laid upon it, her feet to the east.

All this was done after the customs of her people. It was said among them that this was good, for along the waters of Cherry Creek was where she was born, where her grandfathers' bodies were placed in the fork of a cottonwood tree. It was good. Cherry Blossom was not alone in death; already her people were welcoming her. She was with them and they, her. Her family did not speak her name again.

Later, after Cherry Blossom's body had been prepared and cared for, Grey Elk called for his daughter, Autumn Flower, who was younger than her sister by four years.

"Sit here," he said to her. "Sit in this chair where Cherry Blossom sat. Look at the white man dying. Every time he lifts his head for a drink of water, smile at him. Wave your hand as if you were his friend. Maybe offer him some beans. Offer him drink but do not let him drink. Pour it instead in his lap, on his shirt. Give him nothing."

"Father?" she said. "What is this?"

"Do this for me." Grey Elk looked at her. "Do this for me that this White may know that he cannot kill my daughter, that in his last breath he may suffer knowing the evil that he has done to my people."

"All right, Father," she said.

So the youngest daughter sat in the chair of her sister, ten feet across the room from the wounded man. When the big one asked for water, she poured water on his head, then hit him across the face with the ladle. When he looked at her, blinking, his eyes full of disbelief, she poured cold beans down his shirt so that he could smell them and his own stink. As her father asked she kept herself in front of him so that he could suffer continually for she looked very much like her sister. And she did not let him sleep.

Saturday noon the Hardin Stagecoach made the rise south of the Deadman Substation. Had Billy Caldwell counted he'd have discovered that he and Hank were about to be met by twenty-seven men on war ponies, complete with face paint, rifles, bows, spears and somber, ugly dispositions. But he didn't count because there were one hundred fifty-seven more on the ridge north of the substation, standing, waiting. Up and down Cherry Creek were the lodge poles of many, many lodges—more Crow than he'd seen in one place in all of his life.

The realization of what it meant came to him hard and cold for in that instant he knew he was dead. There was no going back, no getting away, and there was no stopping. They'd already crested the South Ridge above the substation. There were riders behind them, to the sides and in front. "Keep goin', Hank," he said quietly, "we're dead men."

To his amazement the coach actually made it to the bridge. He had no idea why he wasn't full of arrows, drawing his last breath. Once across the cottonwood planks of the bridge, they reached the hard packed ground of the company way station. They were met by Pistol and a new team of six bay horses harnessed and ready to go. All around them was a scene of milling horses and somber riders. He had the distinct feeling that if they had any luck left it was running dry.

Not one passenger stepped from the coach. No one got out to look around to discover what was going on. No one thought of their empty stomachs, of eating beans and warm sourdough bread. All were concerned with their hair, wondering how long they were going to keep it and if it was soon going to be hanging from the lodge pole of the nearest buffalo skin tipi.

From his seat on the box Caldwell could see women tending fires and dressing a deer. Some were cooking meat on a stick. Naked children ran about playing games he'd never seen. One wide-eyed child stood staring up at him. Smoke hung in the cottonwood trees waiting for the afternoon breeze to suck it down the canyon to the Horn. Neither he nor Hank was inclined to get off the box. Fortunately Pistol didn't take long in unhitching the tired and spent team.

"I'd keep moving," Pistol said before he led the old team away. "I'd not hang around here more than needful."

Now there was good advice. Caldwell thought.

"Once up on the flat I'd run them a mile or so before taking a breather. These boys 'round here aren't all that happy right now."

Come to think of it, ol' Pistol isn't all that talkative himself.

Pistol had backed the new team up, the tongue between them.

"What the hell ya got goin' here, Pistol?" Hank asked.

Pistol grunted as he attached the trace chains to the single trees. "A burying," he said. "Funeral anyway, not so much a burying."

He stopped in the middle of his task to look up at Hank and Billy sitting uncertain and a bit anxious atop the hard seat of the jockey box.

Hank nodded as he glanced up at the north ridge. "I can see ya invited everyone that was handy."

Pistol handed Hank the reins.

"Purty near. I expect there will be more. Been arriving all night and they just keep coming. Didn't know I had that many relatives. Hold on. I need to attach the tongue to the leads."

Hank thanked Pistol. "Not like we're goin' anywhere 'til you do. Not far anyway. You already buried her?"

"Yes. Up there on the north ridge. You can see her scaffold if you look."

Both Hank and Billy looked at the north ridge and nodded when they found the scaffold.

"Steeple dead yet?" Billy asked.

"No. He's still hanging on, barely. These folks are waiting for him to die. I suspect there will be a great celebration when he does."

"Ya know, Pistol," Hank said, "with this many Crow off the reservation you are gonna have Army troubles. They're bound to come lookin' to see what's goin' on."

"I thought Cherry Creek was part of Crow Country. So many are buried here."

"The way I understand it you're a mile or so off. Don't know where it begins or ends but that's what a feller told me at Crow Agency. That's why I'm sure the Army will be lookin' into this mess. They gots to. Could be trouble, given their willingness to shoot first then raise hell."

"Well, all right," Pistol said. "Not as if I don't already have more than my share of troubles." He smiled. "What's a few soldier boys to add to the stew?"

"Maybe another Indian war."

"Maybe," Pistol said.

CHAPTER FIVE

Pistol wasn't always known as Pistol. There was a time, a year or so before he'd met the Crow Woman, when he was just Josiah Edwin Kern, a traveler in a foreign land, a man who rode a dun horse from Amarillo, Texas by way of Sonora, Mexico in search of his brother. It was a long ride. It took the better part of three months. Time didn't matter. There was no hurry. His horse wasn't fast. But he was steady.

"Ma'am." He touched the brim of his hat, waited for the woman to pass, and stepped inside the two story hotel.

It was the tallest building in Kane, Wyoming. There were others, of course, but it was the tallest. The first floor served as a general store. In its center sat a large pot bellied wood stove. On its right a huge roll top desk served as an office. In the winter a number of chairs were positioned around the stove for folks who wanted to sit and talk. There were always those.

The Neely hotel had a tall false front that did not face the street. It did face a woodpile and a storage yard for broken and soon to be repaired buckboards, buggies, and freight wagons. In the corner of the storage yard was a blacksmith shop. In the mornings after the forge was blazing hot, the metal glowing, and the billows pumping, the sound of hammer on anvil rang loud and clear and woke the late sleepers on the second floor.

"Deadman? Yeah that's Crow country. Goin' there?" The store clerk ran his fingers through his thinning hair and looked across the counter at the rangy man.

"Thought I would," Josiah answered.

"Well, all right," he said. "It ain't hard to find. It's north of here. In a mile and half you'll come to the Shoshone. Cross it. It should be passable this time of year."

He shook his head, pausing.

"I say passable cuz you never know what's happened up river. If it's runnin' yellow, be careful. The river, she ain't forgivin'."

He looked at Josiah, then continued. "Cross her and stay west of the Horn. Half a day you'll reach Crooked Creek. Outta the creek you'll come across the Crow trail. You'll see it. Mounds of rocks mark it clear."

The storekeeper removed his glasses and held them up before wiping them with his kerchief. He went on. "Damned old trail. The Crow used it for a thousand years or so. Pretty rough country. You'll have the east Pryor on the west and the Canyon on the east. Stay betwixt them and go 'til you get there. Be a day's ride or so. Can't get too lost."

The storekeeper replaced his glasses. He stopped talking long enough to look at a woman coming into the store through the front door. He turned his attention back to Josiah.

"Sure that's where you want to go?" he asked. "Ain't what you'd call hospitable country."

"Reckon so."

"Well, good luck to you, then."

The store clerk turned to help another, a young woman. She wore a long, pink, floral, cotton dress. She

31

smiled up at the traveler, paid for her goods, and thanked the store keeper.

She turned then. "Hello," she said to Josiah.

Josiah, smelling of salt sage, pine, and horse sweat, nodded and tipped his hat. "Ma'am."

A man wearing a large grey Stetson hat and thick leather gloves that covered his forearms stepped inside the hotel. "Hey! You! Pistol," he called.

Outside someone was yelling something unintelligible. The man in the hat was looking at him. "You takin' the stage west? If you are, we're a leavin.'" The man turned and was out the door before Josiah could answer.

He looked back at the young woman who was still smiling up at him.

"Well, Mr. Pistol," she said. "I'm Clara Lovell. Do be careful. Keep your hair if you can."

"I will, Ma'am. Thanks."

He walked outside and watched the stage leave. The driver, with ribbons in both gloved hands, was slapping the leads on the butt, yelling as the stage lurched forward. A man next to him, a shotgun across his knees, swore.

"Damn you, Hank. Learn to start easy. You're gonna throw me offa' here and them folks outta' the coach."

Josiah Edwin Kern swung up on his horse and followed the coach out of town. The stage was moving at a trot, Kern at a walk. Soon the stage disappeared from his sight.

He rode north into the timbered river bottom and found himself surrounded by cottonwoods, big and old, young and new; the new fighting for space to live, the old claiming it. Trees gave way to water.

The Shoshone River wasn't running high, nor was it running yellow. But it was running quickly. Pulling his hat down around his ears, Josiah pushed the reluctant dun into the river.

For the first fifteen feet the horse could see the rocky bottom, feel it. Suddenly the bay was swimming and the bottom was gone. The current ran fast and they were swept downstream. Maybe it was the swiftness of the current, or maybe the horse touched the river bed, or maybe they were struck by a floating log. Whatever the cause, the dun suddenly rolled, dumping Kern into the ice cold water. Kern jumped away from the horse, fighting with the stirrups to free himself.

Conscious that the dun was about to kick him in the head, he dove as deep as he could to get under the churning, eggbeater hooves. The current pushed him deeper. His head hit rock; the bottom fell away then rose to meet him in a rush. Instinctively, he grabbed a boulder, the horse's thrashing legs narrowly missing his head and shoulders. Josiah clutched the rock, straining against the current. In dark waters he hung on not knowing if the horse was clear of him, whether he was out of danger. His uncertainty was compounded by his having no sense of how much time had passed. The river was swift and the rock slippery. In the tug and pull of the current he lost his grip and the river swept him downstream. He came to the surface in a rush, bobbing like a duck. Gasping for air, he blew water from his nose, immediately lost in the swirling water.

A hundred yards downstream the dun reached the north shore, belly-dragging its saddle. Kern started swimming. In spite of his efforts it was some time before he was able to touch bottom. Once he reached shore he took off after the horse. He did that running, weighed down by water sloshing heavily in his boots, and wet clothes clinging to his skin. His horse was in a hurry, having no intention of waiting for another ice water bath.

Half a mile farther downstream Kern caught him. That was as far as Josiah Kern traveled that Tuesday.

He had not intended to spend the day lying white naked in the sun. But he did just that until the fierce sun drove him under the cottonwood canopy. Afterwards he spent the time barefoot, in and out of the shade, turning his socks, shirt, boots and pants until they were dry. The saddle blanket he hung from a low branch, then busied himself wiping the moisture off of his saddle, cleaning his saddle gun and riata, musing over the storekeeper's words, 'The Shoshone ain't all that bad this time of year.' That's what he'd said.

His shirt dried first. He put it on, buttoning it up, stopping to listen to the river. He heard the leaves rattling overhead and a robin chirping. Something wasn't right. Back in the shade of the cottonwood he had an uneasy feeling that he was being watched but he saw nothing. He listened. There was nothing out of the ordinary. Still, the hair on the back of his neck was standing up. Growing increasingly anxious, he ventured out in the sunshine and turned his pants and socks over for the umpteenth time, surprised at how warm they were. With the hot sun beating on his back, he heard an intermittent thumping, not like the rat-a-tat-tat of a woodpecker but lower, deeper. It stopped. It started. It stopped again. It was coming from the tree.

Pistol in hand, he moved into the shade, listening and found the origin of the noise on the other side of the cottonwood. Hidden in the contours of a root bole was a mangy, yellow dog. It lay on its side, one large eye looking at him as if to say I've come this far and I'm going no farther. How it got there he could only imagine. There was no movement except for its thumping tail. He was thin, his yellow hair matted and tangled with cockle burrs.

"How long you been there?" Josiah asked.

The dog responded by more tail thumping.

"You sick, hurt, or just starving to death?"

Josiah tossed the dog a piece of jerky. The dried meat landed inches from the dog's nose but the dog didn't move.

"Lord, you're hard up, dog. When did you last eat?"

The dog still didn't move. Even its tail stopped thumping.

Josiah crept closer half expecting the dog to jump and run. It did neither. Out of mercy he stuck the piece of what used to be dried meat inside the dog's mouth against its cold, damp tongue.

"I'm not chewing it for you. For that you're on your own."

The dog simply swallowed.

"I'll be damned," Josiah said and turned his attention toward the river, listening as he looked up and down the shore line. Overhead, lost in the branches of the cottonwood, a magpie argued with itself. Somewhere a woodpecker tapped out a drum roll, looking for termites. Satisfied that he was alone, Josiah placed another piece of meat in the dog's mouth and watched him swallow, thinking that was a good place to dispose of wet jerky, wet hardtack, and sticky rock candy. By morning the dog was gone, as were his supplies.

The first time Kern laid eyes on Deadman, he was a two-day ride out of Kane, Wyoming, tired, hungry, and a long way from Tombstone, Arizona, and Sonora, Mexico. The storekeeper and stage agent had been a couple of days off in his one day estimate. True, Deadman was out of Crooked Creek, but it had taken Kern three days; one day spent drying out, one to find Crooked Creek. It was just that--crooked. And not that much creek. Nothing more. And another day following an old Indian trail marked by stacks of lichen-covered rocks. Somewhere along the trail the yellow dog caught up, keeping twenty feet behind Kern's horse. Kern first spied him at the top of a long yellow hill watching horse and rider. From time to time he'd disappear for an hour or more, always returning, padding aimlessly behind him in the dry, mountain air.

Josiah Kern didn't know he'd reached Deadman when he did reach it. All he had was Bob's one sentence description. The more he studied the area the more convinced he became that he had arrived.

The house sat on the far side of the creek right up against the red rim, behind a log barn and a corral. They were the only buildings he had seen in three days. Upon closer inspection he concluded that the barn could only be Bob's because Bob overbuilt every damn thing from grandma's rocker to a serving ladle. It wouldn't have surprised Josiah one bit if, come winter, the barn was warmer than the house. That was saying something; a man could probably heat the house with a candle. That was Bob. From the south ridge Josiah could see other telltale signs of his brother. Through all of this discovery the dog sat on his haunches and looked at the buildings below, tongue lolling out the side of its mouth.

Josiah yelled "Bob" as loud as he could, listening to the echo as the sound bounced off the mountain of red stone behind it. The dog patiently turned his head and looked up at him. Josiah yelled again. There was no response, only silence. He yelled again. Still nothing. He guessed Bob wasn't home. Josiah looked down at the yellow dog who returned his stare, his round brown eyes asking why he was yelling.

Something was wrong. Josiah loosened the colt in his waistband and the rifle in the scabbard. For additional comfort he patted the stock of his shotgun. Beneath the rider the dun had grown impatient but Josiah held him back. He listened, hearing only an unearthly silence. Even the killdeer and snow birds had grown silent. Down the draw the rock dogs no longer chirped and barked. A magpie silently floated from one cottonwood to the next, its wings extended, flapping. The dog stood on all fours staring down the ridge at the house and barn.

Josiah nudged the dun forward, following the game trail down from the south ridge to the creek bottom. The yellow dog was out front. Crossing the small stream, he rode to the doorstep and dismounted, noting that there were no horses in the corral. There were also no cows, no mules, no livestock of any kind: only grass, tall spindly sunflowers and a host of wild flowers. Across the corral he watched the dog disappear through the open door of the barn.

Everywhere Josiah looked the grass was long, even at the front door where it should have been worn down and dead. Behind the house he could see where Bob had grown a garden. The patch was overgrown. Weeds grew where once stood rows of corn and beans, peas, cucumbers, and winter squash. *Not good*, Josiah thought. *Not good at all.*

The front door was imposing, sun bleached and grey. Josiah thought about knocking. But why? No one was there. No one had been there in months, maybe years. He guessed it had been some enormous space of time.

To reassure himself he reached into his saddlebag and rifled through the contents until he found his brother's still damp letter dated May 11, 1875, Deadman, Montana. It wasn't posted Deadman; in fact, there was no postmark. There never had been. He had received it four years later, had made the necessary arrangements, and started north. Now it was 1879. He guessed May or June. How too late was he? It was a wonder he'd even received the letter. Four years was a long time, especially if you were waiting for a reply.

Without bothering to knock, he pulled the door latch and pushed the door open. It gave grudgingly, scraping across dried red mud someone had tracked inside. The interior was dark, shadowy. The dog ran past him. Josiah stepped inside immediately engulfed by cool, dank air, old, and musty. He heard the sound of dripping water. One by one he opened the inside shutters surprised at finding there were exterior shutters as well. He had to go outside to open those, first releasing each from inside the house. The shutters had been protecting glass panes. *Where had Bob gotten glass?*

The floors were deep in dust so thick he could see mouse tracks where they had crossed the floor--a lot of them. It was easy to follow the yellow dog's trail. The thought occurred to Josiah that Bob needed a cat, a big one. Maybe two. The dog went back outside through the open door.

A pack rat had situated his nest in the oven in the kitchen. Bob had built the oven, lining it with sheet iron. He'd built a stove by laying another flat piece of iron on top of adobe brick. Bob: always creating, making do with the best of making do. If someone had made it, Bob would make it better. Without making a fire, Josiah bet the firebox worked and worked well. He was sure it would have the proper draw and get the most heat available.

But where was his brother? It was clear that he left suddenly. Tables, chairs, dishes in the cupboards, spoons in the drawers, and forks, knifes and ladles were all in place. He observed that most of the furnishings were hand built, even a bedstead with a patchwork of dusty blankets. And a bed unmade--that wasn't like his brother.

Josiah Kern took another tour, looking out the back door, leaving it open. Then he started cleaning. He started in the kitchen. Finding the rat's cache of a stolen spoon, three shiny marbles, and a broken silver bracelet, he burned the pack rat out of his house. He swept the room with a broom he found in a corner behind the stove. He opened all of the windows so the canyon breeze could blow the dank smell out the front door. He dusted. He mopped. He washed the windows, working until he was exhausted.

Ten days later the place looked as if Bob was expected, as if he lived there and would be returning in an hour or two. To the unsuspecting traveler, Bob could have been out picking chokecherries or hoeing in his garden. Any moment now Bob could walk through the door. Josiah knew he wasn't but he cleaned the place anyway, cleaned it twice because he couldn't think of anything else to do and didn't want to give himself leave to speculate on Bob's whereabouts.

The house was something to appreciate. Inside, Bob had built a spring box. Somehow he'd piped water from a spring above the house into the rock basin, then out under the floor planks until it drained into the creek. Josiah thought it a miracle. Water was always running yet never ran over. The spring box itself was encased in stone, shored up with a glazing that Josiah'd never seen before. *Leave it to Bob*, he thought.

CHAPTER SIX

"Hello, the house!"

The yellow dog growled from under the kitchen table. The deep rumble that rattled around in its throat sounded like he was about to tear someone's leg off at the hip. A barefoot Josiah Kern peered outside, standing far back from the brightness of the door. He glanced at the yellow dog lying under the kitchen table. Other than growl, the dog hadn't moved even so much as an eyelid.

A dish rag that had once served as a blue shirt lay on the floor at Josiah's feet. At the sound of the voice he'd dropped it, picked it up, and hurriedly dried his fingers, cleaning them of blood, feathers, and entrails. His right hand was still damp and clammy on the walnut pistol grip. The voice had caught him in the middle of dressing out a fool's hen, cutting brisket away from leg, with the intention of frying the parts of the bird he liked and baking the remainder.

A second pistol remained stuck in his waistbelt. A long knife sat in a dull leather sheath hanging on his hip. Moving quietly to the open door, he saw a big man wearing a grey faded hat, sitting slouched over in the middle of a big Appaloosa horse.

The rider studied him, then leaned over the shoulder of his horse and spat.

"Ah, Pistol," he said, wiping his lips with his sleeve. "Mind if I slide down and sit a spell?"

The big fellow wore leather gloves, cuffs pulled up to the elbows, a Colt .44 on his hip, and a wide leather belt. From where Josiah stood it looked like an SAA Army edition produced for the 1873 trials. Josiah recognized him from Kane. He remembered him standing just inside the Neely Hotel where he'd asked Josiah if he was taking the stage west. It was the coachman with the automatic smile, tobacco stained teeth, a knife scar down his left cheek, and a week old beard that held a red hue. His dark eyes were hidden in the shadow of bushy eyebrows.

"Not at all. Step down. Sit."

Kern thought it interesting that the man had never asked him his name. Just called him Pistol. Kern hadn't volunteered it, either. It was an oddity that existed west of the Mississippi, as though a man's name was holy or something--for business use only and none of your business unless the owner decreed it otherwise. If you didn't volunteer it, no one asked for it.

"Name's Hank," the visitor said. "Mind if I get a drink of water?"

"No. Help yourself. Know where it is?" Out of habit Josiah glanced about, looking up and down the creek, then followed the big man inside, listening.

"Sure do. Ol' Bob showed it to me. Damnedest thing I'd ever seen. Fixin' up the place, I see. Bob sure could use his hands. Gifted, I'd say."

"You knew Bob?"

"I did. You look a bit like him." Hank removed his hat and hung it on a peg just inside the door. "Ya might say I'm a regular," he said. "Ride through every six or seven months. Goin' to Hardin."

The yellow dog hadn't moved. He was still growling from under the table. Hank was staring at him not sure of whether to continue or not.

"So, where is he?"

"Bob?" Hank turned to face Josiah. "Well, he's dead. Thought you knew. You movin' in, fixin' up his place and all. Found him dead right there. Sittin' at that very table he was. Sort of slumped over. A hole right betwixt his lookers. Nothin' else. Just a hole in the noggin. So damn gone I hardly recognized him. If it weren't for the shirt I'd of said it was someone else but I figured it to be Bob. Who else could it be, this bein' his place and all? Nobody bein' around."

He rubbed his beard, staring at the growling dog under the table. "See ya got yourself a yellar dog."

"But you did know him, knew it was Bob? There was no doubt?"

Hank took the water ladle from the hook imbedded in the wall. "I did," he said. "Buried him up the creek. Show ya if you want. That way ya won't go steppin' on a man's grave. Real bad luck that."

Pausing, Hank busied himself with a long drink of cool spring water, taking his time returning the ladle to its hook. He wiped his mouth with his sleeve and glanced at Josiah.

"You know, " he said, "this place's got a rep for dead folks. The fellow before Bob, he's layin' buried up the creek his own self. Couple hundred yards, I'd say. Can't say that I know'd him. Before my time."

Hank sat down in a chair next to an open window and crossed his legs. "You might want to take care. Must be a dozen injun trees up Cherry Creek, and that many the other way. On the ridge there's those burial scaffolds. Three or four, I'd say. It's a damn graveyard--that's what this place is."

Hank pointed at Josiah with a long, bony finger, making a point, then clasped both hands behind his head, intertwining his fingers. "Before Bob, I found that first fellow. No house, no barn then. He was sittin' over under that cottonwood down by the creek, a Henry rifle across his knee. Just dead. Ticker probably. I buried him. Sold that Henry to Johnny Booze."

The yellow dog started vigorously scratching itself.

"Where'd you get that damn dog, Pistol? Sounds like he ain't ate lately."

"A Henry. That's a nice rifle," Josiah said absently.

Josiah Kern sat in Bob's chair half listening to Hank, rubbing his hands together. His brother was dead? He tried to get his mind around that thought. Bob had been right here all along. Josiah didn't know what to think. He couldn't think.

"Had a Henry once," he said. "Got it during the war. Army issued. Never gave it back."

"You don't say," Hank said. "That damn Johnny busted the stock outta' the one I sold him. Not ten mile from here. Know that canyon? South of here? Where up an' down is pretty much the same? He had six mules loaded. The hind one slipped, fell right over the edge, started pullin' the others into that drop. One right after the other. Ol' Johnny had to jump to save his bacon. Damn near killed hisself. Had to climb down in that draw with all those dead mules to get his things. The fall busted the stock on that Henry. But he saved it. Made his own stock. Don't work right though. Just ain't the same."

Hank glanced under the kitchen table at the yellow dog whose sole activity was scratching an itch behind his left ear. Once in a while he'd growl like he'd hurt himself. For the last several minutes he'd been quiet.

"That damn dog sure looks familiar."

Josiah chuckled. "That dog found me over on the river. Might say I was swimming. He showed up while I was drying myself. Fed him some wet jerky, some melting rock candy, and a little soggy hardtack. Afterwards he followed me. Reckon that is the best he'd eaten in a long time."

Josiah had forgotten what he'd been doing when Hank showed up. Suddenly remembering, he said, "Listen, Hank, I've got some of yesterday's beans. I'm fixing to fry up a little fool's hen. I have some bread baking. Care to join me? It's not much but it'll take the edge off."

"Pistol, I'm ready to get after that. Ya' won't have to be askin' me twice. My belly's so empty it done figured someone cut my throat."

"Good." Josiah stood up, paused and eyed his guest. "You wouldn't happen to know who killed Bob, would you?" he asked.

"I don't. Nobody seems to know nothin'. He'd been dead a while. Two weeks, maybe three. He was no pretty sight bloated up like that. There weren't no tracks. Nothin' to follow. Deadman ain't like it's on any map. Nobody comes here 'less they're usin' the Crow trail. And you know that ain't much. Get here by pack mule and saddle horse or walkin'. That's it."

Hank paused before continuing.

"Only folks around is injuns, maybe a trapper or two, and that damn Link Hannon when he's out stealin' a horse to trade over Sheridan way. But he ain't no killer. He and Bob would get together, put up a little timothy hay, sometimes fish down on the Horn, swappin' lies. To tell the truth, they were lucky to catch the worm that baited the hook.

"Things got a little dicey though after Hannon shot up that Morris. But it's settled down some. Folks decided

44

to let Hannon steal his horses, keep his wife and those two kids, and just try not to get themselves killed. Folks figure there's plenty of horses."

Josiah nodded and walked toward the kitchen thinking he hadn't heard anyone talk so much.

Hank followed him, Josiah listening.

"You see," Hank continued, "that bunch come over here to hang Hannon for horse thievin'. He sees them whilst he was cuttin' a little hay. He pulls a Winchester and as they were comin' over the rise, starts shootin'. Clips ol' Morris across the back, cuts his suspenders. Morris got right close to the ground after that. Sorta inspired. There he was crawlin' all the way to Basin City holdin' his pants up with one hand and cussin' like it ain't Sunday. Stayed drunk for a month. He couldn't move while he was a healin'. Course he didn't move much when he wasn't healin'."

Josiah pushed half the fool's hen into the oven along with the bread dough. He saved the other half to fry. "This Hannon fellow, he live near here?" he asked.

"Link? Well, yes sir. It ain't like it's next door or nothin'. Remember that big, bald faced red hill, probably four or five miles back twixt here and the creek? He starts livin' in those parts, about a mile or so close to the river. Easy to miss. You could be looking right at him and miss him twice. Nice fellow. Like I say, he's got a cute little wife, two youngins, a boy and a girl. He's the closest thing to a neighbor you got and he ain't all that close."

Hank stood next to the kitchen wall, leaning up against it, rubbing his jaw.

"You got other neighbors," Hank said. "Not all that friendly, mind ya. If you were to head north ten mile and bend around the corner of the mountain, ride another maybe ten, fifteen mile—that's Sage Creek. Ol' Grey Elk, he lives thereabouts with all those kids of his'n. Likes to winter over there. Likes to summer over on the other side of the Horn on what's called the Bull Elk. Nice fellow if he ain't tryin' to kill ya. Maybe he put it to ol' Bob. Never know. Ain't like him though. Ol' Bob still had his hair."

Josiah looked at his guest. "Bob have enemies?"

"Not that I know'd. Didn't take to carryin' no firearm. And that's right down and damn stupid. Folks'll take advantage. Most think they can. 'Ya ain't got no shootin' iron' I kept tellin' him, that damn fool."

Hank paused, looking at Josiah. "I see you carry a shootin' iron."

Josiah patted the pistol grip protruding from his waistbelt. "I do," he said. "Mostly, I don't care for a short gun. Good for snakes and coyotes. Keeps folks honest. But I favor another. I'll show you."

Pistol half closed the kitchen door, pulled a shotgun from behind it and laid it on the table in front of Hank. The yellow dog looked up at Josiah. The room smelled of baking bread and roasting bird. Accompanying the smell was the sizzling sound of frying fool's hen.

Josiah Kern looked at Hank. "Bob carried a firearm, Hank. The old man would skin him if he weren't well heeled and ready. Always had one in his waistband. One on the hip. Kept a pocket gun. Bet he was packing a throwing knife when you saw him."

Josiah patted the shotgun. "My father gave me this."

"Lord," Hank said studying the weapon. "What is this? Bet if you ain't holdin' it just right it'll tear a shoulder off." Hank ran his fingers along the barrel. "Look at that scroll work. That's some engraving."

He shook his head. "Odd," he said, "I gots after Bob a time or too for not packin'. All the time he was heeled in spades. I'll be damned." He picked up the shotgun and broke it open. "Things ain't never what they seem are they?"

46

"Double barrel ten," Josiah said. "I like to use double ought buck. Rock salt does fine. So do shingle nails if there's nothing else."

"Shingle nails? That'd sure tear a bird all ta hell."

"It's not for birds. It's for lying around in plain sight." Josiah smiled. "It's for sending a message. It says I don't want no trouble. Mind you, I have a Winchester 44-40. But the shotgun sends a clear, unmistakable message in a language everyone understands."

Hank Stumble nodded. "Well, least you're packin' a short gun," he said. "You'll be needin' it. That shotgun will impress. But you'll need a short gun for gettin' by. For snakes and varmints and such. And for just that time. You never know. It'll save your bacon. You keep livin' out here on the edge, you'll need it and you'll need it where you can get at it. That's what I told Bob."

There was a wistfulness in his voice. "So you're his kin?"

Josiah nodded. "Brother."

"Thought so. You sorta look like him. But ya don't sound English. Your brother did. Had that accent. Not you. How's that?"

"I try not to stand out. Figure it's good not to attract attention. So when in Texas I try to sound like I'm from Texas. When in Mexico, I'm Mexican. In Orleans, I'm Cajun. I just listen and mimic what I hear."

"I'll be damned. That's right handy."

Hank stopped talking, looking at Josiah. "Sorry for your loss. Bob, he wasn't much at listenin' but he was a good man. A real good man."

The yellow dog started scratching himself vigorously.

Hank looked at him. "What's wrong with that dog?" he asked. "He looks lopsided, patchy, and not so happy."

Josiah glanced at the yellow dog and chuckled.

"I gave him a hair cut. Sawed the burrs out of his hide. Some places his hair was so matted and long it was like a wool blanket. I cut that off, too. Figured he was tired of sleeping on hard pillows he couldn't throw away. I made him into a shorthaired, yellow dog. He didn't much like the hair cut. But he's cooler now. Gets to the fleas easier."

"I'll be damned twice," Hank said, smiling. "He's sure an ugly bastard."

Josiah wasn't listening. He was remembering that he'd never known his brother to be without a weapon or two. Often he carried a pistol on his hip, another tucked away in his waistband, a pocket or sleeve pistol, and a Bowie knife. He always had a throwing knife, one balanced end for end equally. And he'd keep them close at hand. Who was this man Hank said carried no weapons? It surely wasn't his brother.

After they'd eaten, Hank showed Josiah his brother's grave. The rocks were stacked high to keep the coyotes from digging out the body. For the living there was a view: the cottonwoods lining Cherry Creek, the red rim standing tall and rugged behind. Grass had long ago grown up around the stones. It was a peaceful place sitting in the shade of an old cottonwood.

Josiah looked at the grave, then up and down the creek. He said nothing but he was thinking. *This isn't right. This isn't likely, which is all good except the fellow says the dead man was Bob. That he knew him.*

CHAPTER SEVEN

Sage Creek runs east and west along the northern edge of the Pryor mountains and west into the badlands. It was there on Sage Creek that Grey Elk and his wife of the Bad War Honors Clan spent their winters; they had done so since time remembered. They were not camped there now for their horses fed on the Bull Elk grass along the western slope of the Big Horns east of the river. That's where they were now.

Grey Elk refused the handouts offered at Fort Smith, The Crow Agency, and Hardin. He wasn't dead. He could ride his own horse and hunt the deer, the elk, the buffalo. His people jerked their own meat, picked and dried their own gooseberries, currants, and chokecherries. And there were no complaints among them. What did he need with a can of rancid corn beef? That was food for camp dogs, if they'd eat it. He'd known it to be turned down by many a curly, yellow haired dog who just may crawl out of the brush and bite you on the leg if you weren't watching.

The Agency Crow knew of his refusal and admired him for it, even as they went to receive their own allotments. It is good, they thought. There is one among us . . . still. But in their minds were other thoughts. How does one turn down a can of corned beef, a skinny cow to kill, and a blanket for the winter? The allotment was free. Accepting it required no allegiance. Were they any less for it? No. They were not. In fact because of it they had another wool blanket. Two was better than one. And

49

food? They had something more to eat, no matter a starving maggot wouldn't touch it.

Hank Stumble left Deadman in the early morning, hours before sunrise. The edge of the Big Horn Mountains was just a faint outline, the glimmer of a new day yet unborn. He was riding to Hardin, leaving Josiah standing in the doorway drying his hands on a rag of a dish towel. Josiah watched him, a pistol shoved in his waistband tightening his belt, and a yellow dog sitting at his side, tongue hanging out, growling for no known reason.

In Hank's absence Josiah had no one to talk to except the crickets, a magpie or two, and the homeless pack rat that had retreated to the floor joists. Sometimes at night he could hear him rattling around. The yellow dog was about but he didn't say much. Neither did the pack rat. By sunrise he'd had enough. For once in his solitary life silence choked him. He had no brother, no reason to stay on Cherry Creek. Without dwelling on it he spent the morning locking the place down. He closed the shutters, cleared the ashes from the stove, washed the last of the spoons, forks and plates, swept the floor, and cleaned the towels. He left a crust of bread for the pack rat knowing that as soon as he was gone the rodent would move right back in.

On the day Hank left for Hardin, Montana Josiah Edwin Kern saddled his dun horse and pointed him north by northwest. It was time to move on. The sometime shorthaired, yellow dog followed him twenty feet behind and to the right. Miles later, Josiah stopped to let his horse drink at a spring that bubbled up out of a rock formation on the south side of Sage Creek. The yellow dog found it. While the dun cropped grass, Josiah dismounted and gazed out over the windswept breaks. He swallowed a little water from a tin can someone had left in the brush above the spring. Who'd ever think to find a tin can in such lonely desolation? In the quiet of bubbling, trickling water and wind whispering through juniper trees, he proceeded to curse the heavens, the sky, and anyone who might listen. There was no one but the yellow dog and he didn't seem to mind.

Josiah no longer had a brother. There was a big hole in his chest that left him empty, angry, abandoned and lonely. The feelings were odd, something he'd never faced. His father's death had been abstract and distant. After all, to a youngster what do soldiers do exactly, if not die? Especially in a war. Especially in the King's Lancers. But a younger brother? That wasn't supposed to happen. Not to Josiah.

While the dun cropped grass, Josiah sat on the edge of a flat rock and studied the yellow dog. Idly, he listened to the sound of the leaves fluttering in a solitary quaking aspen and remembered Bob following him to the tavern to find their father. Bob was a head shorter with lighter hair and blue eyes. He was always laughing. His mother had sent Josiah to fetch his father. It was early evening.

"Tell him supper is ready," she said. "Tell him to come home."

Bobby followed after him. His father hadn't been home very long from serving with the King's lancers. Maybe he'd been home a fortnight. He was at the pub where he'd been all afternoon. As Josiah remembered it, the pub was quite a distance to walk; it was a good two miles into Canterbury town. It sat across the lane from a blacksmith and a tannery. Josiah entered the pub through the back door, Bob behind him. He was ten, his brother eight. It was dark inside and smelled of tobacco smoke, ale, rum, and unwashed men. He remembered they were an imposing group, much too big and tall, definitely too friendly.

"Hey, Henry, these wharf rats yours?"

Josiah looked up to see a rotund man wearing a dark shirt peering over the counter at them.

All eyes turned to the two ragtag boys standing in the short hallway that led to the back door. A bull's head with dull vacant eyes, a dry crusted nose, and large horns extending in both directions, hung above their heads. Men filled the room, some bunched up in the center. Men stood, pints of ale in hand, talking in a haze of white smoke. To one side several . . . he didn't remember how many . . . were throwing darts. Out from all of these legs, wrinkled shirts, wool trousers and hob nail boots, their father magically appeared. Upon seeing him Josiah felt so relieved.

"Boys," his father said, "come here."

They walked to him, crossing the dark plank floor, Josiah not altogether sure of himself. He felt the pressure of all those eyes, yet safe because his father was there. He whispered to him.

"Mother says to come home. She says supper's ready. It's time to eat, Papa. She killed a hen and made dumplings."

His father looked at him, grabbed his brother from the floor, lifting him into his arms, tossing him into the air above and catching him as he fell back into his hands. Bobby laughed, his blue eyes dancing.

"Josiah," he said, "I want you to show my mates how to throw a blade."

Josiah remembered the men towering above him. They seemed so very tall and he so very small.

"Throw the blade," Bobby repeated. "Show them."

"You tell him, Bobby," his father said as he laughed and set Bobby down. "Josiah, take your knife. See the board there?" He pointed across the room. "See the center circle? Put your blade in the center."

"Papa?"

"Hey, everyone. I want you to see this." He turned to Josiah.

"Go ahead, Joe. Pull that blade. Now remember what I told you. Don't think. Turn. See. Throw."

"But, Papa--"

"Do it, Joe. Turn. See. Throw. Don't think."

"Okay, Papa."

In the silence he pulled the blade his father had given him from his waistbelt. He tossed it into the air just like his father did, catching the blade between his thumb and index finger. He turned his head and fastened his eyes on the dartboard. Someone laughed. But Josiah's eyes saw only the center of the board. He stepped forward and slung the blade, just as his father said, the way he'd practiced hour after hour. The center was so large in his mind he couldn't miss. He didn't miss. He drove the blade deep into the circle of the dartboard just as his father had asked. Having done that, he looked up at his father.

There was a tumultuous sound of approval from those standing about watching.

"Good boy, Joe. Very good."

His father patted his shoulders approvingly, then left him standing in the room of tall men to retrieve Josiah's knife, Bobby following him. When he returned, he handed it hilt first to Josiah to tuck away behind his belt. Then he picked up his brother.

"Virgil Morgan," his father exclaimed, "there you go, mate. I got a quid that says you can't beat Joe, four out of five, two out of three, or any way at all."

Someone said, "Yeah, Virgil, see if you can beat that boy."

There was an exchange of bets, more against Joe than for him. His father again set his brother down. Bobby jumped up and down with excitement and glee, holding on to his father's pant leg but Josiah was sober. He looked at his father, wanting to be off, to be going home.

A big man, larger and taller even than his father, came out of the crowd. Men laughed, giggled like school boys, the smell of ale and tobacco smoke thick in the air. Virgil pulled a large blade from his waistband, looked down at Josiah, then stared at the dartboard and threw his knife. It stuck with a heavy thud in the second band, off center by an inch. There was a loud "ah" in appreciation.

Bobby had his father by the hand. "Tell Joe to do it again, Papa. Tell him to do it again."

"Quiet, Bobby." His father had turned his attention to Virgil. "Tell you what, mate. Double or nothing. Joe'll put it dead center, right on, twice. Two out of three."

The room grew silent. Double or nothing was a lot of money. Additional bets were exchanged. No one bet on Henry's boy.

"Two out of three, Virgil. Twice dead center."

Virgil nodded. "Double or nothing," he said. "Two out of three."

A murmur came from the men standing at the bar. Toward the front someone came inside, closing the door behind him. Everyone was standing now, every chair empty. The room grew quiet. Josiah so wanted to be gone, feeling lost amid a forest of pant legs. But for his father, he would have run taking Bobby with him. The smell of ale, rum, and smoke was heavy in his lungs, tickling his throat.

"Joe," his father said, "put your blade dead center. Right in the middle. Don't think. Turn. See. Throw."

"Papa?"

"Do it, boy. From twenty-five feet. See that mark on the floor." His father was pointing. "From there."

Josiah saw the mark.

Someone said, "Henry, he's just a boy."

Bobby was saying, "Do it, Joe. Show them." Bobby, laughing, giggling, so alive with excitement, was hardly able to contain himself.

Josiah walked to the line on the dark wood floor. He turned to his father, his back to the board. His father nodded his approval. Taking a deep breath, Josiah turned, saw only the center circle and slung the blade, driving it deep into the center circle just above Virgil's knife.

The crowd groaned. Some cheered. Some said, "Oh, yeah." Mostly, it was a consensus of "I'll be damned!" Everywhere men were taking sips of ale, brushing hair from their faces. Some exchanged money; others made bets. The whole room seemed to shift its weight from one foot to the other.

Virgil glanced first at Josiah, then his father. Turning he retrieved both blades, handing Josiah his. He looked at Josiah, his dark, forbidding eyes hidden beneath bushy eyebrows, offering a grin through stained, yellow teeth. The big man turned to the board and from twenty-five feet stuck his knife in the first circle that surrounded the bull's eye, a half-inch off dead center. The crowd roared in appreciation, clapping.

Bobby was standing beside him, jumping up and down. "My turn, Papa. My turn," he cried.

"Not now, Bobby," his father said. "Right now Virgil is counting all that money he's about to lose. Your turn will come, Bobby. But not just now."

Bobby looked at Josiah. "That's not fair," he exclaimed. "Joe gets all the fun. I want a turn."

In the lamplit room Henry Kern knelt on the floor in front of Josiah.

"Okay, boy. Do it again. Walk to the line and from behind it, turn, look, see, throw. Do not think. Just look, see and throw. Do that and you'll not need a third try."

"All right, Papa," Josiah said.

It was a lonely walk to the white line. Before he got there, he turned and looked back at his father and Bobby. His father was nodding his head as Bobby stood on a table next to him. A large fat man with a protruding belly gasped in amazement as Josiah turned, looked, and threw the knife. He stood a full thirty-three feet from the small circle. But Josiah Kern really didn't know how to miss, and he didn't. The astonishment of the crowd was loud as it reached a crescendo. His father lifted him into his arms.

Afterwards they'd walked home, his father with a wad of money folded tightly in his pocket and a smile on his face. Josiah was quiet. Somehow in his ten-year-old mind it wasn't right. He didn't know why or what. Men, big men, had congratulated him, patted him on the back, glad-handing him. They told his father how proud he should be--a boy like that. Bobby was so excited; it was as if Bobby had won. On the way home they found a tree and his father let Bobby practice throwing his blade. He found the mark two out of five times. Joe never said a word.

Bobby followed him everywhere. He followed him to raid farmer Rice's orchard, to collect the ripening crab apples from his tree in the late evening while their mother slept beneath her woolen blankets. Like highwaymen, they'd left through the open window of their bedroom. It had been a cool night. He remembered his sister sighing in her sleep.

But they were to be disappointed. Sitting on the side of a hill in a clump of trees, they had watched three men strip the tree. They watched them disappear in the dead of that dark night leaving little behind, yet coming back for that little. Joe and Bobby walked home in the starless night through glade and glen like Robin Hood of old, laughing at old jokes their father had told. Laughing at old man Rice charging outside his rock farm house after his apples were gone, firing his shotgun in the air, the three men falling over themselves getting away, leaving very few apples behind.

"We've seen nothing," they answered when questioned by the constable. The boys were surprised that he'd found their small tracks in the clump of trees that overlooked the farmer Rice's orchard.

"We were home in bed," Josiah said in reply. Bobby had nodded in agreement, saying nothing at all.

"It was night. Where else would my boys be on a dark night?" His mother had responded.

But they did know. They had seen the men stealing. They'd done nothing wrong though they had intended to. That didn't seem right to Josiah. But Bobby was right with it. While the constable talked and his mother stood responding and assuring, Lottie played with her Raggedy Ann doll on the oak floor of their father's cottage. Bobby sat in his chair smiling like he had a secret, a secret that was only his.

After the constable left, Mother looked at Bobby. Her look bored right into his eyes as only she could.

"Where were you, Bobby? Now, don't you lie to me, Robert John Kern. Where were you last night?"

"In bed, Ma'am," he replied, solidifying the lie. Bobby had come through for him. They were brothers in apples, throwing knives, lances, and lies.

He'd taught Bobby how to slug it out with Edward Figgens. He taught Bobby what his father had taught him: to feign, to step back, then shuffle forward under the punch. Hold to the inside; slug the gut, the chest, the mouth, and step back out. Do it again. Do it quickly. Never back up. Just look like you might.

Figgens was older and bigger, but he didn't last with Bobby, not that day. Bobby hadn't bothered feigning. He'd just stepped forward slugging Eddy in the mouth; then without any fear he chased Edward Figgens down the street.

Little brother Bobby had hugged Josiah, had thanked him again and again for showing him how to win, for making him so formidable, for making him someone to fear, someone like Josiah. Bobby was happy that day. Josiah wasn't sure it was right, but Bobby was. Eddy Figgens never had a chance.

Those were the things he remembered sitting on the side of a mountain, below Sage Creek accompanied by a dun horse and a mangy, yellow dog.

Feeling like used sheep dip, Josiah mounted the dun and headed north. He rode through juniper breaks and aspen, finding another creek. Angry at himself for his indulgent self-pity, he rode without a destination through unfamiliar territory. He rode through a short canyon and over a rise, then another, and another.

Eventually, he came upon a solitary street defined by six ramshackle, unpainted, and weathered buildings. This was dead center in Crow country on the government designated reservation. It was a place he certainly never intended to be. Everywhere he looked, he saw a Crow Indian or the sign of one. That wasn't good.

The Little Big Horn shoot out had been a mere five years earlier. It felt like it had been yesterday, a fresh headline in *The New York Times*. He felt uneasy. Though five years had passed, no one had ever tamed the Apache; he'd ridden through that country not long ago. Folks there still lived on the edge of worry, thankful each morning for waking up alive.

This town, if it were that, wasn't much. Its solitary street was just a horse trail. Lodges were pitched on both sides, smoke curling out of their smoke holes and the smell of roasting meat drifting on the breeze. It was a trail so twisted that he was forced to ride around holes, between rocks and small gullies. It took longer to get across town than the length of the town warranted. He counted six buildings and a two-holer outhouse hidden in a bramble of skunk brush.

On the street in front of him sat the "Lucky Chance Saloon." For a moment he thought he'd rather be in his dead brother's cabin on Cherry Creek, sitting in the kitchen where "someone" had put a bullet in his brother's head. But that "someone" was not dead. Such unmistakable injustice! Frustration made him restless. Thirty or so lodges made him anxious. What was worse? He didn't know. He dismounted and stood in the middle of the dusty street, uncertain. The yellow dog sat on its haunches beside him, tongue lolling from the side of its mouth, waiting.

Judging from the horses out front, the "Lucky Chance Saloon" sported a goodly portion of the Crow Indian population. Leastwise, the drunks were present. Several were so drunk they hadn't made it off the front steps to throw up. They resided, temporarily, on the steps, unconscious. It was hard to tell whether they had thrown up and then passed out, or the other way around.

Josiah leaned against his saddle horse and looked up and down the street. Nothing was going on. Far down the road, a mile or so, a couple of boys were racing bareback, horses full out, bellies to the ground. Josiah watched them reach the end of the road and plunge into the bramble beyond.

Down the so-called street a young woman stood shaking a red agency blanket in front of a lodge, a yellow sun painted on the side, smoke drifting up from a fire. She stared at him. When his gaze caught her eye, she stopped what she was doing and hurried inside. It was the first time he heard the yellow dog whine.

"What are you thinking, dog? Thinking she's pretty?"

The doors of the saloon that wasn't supposed to be a saloon--illegal on the reservation--sprang wide open. Out came a human projectile who tripped, fell, and rolled into the street beneath the horse's belly. The dun went to popping and getting, jumping sideways to get away from the rolling drunk. Josiah barely hung onto the reins as he, too, was jerked from his feet. He ended up in the dirt, the yellow dog next to him his teeth bared, growling at the Indian lying on the ground beside him.

"Easy, dog," Josiah said. But the dog didn't back away; the growl continuing deep in his chest, his stained teeth showing above a quivering lower lip, his unblinking eyes straining ahead.

The one hundred eighty pounds of saloon outcast, dressed in leggings, moccasins, and a delicately beaded doeskin vest, struggled to his feet. He was unsteady, ignoring the dog as he struggled to stay upright. He brushed himself off, shook his shoulder length hair, and stared at Josiah lying in the dust. He said something long and loquacious, waving his hands and gesturing, then climbed the three steps. Taking a breath he paused, then charged back through the door through which he had just been summarily tossed. The dog relaxed, licking his cheeks with a long red tongue.

Alone again, Josiah picked himself up, straightened his hat, then looked at the dun.

"What do you think?" he asked the stoic horse.

The front door reopened. The man reappeared and, with the assistance of a man on either side, ended up lying in the middle of the street. He landed, his head in a pothole, his right foot propped on the rim, the other wedged under his body. That pothole was large. Telling the story later, Josiah swore a tall man wearing a big hat could lose a small horse within its confines and have no trouble turning around and riding to daylight.

Josiah walked to the middle of the street leading his horse. With his left hand he grabbed the arm of this devoted patron of the "Lucky Chance" and helped him to his feet. Once standing, the inebriated Indian began berating Josiah in the unfamiliar lyrical tongue. Josiah released his grip and the drunk promptly fell back into the hole in the street. The man's tone changed from pissed off indignant to "please, I'm dying, give me a hand." Against his better judgment Josiah extended a hand only to end up in the elongated hole with a moderately drunk Indian, an Indian who spoke very bad Absorkian and no English. The dun and the dog stood on the brink looking down at them.

But that was not the end of it. Between the two, given Josiah's untrammeled ability to stand and the Indian's indomitable will to get inside the saloon, they extricated themselves from the hole. The Indian headed straight toward the front door of the saloon. Josiah followed, the Indian pulling him along.

Inexplicably, the drunk waited for Josiah to wrap the reins of the dun around the cedar hitching rail. The dog sat down beside the post. Both men glanced at the door, then at a drunk leaning against the wall, asleep. Another lay across the steps, his head resting uncomfortably on the edge. The drunk spoke. Whatever he said was just so much gibberish to Josiah but the man's desire to get to the door was clear. Josiah followed him up the steps, around the sleeping form, and through the door.

Inside, Pistol discovered a full house, and not the card variety. It was standing room only. However, as luck would have it, one of the tables had two empty chairs. Pistol settled the drunk into one of them and sat down himself. Across from him sat four men: Crow Indians, all. They stared at him then immediately began talking among themselves. Josiah's companion listened, waved a hand full of disdain and ordered two drinks: both for himself. After all he had two hands and he intended to make good use of them.

To Josiah Kern, all five of his new found companions looked the same. Perhaps this phenomenon was caused by the shadows or maybe the lack of light that struggled vainly to pass through windows: windows that hadn't felt the touch of soap or water since they were installed. One wasn't a window at all; it was just a boarded up hole. Each of his companions had swarthy skin, long jet black hair that hung past his shoulders, and an apparent disposition to drink themselves into oblivion. Josiah thought that he and his companion would soon find themselves under the table and cast into the street, trying to limp back inside past the bodies of those not so fortunate.

The drinks were served in opaque, unwashed glasses, amber in color, or perhaps, inherently dark brown. Not knowing any differently, Pistol assumed one drink was for him, something he deserved after hauling his companion's sorry self out of the street and through the door. He took a swallow. Whatever it was burned all the way down to the bottom of his stomach and sat there in a pool of molten lava.

His companion said something that clearly insulted the four with prior claim to the table. They weren't laughing and one, nearly standing, reached across the table for his throat.

Josiah couldn't be insulted. He didn't know what was said. It wasn't the drink; he'd only had one swallow. Already his skin grew warm. He made eye contact with the waiter/bartender and waved him over. Both glasses were refilled. His companion paid and immediately drank his empty. Josiah left his glass full. Whatever was in that glass, he wanted no more. At least not yet. Later, maybe, if there was going to be a later. The rotund bartender, a huge dragoon pistol stuck in his abundant waistband, did not stop pouring. He refilled the four glasses and then refilled his companion's empty glass a third time.

The bartender, holding the bottle by the neck, looked at Josiah for payment. Josiah glanced at the drunk, noting that the man was no longer drinking; his third round remained untouched. He was out. His head rested on the table, his hand resting short of the glass, the other hand in his lap. A twenty-dollar gold piece lay between his fingers. He was fast asleep. The bartender took the gold piece and while Josiah watched, left change on the table. Spittle leaked from the edge of the sleeping man's mouth.

A deck of well-used cards lay in the center of the table. Josiah stared at the deck a long while before he reached and picked it up, the liquor still warm in his stomach, a bit of moisture on his brow. Josiah wasn't a card player. A game of cards wasn't something he looked forward to with anticipation when he first reached a bar and had a pint. But he'd played.

Slowly he shuffled the cards, once, twice, three times, then set the deck on the table in front of the man on his left, waiting. He was a weasel of a man with a hawk's beak for a nose. He cut the deck. Josiah shuffled again and dealt, setting the remaining deck in front of his comatose drinking partner along with his five cards. Josiah had purposely not dealt himself a card. It didn't seem like a wise idea with four pistol packing Indians surrounding the table and Josiah not understanding a word they were saying.

Josiah did pick up his companion's cards though. He glanced at them, rearranged them to his liking, then set them face down on the table. He looked at the weasel sitting next to him who raised one finger, indicating he wanted a card. Josiah gave it to him. Around the table he went. His benefactor slept oblivious to the play; not asking for any cards, not discarding, unaware of his three dollar bet, or that Josiah was playing his cards for him. The game proceeded, punctuated by his snoring.

The first hand was a winner. Then his friend lost fifty cents. Steadily, here a little, there a little, a few dollars was won. Josiah played each hand without he, himself playing. In the midst of it he learned the Crow words for one, two, three, for I'm out, for I'm in, and call. Each time he won Josiah put most of the earnings in his sleeping companion's pocket, keeping a few coins to lose, some to win, some to pay for the others' drinks while never touching his own. At any one time it didn't look like he had much to bet, or much to lose. Just a little. He'd lose small pots, win the larger ones, and stay out of the really big ones, even if he had the cards. From the looks on their faces they didn't know who they were playing . . . a sleeping drunk or a crazy white man. One after another they left the table in disgust, broke.

Things got dicey once. The man next to the Weasel took offense at the drunk winning and began berating Josiah. Josiah pointed at his comatose companion drooling on the table. The man stopped talking, looked at the sleeping drunk, and began talking to those around him. The Weasel laughed and picked up his cards. Whatever it meant, whatever was said, that was that.

64

Come morning the original four and the seven others that followed them were gone. His companion was awake, mostly sober, with foul, smelly breath and three hundred forty two dollars in his pocket that he hadn't had the prior evening. His drinking money and his gambling money was still in his pocket.

From the look on his companion's face Josiah could see that he was concentrating on the puzzle, probably asking himself what he was doing with a short haired, light-skinned white man wearing a big hat and a week's growth of hair on his face who didn't understand a word he was saying.

Finally, he waved the man behind the bar over. The bartending Indian with the large belly, the big dragoon pistol, and a scar across his forehead stared at Josiah. Josiah noted that the first finger joint of the little finger on his left hand was missing. He came with a bottle but Josiah's companion waved off the offer of more drink and spoke quickly to the bartender while holding his head, rubbing his temples and gesturing with his right hand.

There was a long silence. The bartender nodded, then turned to Josiah and said in English, "He wants to know who you are. He wants to know what you are doing here. Your name. What you are called."

Josiah was about to say Josiah Edwin Kern. He thought of his name. Bob and his mother had called him *Joe* or when he was really small, *Joey*. His grandfather had called him *Edwin*. That was his grandfather's name. But who was he? His true name was long. If you'd never heard it before, or didn't understand English, it was both difficult to pronounce and difficult to remember. It was all a man could remember on a good day in a London pub. Yet Josiah Edwin Kern was who he was; it was the name his mother had given him.

"Pistol," Josiah Kern said in reply. "Pistol."

He could hear his mother saying: *What's wrong with your name, Joe? Josiah was my father's name. Edwin, too. What's wrong with that, Joe? What's wrong with your Christian name?*

The fat man interrupted his thoughts.

"Pistol?" he repeated, staring at him. "He also wants to know what you are doing here and why he's got so much money in his pocket."

"Tell him he invited me to drink with him and he won the money playing cards. Tell him he's really good at it."

The interpreter smiled, nodded, and repeated the answer, talking to Pistol's drinking companion for a considerable time. Finally finished, the fat man turned his attention back to Pistol.

"I told him what you said. I told him how money fell into his pockets. He wants to know if you want it back and if you are hungry."

"Tell him, no, I don't want his money and yes, I'm very hungry."

The bartender said something to the Indian, then turned to Pistol.

"He wants you to go with him. His name is Walking Bull. He thinks you bring him luck."

"All right," Pistol said and stood. He didn't have anywhere else to go and the language he heard sounded interesting to him. He'd learned English from his father, French from his mother, and Spanish from the Mexicans in Sonora. Not that he was proficient in Spanish, but he could get by: ask for a tortilla, some cooked beef and chili peppers. Now he could place a bet in Apsaruke and ask for a card or two.

Once outside Pistol found the dun watching him. The yellow dog rose to his feet. Pistol suddenly felt guilty for leaving both animals alone and hungry all night.

Walking Bull started to kick the dog but Pistol held up his hand, shaking his head, wagging his finger.

"He'll chew your leg off," he said.

Walking Bull pointed at the dog then at Pistol. Pistol nodded. Walking Bull shook his head in disbelief.

Either Pistol looked hungry to Walking Bull or Walking Bull was simply hungry himself. Regardless, Walking Bull led Pistol down Pryor Creek through head high buck brush. Pistol led his dun horse, followed by the ugly, yellow dog. In the morning light Pistol gave the dog some jerky and picketed the dun. Walking Bull waited for him, then both men entered the dark confines of the buffalo skin lodge.

Inside, Pistol was invited to sit on a buffalo hide across a small fire from Walking Bull. He listened to Walking Bull chatter in the language of his people, heard his wife laugh, the yellow dog whining outside, other dogs barking. Somewhere farther away a woman was yelling, her voice shrill and agitated. He saw Walking Bull's woman glance at him then at her husband. She shook her head in disbelief and his daughters laughed, giggling.

He discovered that Walking Bull had three daughters and two sons. The boys weren't present. In the cool, shaded lodge they ate jerky and dried chokecherries as they watched fresh deer meat roasting over a small fire. It was good.

Walking Bull pointed at one thing and another, naming it. Pistol gave each word a try. Always a good mimic, he repeated the sounds over and over, first aloud then to himself, tying the sounds to an object, doing his best to sound like Walking Bull, using a throaty voice. He used each word until it was his, then moved on to the next.

Thus, Walking Bull taught and Pistol learned Apsaruke. Pistol didn't learn the language in a day or a week. After a month he could get by, and after two months he could carry on a conversation about simple things. After three months he was conversant. Languages came easier for Pistol than for most men. Another ninety days and he understood what he said and what he asked and most of the responses. It was easier too because Apsaruke was all he spoke and all he heard. No one but the bartender spoke English and Pistol didn't see him much. After six months it became the language of his dreams, the daily conveyer of his thoughts. When that happened exactly, he wasn't sure. It just happened.

Pistol fell into a routine that allowed for selective forgetfulness. Mornings were spent waking up, eating, bathing, and watching the women; protecting them from an unseen enemy who Walking Bull assured him was there. Afternoons and evenings Pistol rode with Walking Bull in search of deer, antelope, buffalo and elk. Sometimes they did not hunt to kill. Sometimes they located game for hunting later when game would be scarce and hard to find.

Walking Bull told those who asked him that he kept the white man for luck. He, after all, had gone to sleep and won more money than he ever won while awake. Who could say that? Walking Bull's woman was called Young Crane because of her long legs. She was a sister to Crazy Head, the weasel of a man with whom Pistol had played cards. The other three men with Crazy Head who also sat at the card table were his two brothers and his maternal uncle.

They lived together, not in the same lodge but in the same camp. It was a matter of protection and expertise. As a practice Walking Bull hunted while the women were in camp. It was then that Crazy Head, his brothers, and uncles would stay close, making themselves available for the "just in case" danger.

Protection duties rotated. During the time when the women gathered berries, roots, or wood, there were men close by to watch. Others hunted ranging far and near in search of fresh meat. Raiders and thieves from the east and north were always expected. The Lakota, the Cheyenne, the Blackfoot always looked for new horses, more wives, and coups to count. As did the Crow. A lack of vigilance risked death and terrible loss.

"Stay here," Walking Bull told Pistol. "Watch over the women. I will get us something to eat. Water to drink."

Pistol nodded as he watched Walking Bull mount his horse and disappear over the rise. He estimated that Walking Bull would be gone half an hour. Certainly he could watch the women picking berries and the small children dashing about playing games, laughing as their mothers chatted. Below him the creek bottom wound its way upland into the Pryor mountains and the dark pine timber that covered its crest.

Walking Bull's woman, the wives of Crazy Head, and Walking Bull's daughters walked from bush to bush in search of currants, goose berries, and chokecherries. The latter were not fully ripe yet but a few early berries could be found. All morning they had been working steadily. Per their duty, Walking Bull and Pistol had watched from the ridge, looking for signs of intruders, spooked deer that ran for no reason, or birds suddenly flying without cause.

Walking Bull had not been gone fifteen minutes when Pistol heard the frantic screaming of a child. In one stride he was on the dun's back, his Winchester 73 in hand, spurring the horse. In a heartbeat he dropped off the rise, his eyes searching for the cause of alarm, the yellow dog at the horse's heels. Up the creek he saw Walks With Her Dress running across a clearing, her legs churning, carrying her across the grass of the creek bottom toward her mother. A full-grown brown bear lumbered not far behind her. Off to the side two yearling cubs were scrambling away, bleating in panic.

Young Crane ran toward her daughter screaming her name. She dropped her basket and hiked her skirt up as she ran, her shrill voice encouraging Walks With Her Dress to run faster. Pistol spurred the dun into a full gallop, chambering a round with one hand. It was an all out effort to get to the bear before Young Crane reached her: to keep the bear from overtaking Walks With Her Dress, and to keep Young Crane from overtaking the bear. Both mothers were on a collision course.

The girl stumbled, nearly falling as she scrambled. Pistol got a shot off, firing over the horse's head. He fired again and again. Three times. The bear had all but overtaken the child when he fired, catching the bear in the mouth. The shot busted her backbone, dropping her into a quivering heap. He cursed himself for missing three times. Pistol came off the horse running, put another bullet in the bear's head, then reached for the screaming girl seconds before her mother arrived.

"Are you all right?" he asked, pulling her from the ground with one hand, still watching the bear. The girl wrapped her arms around his neck and buried her face in his shirt, sobbing incoherently.

Young Crane arrived breathless and pulled the child to her. Both mother and daughter stood crying, hugging each other, the mother scolding Walks With Her Dress for getting between a sow and her cubs.

"Never, never do that," she said again and again.

"But Mother, I didn't see the bear. I didn't see the cubs."

"I know. I know. Just don't do it. Do you hear me? Just don't do it."

The conversation amused Pistol. He couldn't help but smile as he examined the bear to make sure she was dead. The yellow dog stood off to the side growling, pacing back and forth, looking as if he were about to tear someone's leg off. That's how Walking Bull found them. He looked first at the bear then at Pistol.

"I got hungry," Pistol said to him. "Thought I'd do a little bear hunting so we wouldn't starve while you were gone." Pistol smiled as Walking Bull looked to his wife.

"I'm not just saying it, Walking Bull. Walks With Her Dress spooked this old she bear up and got her to chase her just so I could kill it. Got to tell you, that child of yours can run. Outran the bear. If I hadn't shot the bear momma, your woman would have strangled it herself. Lucky I got a shot off before she got her fingers around its neck."

Pistol smiled. "We were sure hungry. Our bellies thought someone done cut our throats. Where were you? You sure missed a dandy foot race."

Young Crane watched her husband as he listened to Pistol's talk and began to laugh. Walks With Her Dress finally stopped sobbing though she was still breathing hard.

Her father shook his head as he studied the dead bear. "Four times it was shot," he exclaimed.

He wanted to give his oldest daughter a new name that afternoon. He wanted to call her Chases After Bear. But Young Crane said no, he was not changing his daughter's name, that it was not funny, and that she really had not been that hungry.

In late September, Pistol and the yellow dog that growls went hunting elk with Walking Bull, Crazy Head, and his brothers on the Bull Elk across the Horn on the west slopes of the Big Horn Mountain. The hunting was good. Soon enough the women had plenty of meat to dry for winter and enough to fatten the camp dogs on scraps. The yellow dog was shaping up as well. His hair had grown back and he was getting his winter coat. The camp was happy. Mornings were frosty, the days warm.

Memories were made. One memory Pistol would never forget. Crazy Head was straddling an elk cow with his knife in one hand, preparing to cut her throat to properly bleed it. Two arrows had been driven deep in its chest just behind the front leg where the heart sat. It was dead; the cow just didn't know it. Crazy Head had lifted the head and started to cut its throat.

The dead cow jumped up while Crazy Head was clinging to her, trying to finish cutting. Walking Bull rode his war pony on one side to get in front of the frantic cow and keep Crazy Head from getting killed. Pistol rode on the other side trying to get a shot at the now very much alive cow without shooting its rider. The yellow dog kept the race alive by barking and nipping at the heels of the frightened animal.

For over a mile the drama played out. No more arrows were shot into her chest. No rifle shot was made because Crazy Head was in the way, down on the cow's neck hanging on and cutting as fast as he could. Finally she stumbled and fell to the red earth, no longer moving, her remaining blood spilling into the brown grass.

Crazy Head rolled when the cow fell. He jumped up, dropped his knife and began beating his chest.

Pistol asked if he was all right. The yellow dog was walking back and forth growling at the dead cow.

Crazy Head said "no," looking about as white as a dark Indian could. The three began laughing, shaking their heads, wiping their eyes, catching their breaths. It was a hunt to be remembered. It was memories like that that made it easier for Pistol to forget about his brother.

During the last week in October the moon was full. The first snow fell and stayed above the timber line. Winter was not far off.

Among Walking Bull's people were women without husbands, children without parents taken in by their relatives, old women, and old men. The returning hunting parties always left portions of the hunt at the lodges of these less fortunate.

Pistol observed this practice. It was obvious that those without hunters would need more to survive the winter snows ahead. Their fate didn't look too promising to him. The community was an odd mix. Some had plenty, others little. He wondered about it and asked Walking Bull about the practice of leaving a portion of the hunt at the lodges of the needy and of the old people.

"It is the way of the Apsaruke," was his reply.

Pistol believed it was a good way, that it was admirable. And for some strange reason he felt that it was something he could do for his brother in place of vengeance, in the name of vengeance, or because there was no hope of vengeance. He really didn't know why he felt compelled to do it other than it made him feel good. In the end, he hunted for the needy because it needed to be done and because the yellow dog needed to get its exercise.

In the early morning in the month of falling leaves he saddled his horse and borrowed Walking Bull's pack mule. Pistol and the yellow dog went hunting. Later, after dark, after the small ones were asleep and the old ones were huddled in their agency blankets, he unceremoniously dumped the carcasses of two mule deer: one at the opening of one lodge of old people and another at the lodge of a woman whose husband had been lost in battle, leaving three fatherless children.

Before the occupants could scramble to see what the ruckus was, he was gone; off to meet Walking Bull, to tell stories and eat buffalo steak. At night as he slept in the lodge of Walking Bull, he imagined the bellies of people who would eat venison during the time of falling snow and felt good. He didn't think about Robert John Kern.

On the second day he and the yellow dog did the same thing, this time leaving a fat mule deer at the doorway of two different lodges. Each time he rode into camp long after dark, having hunted for people that Walking Bull suggested were in need. For ten days--then for two weeks--he did this, leaving early, returning late followed by the yellow dog.

On the fifteenth day he left the carcass of a bull elk at the doorway of a very old man. Walking Bull had said he didn't know how many seasons the man had lived. He was just old. But this time was different. In the starlit darkness Pistol discovered the man sitting in the doorway of his lodge waiting for him. The growl of the yellow dog told Pistol the old man was there before he spoke.

"I knew you would come. I have seen it," he said to Pistol. "I saw the yellow dog following after you. Why do you do this good thing?"

Pistol was embarrassed. He'd been caught by an old man sitting in his doorway in the dark.

"For my brother. I do it for him," Pistol said. "I seek to honor him after the customs of your people." He saw no reason to lie.

"Your brother? He must be a good man."

Pistol hesitated. "He's dead," he said. "My brother is dead. I wish to honor him. I cannot kill the man who took his life. So I do this to remember."

He could feel the old man staring at him. It was an eerie feeling, as if his ancient eyes searched his soul and laid it bare. It didn't help that it was past midnight, before the moon rose over the Big Horn. The stars brightly lit up the sky.

"The white man at Deadman on Cherry Creek? He is your brother?" the old man asked.

The question surprised Pistol. "Yes," he said. "How did you . . . ? Do you know him?"

The old man shook his head, no.

"It is a place for the dead. The white man who died there was killed for the yellow metal. Another took his life."

The old man looked at the elk carcass lying at his feet. "This is too much for an old man," he said. "My teeth are gone, my mouth sore. I cannot eat this much."

"Take what you need, Old One. Give the rest away."

Pistol watched the man whose grey, braided hair hung to his waist. He studied his wrinkled, weathered face, then reached out when the old one struggled to stand and helped him to his feet.

"How is it that you know these things?" he asked. "Who killed my brother? Do you know this?"

"No one," the old man replied. "Vengeance. It is not important for your brother. This one, your brother? He is not dead. He lives."

The old man stood beside him, his gnarled fingers around his elbow, digging into the flesh to keep his balance.

"Go to where your brother lived. Live in peace. Your brother . . . he is not a good man. By doing this good thing for the old, for the hungry, you are better than he.

"Your brother, he is lost in the dark winds. Giving life is better than seeking another man's death. For your brother, seek no more blood."

The old man stopped talking and stood still as if listening to the silence. Silence seemed to close in around him; the darkness became darker still.

"Go," he said. "Soon it will be dawn. Many will come to help with this elk. I will sit and watch. There will be much to do. Go. Rest well in the lodge of Walking Bull. You have given meat to many this night. Bellies will be full."

The old man stood beside him without moving. He stared up at Pistol without loosening his grip.

"Someone seeks your life," he said, pausing as if listening to voices in his head. "With you it is not expected nor can it be avoided. Beware that you do not lose your life to carelessness. First--no--last, there is a woman. But remember, if you wish to live you must leave this place."

"What?"

"Go," the old man said again. "Go."

He released his grip and turned away without a backward glance, muttering to himself in long, unintelligible sentences, talking to unseen personages that seemed to hover about him like storm clouds.

Pistol left the old man in front of his lodge, at peace with himself but puzzled by the words he'd heard. Followed by an ugly yellow dog, he went looking for a game of cards with Walking Bull and his friends, wondering who the old man was, whether he was just crazy, and what to think about his unsettling words. His brother alive? Couldn't be.

In the dark of the fall night, sitting at a table at the "Lucky Chance," he asked Walking Bull about the old one. Though they had talked much, neither man had touched the liquid fire. With them were Crazy Head and his two brothers, Boy Who Laughs, Dangerous Coup, and his nephew, Killer of Many Deer. These five had played cards with Pistol long ago when only Walking Bull won.

"Who is he?" Pistol asked. "He is very strange. Not just old. He's different. Even when he's alone he's not

76

alone. It 's like he is talking to someone when there is no one. A thundercloud seems to hover over him about to let loose."

Walking Bull looked at Pistol for what seemed like a long time, fingering his glass without spilling. "The very old man? Did you take him meat?"

"Yes. A bull elk. A big one. Had a big rack of horns. This one chased me before I killed him. Listen, the Old One, he was sitting outside his lodge when I arrived. He said he knew I was coming, that he'd seen me and the yellow dog arriving with the elk before we got there. It was spooky finding this old man sitting in the dark. My dog was even spooked."

"The old man has ghost power," Walking Bull said. "He sees lost people, sees things that cannot be found. It is the way with him."

Walking Bull smiled, then looked at Pistol. "You think I am just saying this. Two winters ago there were two young men of the Thick Lodge clan. They had been gone many days. Lost. Their people worried. They thought they were dead, lost to them. Finally, they went to the old man, gave him a war horse, the robe of buffalo, the meat of the buffalo. They asked him to find these young men. He agreed to do this thing.

"For seven days the old man stayed in his lodge. At night it is said he sat in the dark, building no fire. He hooted like the great owl, talking to someone, to many people as if they were with him. There was no one.

"Some say his lodge shook as he hooted. He spoke in a language no one had heard. There were voices speaking that were not his voice. After the sun came up on the eighth day, he rekindled his fire and opened his lodge covering. He told the people that these boys were not lost; that they were in camp and not living among the dead. Everyone knew they were not in camp. In the evening one of the lost ones, he fell into camp. A month later the second was found living with Grey Elk's people on the west rim of the Big Horns."

Walking Bull smiled. "The old one is different. His words are much sought after. They are strong in truth. They are words not to be forgotten nor taken lightly."

Pistol nodded. "He told me that my brother lives. That's crazy. I stood over my brother's grave. I spoke with the man that buried him."

Walking Bull looked at Pistol. "Before the old man said it, the lost ones were not in camp. Afterwards, they were. His words have much power. If he said your brother lives, he lives somewhere. Chances are you will see him again."

"But I've seen his grave, the place his bones rest. The man who buried him knew my brother. He told me he was dead with a bullet hole in his head. He buried him after the manner of my people. If he wasn't dead before, he sure is now."

Walking Bull glanced at Crazy Head, two men, and a boy sitting at the card table, their drinks untouched, watching and listening, their cards face down in front of them. He nodded at Pistol.

"It is someone else who died," he said. "The dead one is not your brother. If the old man said your brother is alive, he lives. Did he say anything else?"

Crazy Head interrupted. "He is called Old Dog. He knew my father's father before my father was born. In the lodge of my mother it is said that he speaks with the dead. His words are valued. His words are to be trusted."

Pistol smiled. "Yes, well, he told me to return to the lodge of my brother and live in peace. He told me to seek no more vengeance and that someone was trying to kill me. He said that I should leave here if I was going to live.

But first he said there was a woman. Can't say that it made a lot of sense."

Crazy Head smiled. So did Walking Bull.

"Sense? A woman?" Crazy Head said. "Soon you will not be sleeping alone. That is what he told you. Soon you will be whispering into a woman's ear, causing her to smile in your blankets." Crazy Head chuckled. "If the old one would say that to my nephew he would be happy, not sitting here playing cards with old men."

Everyone laughed.

Crazy Head picked up his cards, looked at them, and took a small sip from the opaque glass. "I will take one," he said, the grin holding to the edges of his lips. "A good one."

CHAPTER EIGHT

In the sixth month after Pistol and the ugly yellow dog had left Cherry Creek a large celebration was held on the flat north of the west ridge of the Pryor Mountains. The lodges of many of the people Absaruke were set upon the plain. For over a week they had gathered. Many more arrived each day until both sides of the creek were occupied. Some said five hundred people, others a thousand. No one knew because no one counted. They just looked and guessed.

Such a gathering had not happened before in the remembrances of the old people. There were games, food aplenty, and much celebrating for they had enjoyed many good hunts. Their parfleches were full of dried meat, chokecherries, and currant berries. They sat about their campfires, ate fresh buffalo meat, and talked.

Walking Bull's lodge was among those pitched on the flat north of the six buildings. It was said among the people that Pistol always found hospitality there. For had he not fed the old people, the women without husbands, the children of lost parents? Had he not kept nothing for himself? Was not his generosity renowned? Was not the name of Pistol spoken in great admiration in the lodges of the Apsaruke? With Walking Bull, Pistol was an honored guest, and deservedly so.

It was said Walking Bull always won at cards when his friend looked at his cards. It didn't matter whether he knew what was in his hand. He merely had to look. Others said it wasn't so. Some said it was the dark drink of the white man that clouded their brains and winning at cards was an imagination sickness. Crazy Head's people said that Walking Bull no longer touched the drink. Everyone knew that Pistol refused the dark liquid. Such was the gossip voiced among the campfires of the People Apsaruke as they wondered about him.

Others found evil. They saw a light haired, light skinned white man devil who lived in the lodge of Walking Bull, taking advantage of his hospitality. It was his people with whom the Apsaruke fought continually, who in 1869 imprisoned them on a reservation with imaginary borders, taking away the old trails south along the Big Horn River. He was a white man and everyone knew that white men were drunken thieves who lied continually. Pistol was white. What more need be said?

This eternal search for evil, looking behind every bush and twig, was personified in He That Rides Boldly. Not that He That Rides Boldly was evil for he was not. Rather, he was vigilant to discover evil: quick to root it out. It was a trait fueled by jealousy and, perhaps, embarrassment. For in him was a suspicion that not all good men were born Absaruke. He gave this suspicion no credence. His conclusion was simply Pistol was white and all whites were evil. Thus, Pistol was evil.

On the fourth day of celebration a challenge was issued to Pistol to participate in the warrior games. Ironically, the challenge came not from He That Rides Boldly, but from the friends of Walking Bull, those who sat at the card table at the "Lucky Chance." Pistol respectfully declined, wanting no part of it.

Walking Bull explained to him that he could not decline. It was not permitted. Others would not regard him as a warrior who could protect his family, should he have one, and should the need arise. His gifts, his generosity would be of no value if he could not walk with warriors, his head held high, his hair long. It was necessary that he stand honorably among such men. Walking Bull himself considered him one of the people, even as his brother, but that was not enough.

Through it all the yellow dog followed Pistol around growling, a sound of displeasure that started deep in his throat. For the most part it forced people to keep their distance, not wanting to be bitten.

On the fourth day, in spite of Pistol's reticence, he found himself on the playing fields with Walking Bull and Crazy Head, his brothers, his uncles, and his nephew. The six competed among themselves, laughing in the fall sunshine, telling stories on each other. They talked of what they had done together, the hunts they had experienced, the elk and buffalo they had killed and the speed of their horses. After all, these were games in a time of great celebration.

On the fifth day, Pistol showed up with his friends for the honor and good name of Walking Bull. The games on the fifth day involved a series of skill contests.

Everyone who was anyone became involved, and more especially He That Rides Boldly. Every time it was his turn to perform the crowd grew quiet for his performance was something to watch. To throw a spear farther, to shoot an arrow more accurately, to shoot a rifle from horseback and hit the target--these were feats of superior skill. To break the gourd, to wrestle, to play the stick game--these were warrior games meant to establish and enhance warrior skills. The young men had played them since birth, since they could walk, before they could run.

He That Rides Boldly was very good at these games for he was a superior athlete, a strong warrior, the owner of several fast horses. Many of the enemy had died at his hands. To see him perform was an opportunity to see the best, to see a true man among the Absaruke. Everyone wanted him to succeed. Indeed, they expected it.

In these games He That Rides Boldly singled out Pistol as the butt of his derisive comments. He voiced it around that Pistol was less of a man, a weakling, a toothless old woman who walked in men's clothing followed by a worthless yellow, and certainly unhappy, dog. Characteristics cited, in short, because Pistol had been reluctant to participate. "Was it not so?" He That Rides Boldly proclaimed. These assessments were supported by the fact that Pistol not only declined to participate but had chosen to stand among the women, the children, the old, and the infirm to watch the contests.

These words angered his five friends. In their minds Pistol had nothing to prove. None of them did until Walking Bull, himself, was openly criticized for harboring a coward in his lodge. He was ridiculed for befriending one who, as everyone believed, had no stomach for combat or warrior skills, no stomach for doing those things that men did without flinching. This unified them in their anger and instead of the friendly contesting among themselves, they began to compete against He That Rides Boldly and those with him. They did so successfully.

Pistol reluctantly became a participant in these contests. On the last day of the celebration many dropped out, preferring instead to watch the head to head competition between He That Rides Boldly and the white man from Walking Bull's lodge. The yellow dog continued to growl as he followed Pistol Clearly, he was an unhappy nuisance, always underfoot, something to be avoided.

With a bow Pistol wasn't very good. His arrow in flight had no distance and missed everything but the ground. Even the children were better archers than he. He That Rides Boldly was much better. To the latter's dismay Pistol openly honored him for his skill. This graciousness endeared him to those who watched, more especially his friends, but not to He That Rides Boldly.

With lances it was a different story. Pistol knew lances, for his father had been a lancer. He had been insistent about proper technique and had taught his sons well. Pistol did his father proud. He would have relished Pistol's performance had he been there to see it. Instead he was dead, killed on the bloody fields of battle, killed as he rode with the men of the light brigade, cannon to the right and left.

Because of the hours of practice under his father's watchful eye, Pistol threw farther and with greater accuracy than He That Rides Boldly. He especially enjoyed winning this game for Pistol did not enjoy losing. His brother Bob could attest to this trait. His five friends were equally joyful and loud, amusing the crowd with their antics and boisterous comments.

Pistol commented to Walking Bull, "Maybe I should not have done so well. I do believe I have embarrassed your friend."

To this they all laughed, slapping him on the back.

"He is not my friend," Walking Bull answered. "But you have gained the appreciation of the young women. Your name is spoken in admiration. Already I have heard it."

Crazy Head laughed, saying, "Pistol, remember Old Dog's words. One of them in this crowd is watching you right now, even as we speak."

"What would I do with a woman?"

"You need to ask?" Walking Bull said.

"No, I reckon not." Pistol grinned. "I think I have a pretty good idea."

Pistol caught the crowd's mood. It was hard not to feel pleased. He had surprised the many people who watched; Pistol was supposed to lose. Winning was a surprise bonus. With the laughter, the kidding, and the yellow dog voicing its displeasure, he was relaxed, easy going, and performed well. For him each contest was just a delightful game.

Often he laughed at himself. His friends laughed with him and would not let him hide in the crowd. It was simply too much fun seeing He That Rides Boldly lose at some games. After all, he had started this. It was he who repeatedly dined on his own words.

Pistol excelled with a rifle and a pistol. At wrestling he was exceptional, another family skill taught him during his early youth by his father. He That Rides Boldly won at those games he'd played since he could walk, since he had been old enough to sit a horse bareback. At those games he was practiced and efficient. Pistol won those games his father had worked his sons at until they hated him for his obsessions.

Both men won and lost for they were evenly matched. For He That Rides Boldly losing at anything was not an everyday event. It had never happened. He'd always been acknowledged as the best. To his dismay the crowd, led by Pistol's five noisy friends, was solidly behind Pistol, not him. For the first time winning was difficult and winning at everything was impossible. To make things worse, his opponent really didn't care, and he did.

Competition, like anything else, grew old. By the end of the last day Pistol was ready to wander off with his friends. He had had enough. He wanted to relax, tell stories, and enjoy the evening. It had been fun but he was hungry and thirsty. Enemies he did not need, did not want, and was more than willing to avoid.

In the afternoon the appreciative crowd left the playing fields feeling good about themselves. The games were over, the time of celebration past. Their minds were now on more important matters: where they would winter and whether their parfleeces were sufficiently stocked with dried meat and chokecherries for the time of deep snow and blowing cold.

For He That Rides Boldly defeat stung. Winning didn't feel as good as it had in the past. Having been thrown and bounced off the grass by a superior wrestler in front of family and friends hadn't helped. His own words rang hollow in his ears. The "old toothless woman" was not as old as he had thought. Indeed, she had some bite. Everyone saw it. This disparity between what he wanted to be true and the truth made his words hard to swallow, difficult to live with. It did not help that the five "unholy" friends of Pistol had repeatedly let him know that he'd been beaten or played evenly by a "very old, very toothless, woman and his yellow camp dog."

To He That Rides Boldly contests were always more than just games. They were who he was. Consequently, he was sensitive to his several losses and had grown more so with each passing hour of each passing day. The five sensed it and had rubbed it in. Pressure to win and win each time by large margins had made the scenario impossible. In the end it was He That Rides Boldly who had everything to lose and lost. It was said among the most casual of observers that even when he won he lost.

"No," he shouted to the retreating crowd. Those closest turned to see what the commotion was about. "He and I, knives," he said, pointing at Pistol. "I will show you this one is a toothless old woman."

Pistol shook his head "no," immediately finding Old Dog's words screaming in his ears.

His friends were equally angry. "Sore loser," they cried. "Let it go."

The challenge embarrassed Walking Bull who immediately confronted He That Rides Boldly. Pistol had participated in the games solely because of his encouragement. Mortal combat with the "loser" was not supposed to be his reward for having fun.

"These are just games," Walking Bull said to He That Rides Boldly. "The games are done. It is over. Finished. We had our fun."

"What is this?" Crazy Head said to He That Rides Boldly, deriding him. "Are you not satisfied? You lost. You won. What more is there? Even a child knows he cannot win all of the time."

All five were in agreement with Pistol. It was time to eat buffalo steaks, to swap lies, and tell stories, both good and bad, to laugh long into the night. It was time for saying goodbye, see you in the Spring, be safe, may the wind be at your back. It was not time for a fight to the death.

"Over? It is never over. Not as long as he lives," He That Rides Boldly retorted. "He is a man. I am a man. I have challenged him. Is he not an old woman? Is he not a white eyes? Should he not wear a dress in Walking Bull's lodge? Since when do we feed our enemies?" He That Rides Boldly glared angrily at Walking Bull and spat upon the ground in disgust.

The perceived "loser" forced the fight even as he choked on his own words. He pressed it, challenging Walking Bull's honor. His raging voice made him impossible to ignore.

Pistol again heard Old Dog's words repeated over and over. Warning bells rang incessantly. "Someone wants to kill you," the old man had said. "Be aware. Be on guard. It will come when you least expect it."

A disgusted Walking Bull scoffed at He That Rides Boldly, belittling him for his words. He asked, "What is there to win by meeting your challenge? What? Before everyone he has already defeated you. What more is there? It is you who has no shame."

Among the crowd someone was heard to say: *Enough!* Another cried, *Already, this is too much.* A third: *It is a game. Only a child's game.* The cries continued: *What good can come of this? Nothing was the repeated answer.*

Washing his hands of the growing affair, Pistol turned, walking away, his friends with him, the yellow dog following. They only hesitated, waiting for Walking Bull who was engaged in verbal conflict.

"See?" cried He That Rides Boldly. "The old woman runs as does his yellow dog. He is what he is. A coward. We must rid ourselves of this scab, this open wound."

The public assertion angered Walking Bull even more. "You fool," he said. "What has he to gain by meeting such an empty challenge?" Turning his back on He That Rides Boldly, he said, loud enough for all to hear, "Such a hollow challenge." He started to walk away.

Pistol and his friends stopped their slow retreat, looking at Walking Bull, watching, listening. *This is not good*, Pistol thought. *Nothing can be achieved. This will not end well. I should leave. Right now.*

He That Rides Boldly spoke loudly. "I will tell you. Listen, everyone. If I lose to this coward, this toothless old woman, I will be dead. Is it not so? In defeat I give him all I have. If he loses, and he will, he will be dead. If he runs, he leaves the people immediately like the camp dog he is, his tail dragging between his legs, never to return. When he does this, I will follow him and I will kill the coward. I will hang his scalp from my lodgepole."

Again he spat, standing, his arms folded across his chest in defiance. "We must rid ourselves of this scab. I will do it."

Pistol shook his head in disbelief.

How simple it had all become. He That Rides Boldly has effortlessly made it so I can't stay and I can't go. I like it here. All because of his silly pride, because of embarrassment, perhaps because of the color of my skin. I hear he is a good man. I've never heard anything bad said about him. Come to think about it what I have heard was good. He just talks too much, brags too much.

Pistol smiled at the irony.

My friends certainly haven't helped. They forced him to eat his words. And they were bitter words. And all because I helped a few people, and fed some hungry widows. This is just nonsense. One thing is clear, I am not ready to die just so this idiot can feel good.

Pistol took a step toward Walking Bull. To all who had been watching that step was his acceptance of the challenge. Without so much as a word, the crowd encircled the three men, giving them room, waiting. On the edge of the crowd Walking Bull and Pistol stood together. Fifteen feet away He That Rides Boldly was surrounded by his friends and admirers.

Many who had left for their lodges returned.

Walking Bull smiled ruefully. "I am sorry, my friend. I would take your place if it were possible."

Pistol nodded. "You didn't cause this. It would happen anyway. I heard you ask but I didn't understand his reply. He spoke too fast. Beside walking away from here with my hide, what do I win?" Pistol paused, staring at He That Rides Boldly. "If by some chance I manage to kill this man and not get killed myself?"

"He has six horses, a new wife. He has one son, two daughters. They are very young. He has a lodge. You get this. He says if you win, this is all yours. He also says that your death is soon, that we should not be concerned with the possibility of you obtaining such wealth."

"I get his wife and kids?" Pistol started laughing. Heads turned. "Could this get any worse? Like that would happen. I kill her new husband and their father. Do you really think they'd go with me? How likely is that? It is a gift not given."

"The young ones are not hers. I think Chokecherry Blossom will not make your life worse. I think she will make your life worth living. Old Dog said a woman. Maybe this is she."

"I don't think I need worry. She will not be with me especially if I kill her husband. Besides I haven't won. Not yet. So other than my hide I get nothing." Pistol laughed, then stopped talking, eyeing his opponent. "Well," he said slowly, "let's get to the dying. I'm getting hungry for buffalo steak, the meat still red."

Walking Bull smiled, pulled a long, heavy, knife from his belt, and handed it to him. Pistol took it, balancing it in his hand.

"Not bad," he said. "James Bowie make this for you?" It was a feeble attempt at humor.

"I have not heard of this man."

"That's all right. He made knives like this one. Maybe he had them made. Some say he used folded steel. It is said they last forever holding an edge."

They were joined by Crazy Head, his two brothers, his uncle, and his nephew. Together they watched He That Rides Boldly prepare himself.

"Watch this one," Walking Bull said to Pistol. "He likes his left more than his right but uses both equally well. Be careful."

"Oh, I am all about careful."

Walking Bull backed away. All five of Pistol's friends merged into the circle of spectators.

Pistol found himself standing alone, face to face with his adversary. Two men, two knives in the hot afternoon sun on the rocky plain a few miles north of the west lobe of the Pryor Mountains.

It started. He That Rides Boldly crouched, circling to his left, his knife in his left hand. Pistol stood upright, hefting the shank of the Bowie knife in his right, his right foot closer to his adversary. Pistol's every movement was calculated to simply keep his adversary in front of him. *What now?* he thought. The voice of his father told him to wait, to be patient. Pistol resolved to pay heed to that advice. He watched He That Rides Boldly circling, feeling anything but patient.

He That Rides Boldly lunged forward, his knife hand in front. Pistol didn't move for his adversary was too far away to do him any harm. But it was coming, the distance closing as He That Rides Boldly continued circling. The noise of the crowd died down to a whisper as it held its collective breath. Then there was no crowd, just two men circling--nothing else and no one else, a life hanging in the balance.

Suddenly He That Rides Boldly closed the distance quickly, lunging forward, leading with his knife hand. Pistol surprised him. And himself. Instead of retreating, he sprang forward, right foot in front of left. Parrying with his left hand, he seized the extended left wrist of He That Rides Boldly, knife and all, jerking him off-balance. At the same time he pounded He That Rides Boldly's jaw with his right fist, still tightly gripping the shank of the Bowie knife. Twice he struck with short jabs. His opponent's jaw bone absorbed the full force of the blows, teeth loosened, bone gave way. Pistol immediately retreated, wondering how he did that and how he was so lucky to still be alive. But he knew why. His father had suggested it. "No one expects you to grapple in a knife fight, not and slug it out. You 'll find they are worried about the knife, not expecting it."

In front of Pistol, He That Rides Boldly stumbled, momentarily losing his balance. Pistol backed away and was watching him. Deftly He That Rides Boldly switched his knife to his right hand, striking across his body. But again Pistol wasn't there for he'd moved, maintaining distance between them.

It became increasingly clear to Pistol that this fellow hadn't lost any knife fights. He watched in admiration as he switched directions, now circling Pistol to his right, holding the blade in his right hand. He worked his jaw as he moved, shaking his head to clear it. Suddenly he stopped circling, clearly agitated. He motioned for Pistol to come to him, to be the aggressor, his right hand extended out from his body full of sharp, unbending steel.

Pistol watched in amazement. *He thinks there are rules,* he thought. *There are no rules. No, I'm wrong. There is one rule. Stay alive. Don't get killed.*

Pistol remained upright, looking vulnerable. He shifted the Bowie knife to his left hand. He spoke softly to He That Rides Boldly calling him by name, keeping his voice even, calm. He'd had enough.

"We don't have to do this," he said. "I am willing to walk away. I want to walk away. I bear no evil against you. I have nothing that I need to win by killing you. I don't want your wife, your son, your daughters. They need you. There is nothing you have that I want. There is no need to do this."

He That Rides Boldly laughed, blood forming on his lips from a broken tooth, a broken jaw. "You are a coward," he hissed.

"If you think so, all right, but you are leaving me no choice. I do not wish to take your life. I do not wish to fight with you. Neither you nor I have anything to gain. Think of your woman. Your son. Your daughters."

"A coward always has a choice." He paused. "My woman is not your concern."

"But she will be if you are dead."

"Coward," He That Rides Boldly hissed.

Pistol stared at his opponent standing slightly crouched in front of him, the afternoon light in his eyes. Pistol took several steps backward, wanting and needing distance. He said, "You are a brave man who gives me no choice. For this I am truly sorry."

With his right hand, Pistol pulled his throwing blade from his belt, tossed it into the air, catching the blade between thumb and index-finger, momentarily balancing it. Then he slung it hard as he had done ten thousand times before, spinning it, end over end over end. This time he wasn't aiming at the center circle in a pub with no name. This time his brother wasn't cheering for him nor was his father collecting bets.

The second he released it Pistol hesitated, saddened by what did not need to be, holding Walking Bull's Bowie knife in his left hand "just in case." But there was no "just in case"; there was just death. Pistol knew it.

Surprised, He That Rides Boldly dropped his knife and grabbed his throat. The throwing blade had sliced through the soft tissue and embedded itself deep in the bones at the back of his neck. Blood spurted between his fingers. Slowly the warrior collapsed, falling to the trampled grass, the red clay earth catching him. His blood spilled profusely, his heart pumping it out rapidly. He tried to breathe but choked. He tried to move his arms, his lips. They grew numb and he could not.

Pistol appeared over him, kneeling beside him. "You are a brave man," he said. "Your people will miss you in their councils and on the field of battle."

He That Rides Boldly slowly blinked his eyes in the bright sunlight; then he was dead, his body limp. Pistol pulled his throwing knife from the man's throat, wiped it on the buckskin vest of He That Rides Boldly, and rose to his feet. Walking Bull stood beside him. His friends crowded about him for protection. There was no need. One by one they came: the men of the tribe--the warriors--men held in honor, fighting men. They touched Pistol, his sleeve, his arm, and said nothing, walking away. Behind him the people of the dead man's clan collected his remains, bearing the body away. Only the yellow dog kept his distance, whining, growling intermittently.

Who would believe it? Pistol thought. This death would drive the people away. No one truly had the stomach for it. They'd wish to forget. So they would leave. There would be no stories told. No buffalo steak cooked over an open fire. Not today.

"Walking Bull," Pistol said quietly, "I have got to get out of here."

"I understand," Walking Bull said. "I will tell your woman to make ready. We will help her."

"My woman? You can't be serious." He looked at Walking Bull, knowing what he was thinking. The words of Old Dog were ringing in his ears.

The six men started walking, followed by the yellow dog. Walking Bull continued. "Yes, your woman. Come we must prepare, my brother. I have something for you. Come."

Pistol followed Walking Bull and his friends through the disbursing crowd, looking neither right nor left, wondering if this day would ever end. He wondered what was on Walking Bull's mind, glad for the company. Mostly he wondered about three children and a woman who had just witnessed him kill their father and husband with a throwing knife.

When it was clear that no one else was seeking Pistol's life, Crazy Head and his family departed.

Everywhere were the sounds of breaking camp, the barking of dogs, the catching of horses. Within hours nothing remained. No lodge pole was left standing, no pony loose, no child unclaimed. In the midst of the cacophony of sound, Walking Bull presented Pistol with his best war pony.

"Oh, no," Pistol said. "You cannot do this."

"Oh, yes," Walking Bull replied. "Your generosity is sung in camp songs. In legends it will be told over camp fires. To my brother I must give as my brother has given. This is my best. The one I trust with my life. It is yours. I know he will protect you as he has me."

"Jesus, Walking Bull."

"What is this? Who is this Jesus you speak of?"

Pistol hesitated. "He's a guy who was great at giving. Like you."

"Ah," Walking Bull said. "Come. I will take you to your woman. She waits, as do your son and daughters. I think she will go with you."

"Listen, Walking Bull, is there any way out of this? After what I did she's not going to like me much. Not at all. This get together has no possibility of succeeding."

"No," he replied. "Not really. Her husband is dead." Walking Bull smiled at Pistol. "You won," he said. "It was the bargain. Not to mention that winter is coming and she needs a man. Someone to hunt. Someone to protect."

"Doesn't she have to agree to this? Don't I have to agree?"

Walking Bull turned and looked at Pistol. "What is there to agree to? The woman needs you. Not only will she be good for you, you will be good for her. And she probably likes eating. Most people do. I think she needs you. She might not know it but she does."

What are you talking about? Pistol wondered.

In those times that stretch men's souls, that stretched Pistol's more than he could imagine, he walked leading two horses; one, a really good war pony, and the other, a dun, a Spanish mustang who never quit and wasn't much to look at. He followed Walking Bull, waved when he was waved at, smiled when he was smiled at. He thought that he'd get through it. Somehow. After all what is difficult about greeting a woman whose husband you just killed, speaking civilly to children whose father you had just bled on the grass?

Oh no, he thought, *the woman . . . this woman . . . she'd probably been standing in the crowd watching. Lord.*

Pistol hoped she knew her husband's death had not been his intention. He wondered if she had any kids.

No, she was just married. What was he thinking? *She could still have children.*

Could things get any more complicated? Well, now she was just married again. Whose daughter was she? What will they say? These other people? And what about those kids? Walking Bull said that they weren't hers. Whoa, kill a man, inherit his son, his daughters, his wife. Who won this fight, indeed? I could just leave her. I don't have to do this. She isn't really my problem.

The lodge of He That Rides Boldly had been struck, the travois packed. There were six horses, and with his two, eight. All waited, standing on the soon to be deserted plain. Two horses to pull, the others for riding or for packing. Walking Bull's daughters were helping, finishing up, making ready for his departure even as he arrived with their father.

Walking Bull had not exaggerated. If anything, he had not told the whole truth. The woman of He That Rides Boldly was incredibly beautiful. Her raven hair was short after the custom of her mother's people. The black strands framed her face, accentuating her round eyes, her eyebrows, the curves of her face, her lips. She was taller than he expected; he guessed five foot seven inches, and more leg than torso. Her age--probably in her early to mid-twenties. There were no beads on her doeskin dress.

He thought Helen of Troy had nothing on her. It was difficult--no, impossible--to take his eyes from her. And he'd just killed her husband. *Lord, this is going to be difficult.*

Walking Bull seized his shoulders. "Until we meet again," he said, smiling. "Where will you go?"

"Deadman," he answered. "That's what Old Dog told me to do. So far he's been right."

"Good. I will see you there in the Spring. Have a good journey. Do not worry," he said with a smile, "her father does not know. Not yet."

Walking Bull laughed as he walked away following his daughters, his son walking with him. They left Pistol standing alone with eight horses, a young woman, and three kids. Pistol thought that to his departing friends he was now a very wealthy man. He wondered who her father was and decided that he really did not want to know right then. His plate already was too full.

What do I say?

CHAPTER NINE

In the silence left by the departure of Walking Bull's family, Pistol stared at the young woman, at the three kids, at the horses, then back at the woman. After five months of practice he managed to say hello in the language of her people. The words didn't sound right. He hoped they did, but they didn't. His greeting was met with stoic silence.

Finally, he said, "I'm called Pistol by those who know me."

"Peestal," the two girls repeated, their faces in a frown, their voices soft whispers. The woman and the boy did not respond; their faces held no expression.

"Yeah, well . . . I'm sorry. I hardly know what to say. My use of your language is weak but I'll do my best." He stared at the four.

"Where are we going?" The woman asked abruptly.

There was no fear in her. She seemed all business. It was a quality that he couldn't help but admire. Fearless. He didn't feel fearless just then. If he could have bolted and run, he'd have done so. He kept thinking how he didn't need this and wondered where the yellow dog was.

"I'm headed for Deadman," he said. "Do you know this place? It is some distance. It is where I live when I'm not living somewhere else.

"Listen," he said, "This is not easy. I do not force you to come with me. This must be your choice and not mine. I am sorry for what just happened. Truly, I did not mean it to happen. I wish it hadn't."

She nodded. "I was born there," she said, "in the place called Deadman, in the month of blossoms, on Cherry Creek. It is the place of my grandfathers and their fathers. Where the dead live in peace."

Geez, he thought. *I do live in a graveyard.* He found himself relaxing, breathing in and out, waiting for all hell to break loose. It didn't.

What are we talking about here? Surely she doesn't want to go to Deadman with me? Not after what I did. Not with me!

"You know the place then. Do you . . . what are you called?" he asked trying to be pleasant, not sure that he was being successful.

Why did I ask her for her name? I already know it. I am such an idiot. Ok. Let's think. Let's get a handle on this situation. She is just a young woman. They are just kids. But they have no one. They are alone. Now what do I do? You can't just leave them alone . . . with no one to protect them. What would happen?

Pistol paused, thinking. He looked around. Everyone was gone. *What have I gotten myself into?* The wind picked up. He looked at the young woman, trying to find answers when there were no answers to be found.

"Chokecherry Blossom," she said.

It seemed one word to him and it was a beautiful word. "Chokecherry Blossom," he repeated. "That is what Walking Bull told me."

"Why did you ask if you knew?"

"Good question. I'm not sure I know the answer. I didn't know what else to say. Please, forgive me. This morning I didn't wake up thinking I was going to be married and be responsible for a wife and three children. I didn't think I was going to get in a knife fight. I am new at this."

He paused, thinking they should get started.

Started? Well what else am I going to do? Staying here can't be too good. We got to get out of the open.

"Let's not burn any more daylight. We can talk later." The words rolled slowly off his tongue as he tried to formulate them in another language. "If you are coming with me, we should begin the journey." *Yes, I really mean that! What else am I going to do?*

She stared at him.

How inane I must sound. "We best be making tracks," he said. "How do you say it? Moving across the grass. The sun is not long for the sky."

She shook her head as if she was trying not to laugh at him. Instead an amused smile faintly appeared on her lips and just as quickly disappeared.

Pistol had the idle thought that she didn't look like a grieving widow but he put it out of his head. Her grieving wasn't his business. It was something he might help her through, if he could, but how would he do that? He was the cause of her sorrow. Besides, he was still trying to get through his brother's passing and not doing a real good job of it himself. She was staring at him.

"What is the boy's name?" he asked thinking he'd change the subject.

Her response was immediate. "He is called Scolds the Bear. This one, she is called Gazes at Stars. The young one is Chaser of Rabbits."

Pistol looked at the boy and his sisters wondering what it would take to put smiles on their lips, wondering if it were even possible.

They traveled eight miles the first day. Cherry Blossom seemed to know where they were going so he rode the dun wide of their passage, scouting both sides. Sometimes he caught up with the procession. Twice he waited for them to catch up with him.

He repeated the task even when it wasn't necessary. It was difficult to be near their imagined grief. It reminded him painfully of the sergeant standing in front of his mother, ramrod straight at full attention.

"The King's Lancer will not be coming home," he said. "The King sends his regrets, his gratitude. Your husband was a true hero."

When all was said the words were hollow, meaningless. They certainly didn't mean anything to him. What did "Your Lancer isn't coming home" mean? Who are you to tell us that? Get off our doorstep! That's what he thought, though he didn't dare say it in front of his weeping mother.

The officer handed his mother some medals, a letter of commendation, some buttons from his father's tunic, his father's tobacco pouch and twenty-three shillings owed him on the day of his death.

Pistol could only imagine how the two girls and the boy felt, but he knew how he had felt long ago. And it was he who killed their father. It wasn't someone called a Cossack in some foreign land he'd never heard of, for some reason he couldn't fathom. No matter how he tried he couldn't help the strong feeling that nothing was in balance, that things were way out of kilter, that there was nothing he could do.

They made Sage Creek the second day. Cherry Blossom wanted to stop, to stay on Sage Creek.

"Why is this?" he asked her. "Why should we stop here?" He was surprised that he understood what she said to him.

"We need to eat. We need meat. And this is a good place for this."

All right, he thought. *I'll see what I can pull out of the brush.* Pistol didn't leave immediately. He stayed long enough to overhear her speaking to the smallest girl.

"Take only a few berries, no dried meat. We do not have much. There will not be any until your grandfather gets here," she said. "Do not fret, little one. Your grandfather will be here soon."

He wondered how it could be that late in the year and her parfleches not full, even overflowing, with dried venison, dried chokecherries, buffalo, elk and moose.

The young woman, Cherry Blossom, was not as certain and confident as she appeared. She felt entirely unsure of herself and really unsure of the man who had dispatched her late husband in front of her very eyes. She had heard things, heard of his generosity. She knew of his friendship with Walking Bull. What was that all about?

Now she had seen him in battle, heard him plead with her husband, saw him meet his advances, spill his blood on the grass with hardly any effort. She had seen it. It was just the throw of a knife. So very quickly everything had changed.

In the crisp late Autumn air she had more pressing things on her mind--more pressing than the death of her husband. Winter was coming. It was coming fast. All of her parfleches were empty, a deficiency due to her dead husband whose name was not to be mentioned. He had told her often not to worry. But she worried anyway. She could not help it. For weeks she had witnessed the signs of the beginning of winter. The time of snow was upon them, though it had not yet fallen at the lower elevations. Already the far away Medicine Mountain was white with snow that would stay. There was no possibility that they had enough food to last through the winter.

But her father was coming. She hoped he would be here soon. To complicate her life, she traveled with a white man and three children. Bad had turned to worse and Cherry Blossom was looking for solutions. The white man was more of a problem than anything else. Something had to be done and quickly.

She told herself he wasn't her concern; she was not married to him; no promises had been exchanged. Yes, he had killed her husband. By the throw of a knife she had been won and lost. She had heard the words of he that was not to be named. But those were his words, not hers. She had been there. Hundreds of the people had seen it, heard her dead husband's promises. Many had wished her well. Many thought her fortunate. What was she to do? Help was coming. But when would it arrive?

She considered the boy and the two girls of her late husband. Right then she did not like him very much. Stupid was not the only word that described him. She also remembered the words of her father when he had spoken to her of him and his marriage proposal. So easily had her father applied the words "young and foolish" to her. It was now very clear why.

I am in trouble, she thought. *Very bad trouble. It is my fault! I caused this.* Her heart of hearts had known it for months. Now there was not much time to solve her immediate, pressing problems. Something had to be done and quickly. She thought about this Pistol, thought about her father, thought about Pistol being a white man. And Deadman? She never intended to go there. But Sage Creek—soon her father would be there for that is where he wintered. She would simply wait until he arrived. After her father's arrival, she would take the son and daughters of her deceased husband to her mother's clan and hers: the Bad War Honors where the parfleches were full of buffalo and elk meat. Soon her father would return from the west side of the Big Horn. Soon, she hoped.

Something unexpected happened on Sage Creek.

In the morning, after their arrival, Cherry Blossom suggested to the white man that she needed meat, not expecting to get any. What did he truly know of the ways and needs of the people? But this man, Pistol, nodded, saddled his dun horse, and was gone. Just like that. Even his ugly yellow dog went with him.

In his absence Cherry Blossom stared out across the valley to the Big Horn imagining that her father was already on his way. She took comfort in that fact. He would be there soon, her problems solved.

In the evening, however, the white man brought back a four-point buck, three rabbits, and a sage hen. Cherry Blossom was surprised, even shocked to see him. Ironically, she was more surprised to see the rabbits and sage hen dressed out; this was truly odd. And there was so much meat. An immediate burden had been lifted from her heart. Literally, she did not know what to say.

"You look surprised," he said to her from his horse. "Is this not what you wanted?"

"It is what I wanted. I am surprised," she said, "because he that is not to be mentioned hunted much without success. You hunt for a half a day and have much success. How is this?"

"He that is not to be mentioned? Why is he not to be mentioned?" Pistol watched her.

His eyes made her feel uncomfortable. "My husband who is dead. I . . . he was not a great hunter. That is what I mean."

"Why don't you use his name?"

"It is not good," she said. "It brings bad luck, ill fortune. It must not be used. He is on his way to where he is going. We must not interrupt that journey by saying his name. Calling him back. He should not return. It is not good."

Pistol nodded, then dismounted from his dun horse and removed the rabbits from the saddle horn. He'd strung them together on a leather strap. In this condition he handed her the rabbits and the sage hen.

She could not help but smile. Relief washed over her again and again in waves. She had been so concerned, what with winter so close. *No, it was no longer close. It was here.* She paused, thinking she must build a fire and gather wood for there was fresh meat to roast. *To night we eat,* she thought.

When she returned, her arms full of wood, she saw that Pistol had hoisted the buck, hanging him from a cottonwood limb, preparing to skin it. Cherry Blossom's shock immobilized her. For a moment she was unable to move her jaw, to speak a word. She dropped the wood she carried, the remaining sticks falling from her hands, landing in a disheveled heap on the ground.

Not knowing how to think about this, she responded angrily. "What are you doing?"

Pistol turned to her voice, skinning knife in hand.

She stared at him, anger spilling out of her like water from a bucket.

"Why? Shouldn't I skin. . . ?" he asked. "Doesn't it need to be done?"

What a stupid question, she thought.

"This is my work," she said. "This is for me to do, not you." Emotion carried in her words, in her voice, by the way she was standing, hands on her hips, chin up, eyes flashing. "Who are you that you have no respect for what I am? For who I am?" Her vehemence surprised even her.

Without hesitation Pistol stepped away from the deer and sat down on a fallen log, staring at her. He stuck the skinning blade in the white trunk. "You're saying that skinning and cutting up this buck is only for a woman to do?"

"Yes. This is so. For all time this is so. It has always been this way. You insult me."

Did he think her incapable of being what she was, who she was? If she was not the skinner, who would she be? If she did not gather the firewood, cook, pack when it was time to move, bear children, then who was she? What was she? She grew more angry. And who was he, anyway? He had killed her husband and now was doing her husband's job better than her dead husband. In the fury of it she tried to sort out her feelings.

"Well, Chokecherry Blossom," he said, pausing, not a little amused. "I apologize to you for doing something that is for a woman to do. I guess. What you are saying is that I could sit on my haunches and watch you work. That would certainly be good for me. Is this what you wish me to do?"

Now she was apprehensive, looking for the trap. That is what she wanted but he was offering no resistance? She nodded, unsure of herself, fighting to hold her anger inside, to cherish it.

She said, "You hunt. It is for you to know where the buffalo walk, where the deer and elk eat. It is for you to keep us safe. To protect us from our enemies." Of these things she was sure. She knew who she was for she knew her job and she was good at it. Had not her mother taught her?

"All right," he said.

Cherry Blossom nearly choked.

He said, "Truly, I have much to do and you have much to do." Again he paused. "Cherry Blossom? If I help you a little when I have the time, if my work is done, then your work will be finished sooner. It will be easier for you. Is not this good?"

Cherry Blossom stood, reconsidering his words, suddenly even more uncertain. *What? What is he saying?*

"If you have no work we can sit beside the fire, eat, drink, tell stories, and laugh. You can teach me the language of your people. I need to know about this boy, these girls . . . what I should do. These are things I have never done before."

Cherry Blossom continued to stare at him. *I cannot live with you*, she thought. *Such would be impossible. There will be no "learning" here. Besides Father will not allow it. Certainly he will not approve. Most likely he will kill you. He barely approved of he that was not to be mentioned and the dead one offered him many horses and buffalo robes for me.*

Only after she had married him did she understand why she should not have and that her father had been right. *No. No, this is not happening.* For her it was Sage Creek and no farther. But like her father's grandfather's grandfather, the white warrior had brought meat into camp. If anything, he was a hunter. Her father would say that is the most important trait. After all, a woman could overlook many things with a full belly. Her dead husband had been just plain lazy.

Her father had known. He had told her. He knew that the man was more show, no substance. "There are other men with less who would be better." That is what he had said, but she had not listened.

I will listen now, she thought. *But this one? This white man?* In front of hundreds he had stolen her from her husband, killed him and then taken her by force, taken his son, his daughters. *Well, that was not entirely true.* There on the high plains of Pryor her people had abandoned her to him. It happened so fast. It was so unexpected. It was not how it was supposed to happen. He who was not to be mentioned had been a warrior, strong, quick, aggressive.

107

A defender. He should have won. *What had gone wrong? Something.*

One moment she was the young wife of a true warrior, a lazy warrior who sometimes drank too much. *No, he was bad. Really bad.* His laziness and his drinking hurt her and hurt the family. It turned him ugly, so ugly that he often beat her. He had forced her to do unspeakable things, hidden things. Already she had planned on leaving him. Now he was dead. *I do not need this*, she thought.

What is wrong with me? I stand on Sage Creek with much meat at my feet. No. No. I will not. Will not what? I am getting out of here. It is here and no farther. That is what. This white man . . . he will go. He will not stay. Probably he will go get drink. Like he that is not to be mentioned. And when he does? I will disappear. I will wait for my father. That is what will happen. Father will be here soon.

Indeed, just as she thought, on the third day Pistol left her alone with the children. But she was cautious. *He may look like he is hunting but this is not to be believed. He watches me from a hidden place. From where? And why?*

That evening he returned. For the second time she was surprised; so surprised she could hardly speak. At her feet he dropped two male deer carcasses. It was more meat than she had seen in weeks. It was meat she needed to dry for winter, meat she desperately needed. It was the difference between surviving the winter or not.

On the fourth day, to her continued incalculable amazement, her "new temporary husband" brought her yet more meat. This time it was two does.

He who was not to be mentioned had brought her new blankets, no meat. He had been so busy sitting around talking with his admirers and his friends that he had been too busy to hunt. He had been with other women. She expected him to be that way. He was who he was.

In the last two days she had acquired five deer carcasses, rabbits, and a sage hen. *Escape?* she thought. *Escape from what?*

In the evening, when the sun had turned the clouds hanging over the Pryor Mountains red clear to the mountains in the west, this man Pistol watched her cut up the meat he had brought her just as he said he would do. She worked, wanting to be angry at the hunter. But he was not letting her. His friends had said he would do good things. Her friends had told her he would--that her fortune had changed. Not once had she believed them. But then she had not been working on five deer carcasses.

Pistol looked straight at her. "It is important to me," he finally said, "that I spend time with you, that I learn things, things that I do not know. I believe we need to know each other if we are to live together."

What? His words immediately troubled her. It wasn't his awkward use of Apsaruke, neither the words nor the unfamiliar grammar. It was the meaning they conveyed.

"All right," he finally said when she said nothing. "Let's do it as you would have it done." He stopped talking, waiting for her to respond.

She could only stare at him.

"I am not sure," she finally said. It had been so quiet, the silence so heavy, she had to say something. "I am not sure. Maybe your way is better than the ways of my people." *What am I saying?*

Pistol nodded. "Shall we give it a try? I could help you."

Who was this man? This white man who brought elk to the old people, who defeated her dead husband in the skills of warriors? Her dead husband had truly been a great warrior, a fearless man, and yet, so easily defeated by a white man. Perhaps this one was just lucky.

"But . . ." *But. But what?* "All right," she finally said.

Immediately, he began helping her, cutting the thin strips of meat for drying. The cautious Cherry Blossom watched for the trick, the trap that wasn't sprung. They skinned and quartered the two does, he telling her of his day hunting. He told her of the two black, almost grown cubs stuck up in a short juniper tree falling out of the tree on their heads watching him. He told her of the buck he let go, of a creek full of chokecherry trees and currant bushes. He shared his observations: how the black birds suddenly had flown away, and that it might be a long, cold winter.

She couldn't help but laugh at his antics, his stories, and his poor use of language. Unwittingly, she began to relax. In the quiet she helped him speak. She told him stories of her people: her mother, and of her father, Grey Elk. He seemed to pull these words out of her. She spoke of what was important to her, to her father.

Cherry Blossom cooked. They ate rabbit and fresh venison. The bellies of the young ones were full as they slept in their blankets. After they finished eating, he took his horse, as if to leave. It was dark; the sun was a long time gone.

"Where is it you go?" she asked.

"To have a look around," he said. "To see if we are safe. To see if there is anyone who might cause trouble."

Immediately she thought this is a lie. She imagined he had some restless feeling that he could not explain so he said these words. In his absence she sat, stared into the fire, and waited. But he did not return. Finally she retired to her blankets and robes, apprehensive. Sleep overcame her worries.

At first light she found him asleep beside her. A loaded pistol lay on his chest, a rifle at his side. When he awoke she told him of their need for more meat for the winter, why it was important, and that their parfleches were empty. He nodded and left camp.

That day he brought her two bucks and another rabbit. That evening she went to bed tired and sore, especially her wrists and fingers. They were sore from cutting meat to dry, sore from making racks to dry meat. As before, the man left in the evening. She drifted to sleep no longer in fear of him. She didn't even bother wondering where he was.

In the morning she found him lying next to her, sleeping, breathing deeply. The same loaded pistol lay on his chest; his Winchester rifle was still within reach. Even in sleep there was a readiness about him, something deadly.

She did not wake him. She had work enough to do, pleased that he hunted. It was the first time in months and months that she had more meat than she could immediately accommodate.

She prepared the drying racks and laid the thin strips of meat across them. In the Autumn sun she thought about her father. Even now he was making his way from the Bull Elk. He should be fording the river. Soon he would be here. What would she tell him of this unsuspecting white man? What should she tell him?

CHAPTER TEN

Scolds the Bear's father had spoken brutally of the white man, had called him an old woman, and worse: a coward, a liar, a thief. His friends had said, no, no, he was not an old woman. Did he not live in the Lodge of Walking Bull? Had he not provided a bull elk for the ancient one, Old Dog? These are things he did not need to do. No one had asked him. Yet had he not cared for the widows? The old? Those without?

No, his friends said. Pistol was not an old toothless woman. His friends had seen him stand up to Scolds the Bear's father, never flinching. And he had not desired the fight. And he said so, yet he fought fiercely, having no fear. His father was truly a great warrior, not taken lightly. No one doubted his bravery, his courage. Yet his father was dead, killed on the playing fields in front of all of his friends.

Scolds the Bear was not sure what he should feel or do. He picked up the spear his father had made him and walked toward the waters of Sage Creek thinking he might kill a grey rabbit. In the cold water he saw a large rainbow trout darting through the waters. Hiding under a shelf of rock, it moved silently in the shadows. A fish that big would be good. Scolds the Bear hefted the spear and threw it at the trout, missing him. He scrambled to retrieve the spear as it floated on the current and thought again about the man called Pistol.

After reaching Sage Creek he had asked Pistol why he killed his father. Pistol had said, "I didn't feel like dying that day. Your father sought my life." Pistol had looked at him, speaking slowly. "Your father was not a bad man," he said. "He was just wrong. Wrong one time. He was unlucky."

Then Pistol told him, "Do not dishonor your father by thinking ill of him. He was a brave man, a man of the people. He was your father: a strong warrior who sought good things for the Apsaruke. Do no dishonor to him. Speak only good things of him."

It was strange the things he said. He had killed his father in battle yet he did not speak ill of him. That was many days ago and Scolds the Bear had not made up his mind.

"Do you wish to know how to throw the spear?"

Scolds the Bear whirled around, turning to the voice, and found Pistol standing behind him watching. The boy was embarrassed. The white man had walked right up behind him.

"There is a right way," Pistol said. "There are many wrong ways. Do you wish to know the right way?"

What was he to say to that? Of course he wanted to do it right. He replied, "I wish to do it correctly after the manner of my father."

"I cannot teach you to throw a spear as your father did. I do not know how he did it. But I can teach you after the manner of my father."

"Was your father a warrior?"

"Yes, he was. My father served in the army."

"Is he living?"

"No. He is not."

"He was a warrior?"

"Yes. He was a Lancer in the King's Calvary. He carried a spear in battle. He died fighting."

113

"Did he die bravely?"

"Yes. Like your father."

"Like my father?"

"Yes."

Scolds the Bear looked up at the tall, thin man, Pistol, and thought about it. "All right," he said. "Teach me what your father taught you."

And that morning Pistol taught him how to step into his throw, how to bring his hand and wrist over the top, how to hold the lance, how to release it. Then he practiced with him. Pistol told Scolds the Bear that this was how his father had taught him, how he had practiced with his father and his brother.

When the sun was at its zenith, he stopped speaking of spears. "Practice this every day," he said. "Practice so that your mind and your muscles will not forget. Tomorrow we will do this again, just as my father did with me and with my brother."

Pistol turned from him to go to the lodge. Scolds the Bear knew he was going to join his mother. He had done so yesterday and the day before. Several times Pistol went with her and his sisters to pick goose berries on the banks of Upper Sage Creek. What a strange warrior, this man.

"Scolds the Bear," Pistol turned to face the boy, speaking to him, his voice smooth and easy. "When you fish with a spear, aim just below the fish. Not right at him, not above him. Just below him. You'll catch him if you do this. Just a trick you should know. And boy, if you don't like chasing your spear through the water, tie a string to it. Tie one end to your wrist, the other to the spear."

Having said this, Pistol turned away. Now he was going to talk with the boy's mother about words, and birds, and how to speak. Scolds the Bear thought this man liked being with her.

In the afternoon his sisters, Gazes at Stars and Chaser of Rabbits, hurried to tell him news. They told him that Hunter for Old Men, for that is what they called Pistol, was going to teach them and Scolds the Bear how to throw a knife and a spear. Also, how to throw a man down, step on his throat, and put an end to him.

"What did Mother say?" he asked.

"She told him that this was not something for girls to learn. That it was his job to protect, to slay the enemy who would harm us. It was not a job for women.

"He said that was true. He said that if he was not where we needed him to be, if he were hunting, that we needed to be able to defend ourselves against those that would harm us. He does not want any son or daughter of his unable to defend themselves in battle. That is what he said. He said his father taught his sister to defend herself against all who would harm her."

"What did Mother say?" Scolds the Bear asked.

Gazer at Stars looked at her brother and smiled. "Mother looked at him like he was crazy, like he had lost his mind. We did not know what she would do.

"Finally she agreed that he must teach us all that we might not be harmed, that we may be fierce in battle. She told us of her older sister being taken from the lodge of her husband by Lakota raiders and how Grandfather has looked for her everywhere. She said no one knows where she is or if she is alive and that Grandfather mourns for her always.

"She said that her new husband must teach us the ways of the warrior that our lodge might be strong against our enemies. Mother said that you never know what is needed. That is what she said. I do not know what she meant."

115

Gazer at Stars was excited. Scolds the Bear could see it in her eyes, in the way she danced about, and in the pitch of her voice.

"He said he would teach us," she said. "Hunter for Old Men said he would start tomorrow. So tomorrow we start."

Chaser of Rabbits pulled at Gazes at Stars' arm. "Come," she said, "we must do our work so we will be ready." Both were off and running toward the lodge to gather wood to burn for roasting fresh venison. They ran to find Hunter for Old Men to watch over them as they worked.

CHAPTER ELEVEN

After they moved from Sage Creek, they camped on the head of Dryhead Creek above the buffalo run. They waited for the venison to dry in the late autumn sun. It was there Cherry Blossom realized her mind was changing. This man continually surprised her.

One evening after they had been on the creek for over a week, he questioned her.

"What is the custom of your people on men? On women?" he asked. "On marriage? On wives and husbands?"

The question did not surprise her for he had not taken her to his blankets as she had thought he would. He hadn't even tried. She looked at him a long time without answering him, the firelight flickering off her face. This was a conversation she had never had with he that was not to be named--not even before their wedding ceremony. They had never discussed the arrangement before they were a couple living with his dead wife's children on Buffalo Creek with the people of the Greasy in The Mouth clan.

"Is this a hard question?" he asked when she did not answer immediately.

"No. It is not hard. It has many answers. Before I was married to he who is not to be mentioned, he paid a large dowry to my father: fifteen horses, many skins of the elk and buffalo. It was considered a large price--a price given because of who I am. I had sixteen summers then."

"Wow."

She looked at him, no longer afraid. "What is this 'wow'?" she asked.

"It means I am very impressed. It is about admiration."

"This is good?"

"Yes. This is a good thing. I am impressed at the bridal price. Now that I know a little about you though I'd say he who is not to be named didn't pay enough."

She smiled. "There are those," she said "from other tribes, other men, who wanted me. I could be stolen if my husband is not strong in protection. My older sister . . . this happened to her. She is gone. She just disappeared. He who is not to be named always stayed where many people lived for protection. Not like my father. My father lives where he wants. Men live in fear of him."

Pistol nodded.

"Like you," she observed. "You seem to fear nothing. My father is like that." She paused, thinking. "I could leave you. You know this? I could return to the lodge of my mother and her people, the Bad War Honors Clan. This has been done. I could do it."

He responded, "You could. Yes, you could do this. If this is what you want, you should."

That brought another question to her mind. "Would you follow after me?" she asked. "To take me back?"

The question seemed to surprise him. "No," he said. "I would not follow you. Leaving me is something you can do. You have a right to do this. If you live with me it must be because you want to. My father said it was his duty to keep my mother happy, to keep her smiling. If not, he was a bad husband. Truly he'd be a man without honor, without pride."

"I have never heard of this. Is this the way of your people?"

"No. I'm sure that everyone is different but it is the way of my father. His way is mine. My father taught me that there is no other way."

"You are a strange man."

"And you are a beautiful woman," he said, looking at her.

She studied his eyes, enjoying his appreciative gaze. For a moment she stared beyond him at the diminishing horizon, watching the east Pryor slip into the evening shadows.

After a few moments she asked, "Will you beat me when you are drunk?"

"No," he said. "I do not drink. Listen, Cherry Blossom. You are like the butterfly. I can only keep you if you want me to. Each day, every day, I must make your life good so that at the end of the day your butterfly wings will carry you back to me. Because you want to be with me."

"These are beautiful words. I have not heard them before."

Embarrassed, he grinned. "And I haven't said them before, not in your language or mine."

"I am a butterfly?"

"Yes, you are that."

"Your butterfly?"

"I would like you to be."

"I will stay with you."

The conversation was never brought up again. And that is what he called her when they were alone--Butterfly in the language of her people--she being of the Bad War Honors Clan of the Apsaruke Indians. She never again thought of leaving him, not even when her father looked at her as if she had lost her mind.

It was two weeks after the games on the Pryor Flats. They had moved the lodge on upper Dry Head Creek. The evenings were cold and getting more so. Pistol suggested that they should move to Deadman before the snow fell and stayed on the ground. She was preparing for the move when her father found her. Pistol and Scolds the Bear were hunting. The girls were in the way, learning how to help. She had looked up from her task and discovered her father and Long Nose sitting on their horses, staring down at her. He looked at her as only her father could. He was not pleased.

Later he walked with her along the waters of Dry Head Creek, the girls following, walking in tall brown grass, giggling to themselves.

"How could you do this?" he questioned her. "He is a white man."

"I have a feeling for him, Father. He makes me smile. I want to make him smile." She glanced at her disbelieving father. "Father," she said, "do not hurt him. He is my man. I want him for my man."

She paused, looking again at her father knowing he was not convinced. "It is coming winter. Did you see our parfleches? They are full of deer meat, dried chokecherries, and currant berries. He did this because I asked him to. In my lodge there are many blankets, the robes of buffalo, and doeskin for dresses. It is warm in his lodge." She paused trying to think of something that would impress him. "Father, all of his enemies are dead. Who among our people can say that? Please do not hurt him, Father. I know you can," she said. "Please do not. I need this."

Her father looked at her a long time, so long that it made her uncomfortable. She worried at what he might be thinking and grew anxious. Finally he nodded.

"I heard he killed he who is not to be named with a knife, by throwing it?"

She nodded. "He is a friend of Walking Bull--like a brother, I think. Not after the ways of the people but as between men. They talk like brothers. Father, he fed the old people, leaving much meat at the door of their lodges. He fed the widows, the sick, and the children without fathers.

"He defeated he who is not to be named at the games and killed him with a knife, making no effort. Before he did this thing, he asked him to stop, to not fight with him. He told him he did not have to die. He complimented him for his bravery. He that is not to be named scoffed at him, called him an old woman, a coward. He should not have done that, Father. It was not true. He is like you, Father. He fears nothing. And like you, all of his enemies . . . they are dead."

Pistol continually surprised her. Each day it was something different. Once he asked her how Scolds the Bear got his name. She told him about the name, told him that when Scolds the Bear was very young he was with his mother gathering wood for the cooking fires. He had found a small brown bear in an aspen tree and tried to convince the bear to come down from the tree and play with him. The bear would not so he scolded him and scolded him, throwing rocks at him for being afraid. The bear just climbed higher and higher and Scolds the Bear became angrier and angrier. She told him it was fortunate that Scolds the Bear was discovered by his mother before the bear's mother found her baby. His mother gave him that name afterwards.

Her new husband was a strange man, not at all like he that was not to be named. On more than one evening she found him sitting on a boulder above the creek

121

listening to the killdeer. He always moved over to make room for her to sit with him.

The first time she joined him she asked, "You have been married before me? With another who loved you? Have you sons and daughters with her? Does she live? Is she far away?"

He looked at her. "No," he told her, "you are the first. I have no sons, no daughters. Not until now. It is something I am learning. It is–how do you say it?– difficult."

She put her hand on his shoulder for a moment waiting for him. He kissed her, touching her cheek with his fingers, her lips with his. It was a kiss she remembered when she had forgotten all others.

"You have done this before?" she asked, touching her lips with her fingers.

He nodded.

"You are good at this," she said.

He smiled.

"We should do this more," she whispered.

And they did. Much more.

Sometimes she joined him as the sun was setting over the Pryor. Violent reds and pinks would cover the skies where the summer thunder heads had gathered and drifted, colors reflecting off the canyon walls of the Big Canyon and along the Bull Elk Ridge. They sat holding each other. It was then that she realized why the Great Father had made sunsets and why it was that her husband watched them. And why she joined him.

Sometimes when he returned late at night from wherever he rode Walking Bull's war pony, she would snuggle up close to him, smelling the scent of sage and juniper in his clothing. She felt safe: safe that he was home with her, safe that his rifle and knife were close at hand, and that his pistol rested under the pillow she made for his head.

She slept well. There was no worry in her. Her new husband knew how to use these weapons. All of his enemies were dead. Men respected him, considered him a warrior not to be trifled with. Cherry Blossom considered these things and slept well knowing that this strange white man loved her more than all the flowers he brought her.

CHAPTER TWELVE

They lived on Cherry Creek in the place called Deadman, so named because it was a place where the bones of the dead rest. Weeks after her father and Long Nose had visited Cherry Blossom, Pistol sat on a log watching the boy and his sisters throw one rock after another into the creek. He observed the boy at play, a gold coin swinging from the leather string around his neck.

"Scolds the Bear," Pistol called. The boy turned to Pistol with a quizzical expression on his face. "What's that you have around your neck?"

"Something."

"Something? What? Where did you get it?"

"Thistles gave it to me."

"Thistles? Who is that?"

"My father. He who is not to be named. I have given him a different name because the true name of the dead is not mentioned. It is not safe."

Pistol nodded, "Yes, this has been explained to me. May I see it? The something you have around your neck."

Hesitating, the boy removed the coin from his neck where it had dangled on a buffalo hide string. He looked at Pistol before handing it to him, dropping it reluctantly into his outstretched hand.

Pistol smiled at him, then studied the coin, rubbing it on his trousers before examining it in the sunlight. As he performed the examination, he glanced at the boy.

"Worry not, my boy," he said. "I will give it back." And having said that he promptly handed it back least its owner doubt him. "Where did . . . where did Thistles get it?"

"I do not know."

"You looked like you didn't figure on gettin' it back."

"I thought maybe you would keep it. Thistles told me that white men are blinded by yellow metal. They kill for it. It drives them crazy. He said I should never show this to a white man or he would kill me for it."

Pistol laughed out loud, ruffling the boy's thick black hair. "He's probably right. Some men do go crazy when they smell gold. They certainly do crazy, stupid, things-- things they shouldn't do. They believe gold gives them power. They think it is important. They don't know, boy, that power comes from who you are and what you do."

"What is important?" Scolds the Bear asked, looking up at him, squinting into the sunlight.

Pistol laughed again. "Boy, I think you are important. I think your sisters are important. I really think your mother is important. I like a good horse and plenty to eat and a warm place to sleep. I like a good story. Does that tell you who I am? My father thought my brother and I were important. He gave my brother a coin like that one. My brother treasured it because my father gave it to him. Like you do because Thistles gave you a similar gift."

"Do you think this one belonged to your brother?" The boy's voice was slow, full of apprehension.

Pistol shook his head no. "I don't think so but I don't know," he said. "I don't even know if Thistles knew my brother. Do you? Did Thistles ever tell you where he got the coin? Wait, you said you don't know. I already asked you that question."

The boy answered the question anyway. "No," he said. "Thistles was gone a long time raiding against our enemies, the Teton Lakota. When he came back he had ten new horses and he had coins of the yellow metal. He gave me this one. He had one for each of my sisters and one for my mother, the one who birthed me. Not my mother today. She was not with us then. But she has one too. He gave it to her."

Pistol glanced at the girls playing, running up and down the creek. The boy had replaced the cord around his neck and played with the coin, rubbing it between his fingers.

"Where did your father get his?" the boy asked. "Maybe it was from the same place." He looked at him, the sun no longer in his eyes.

"No," Pistol said. "It wouldn't be from the same place. My father never lived in this land. He lived in a place called England which is many days, many moons, and several winters beyond where the sun rises. It is across a large ocean. This coin is made of Spanish gold. See the markings? That's how the Spanish people made a thing called money. I don't know how Thistles came across it but that coin is a long way from its home."

Sitting on a flat rock, Pistol stared up at the ridges and spires of the East Pryor.

"The place where my father lived is more than ten thousand miles from here. If you were to start walking today, you wouldn't get there for more than two winters. It's a long, long walk."

"That is really far."

"Yes, it is. That coin you dangle around your neck has great value to the people who made it. You could purchase many buffalo skins and many horses with it.

Thistles is right, Scolds the Bear. Men will kill for it. I agree with what your father said. I would show it to no one if I were you. It would not be safe."

"I will not."

"Good. In answer to your question, that coin is not my brother's. He only had one. Your father had four or five, maybe more."

"This is good?"

"Yes, it means that Thistles probably did not kill my brother. That is good for me to know."

"Is your brother dead?"

"He is. His bones are buried a little ways from here."

"What do you now call him?"

"Call him?"

"The new name now that he is dead?"

"Bob, I guess."

"Who killed Bob I Guess? Was it a warrior? Like Thistles?"

"I don't know. No one does. When his body was found, he was already dead for many days. So no one knows."

"Someone does," the boy said. "Someone always knows."

Sitting in the warm fall sunshine, they were joined by Cherry Blossom. Pistol moved over to make a place for her. Gazes at Stars and Chaser of Rabbits were again throwing rocks into the rushing water. It seemed they were trying to fill up Cherry Creek one rock at a time.

Scolds the Bear sat fiddling with the gold coin. "Did your brother, Bob I Guess, like gold also?" the boy asked.

"I don't know. He kept the one piece my father gave him around his neck like you. The old man, Old Dog, said he died for the yellow metal. Somebody must have liked it."

"You have a brother?" Cherry Blossom asked, surprised. "There are more than one of you?"

"I do. I was looking at Scolds the Bear's coin. My brother had one like it. I told him about it. I asked Scolds the Bear where he got his."

Cherry Blossom glanced at the boy absently playing with the coin around his neck. "Everyone has one of those," she said. "The girls have one. I have one. My father has one. He who must not be named gave them to everyone. They are pretty if you rub them."

"Pretty, huh?" Pistol smiled to himself.

"You are laughing at me?"

"No. I am just thinking how my father, my brother, even my mother, thought the coin so valuable."

"Valuable? You are just saying it? A piece of metal cannot be eaten. It does not keep me warm in the winter when the snow is deep and the winds blow cold. It does not burn. Horses are valuable. So are buffalo robes and meat drying in the sun and wood for camp fires. Babies are important. These things are valuable. They have meaning."

Pistol nodded. "Clearly, my little butterfly," he said, "they were mistaken. Among the People Apsaruke these coins have no value or little value. Not compared to a horse to ride, meat to fill the belly, or a blanket to wrap around your shoulders when the cold wind blows."

"Yes, clearly. It is so," she said. "Clearly."

CHAPTER THIRTEEN

Pistol began the training of his new son by taking Scolds the Bear hunting. They hunted the elk, the buffalo, and the deer. He taught him how it was done: where they were to be found, and how they were to be killed. He taught him to read tracks and how to wait patiently. As he explained it, if Scolds the Bear knew where to wait the animal would come to him.

These are the things Scolds the Bear told his mother, Cherry Blossom, when she asked him. These things made her feel good. They were good things to know in the land of the Apsaruke. Pistol was learning, also. He was learning how to be a father.

Pistol asked Cherry Blossom about Chaser of Rabbits, about her name and the songs she sang to herself over and over again. She told him that as a very small girl, living in her mother's lodge, she found a nest of small grey rabbits in the juniper trees above Buffalo Creek. They were small, as was she. Gleefully she chased them. But she was too slow to catch the hopping bunnies. She laughed in the warm sunshine as her mother watched, keeping her safe. The songs she learned from her grandmother as she held her in her lap wrapped in a buffalo robe in the cold of winter. The girl sang them over and over again wherever she happened to be, whatever she happened to be doing. She always had a song in her heart and on her lips.

As a gift for Chaser of Rabbits, Pistol had taken the skin of grey rabbits and made her a doll with white bone eyes and rabbit feet. Chaser of Rabbits carried it with her everywhere she ran, singing her grandmother's songs, carrying a smile on her lips. She watched for Pistol to return, a surprise hidden in his pockets--one for her and for her sister.

He asked Cherry Blossom about Gazer at Stars. She told him that when the girl was a baby, she had kept her mother awake on hot summer nights. When she did not sleep her mother hung her cradle board outside where she could see the starlit sky overhead. The baby would gaze at the firmament overhead, the mass of shining stars that lit the sky. She would coo the baby sounds of happiness for hours while her mother slept. Thus, her mother named her Gazer at Stars.

Pistol traded her father a horse, three uncured buffalo hides, and two elk hides for two cured, tanned doeskins. Both were soft and pliant. Cherry Blossom wasn't so sure it was a good deal. But Pistol had something special in mind. He gave the doeskins to Cherry Blossom and asked her to make the girl a dress after the manner of her mother's people and to decorate it with beads in the pattern of the stars of the summer night sky.

The girl took the dress off only to bathe.

When the weather was good Pistol taught the children the manner of the spear and the blade--how to throw each. Afterwards he watched them as they practiced. After the snow fell into the cottonwood trees along Cherry Creek, burying the brown leaves beneath the drifts, he did other things. Everything in its time and in its place, he said. Always they practiced. He made games for practice and rewards for success. Always they were told how beautiful they were to him, how they warmed his heart, how he wished for their happiness.

Cherry Blossom watched and listened.

The lodge of Pistol was wondrous to Cherry Blossom. Inside the log house cool water ran into the spring box, never filling up and always fresh. The cooking stove was warm and held the heat. It kept the log cabin warm against the winter winds that ran down the canyon. She was glad when spring came and the snow melted. Cherry Creek became a roaring torrent of snow water. It was then that Pistol opened the shutters inside and out, raised the glass windows, and the fresh breeze of Spring spilled into the log cabin.

CHAPTER FOURTEEN

Robert John Kern was not an evil man. Albeit he did like being alone, 'alone' didn't make him evil. He liked building things--constructing something that had never been seen before. On Deadman he was caught up in devising a system for running water into the house and out so that it ran all of the time. If he had wanted, he could have kept live trout inside; fresh fish swimming around in his "trout box." He could have eaten them fresh every day. He didn't do that, but he could have. Certainly he thought of it.

There were other things he thought about building when he had nothing more important to do and had the luxury to sit and think. Sometimes he thought about his brother, Josiah. Everyone except his mother called him Joe. Robert John Kern revisited his past from time to time and spent a few moments in that long ago when he was called Bobby and had an older brother to look up to.

As a nine-year-old he beat the hell out of a kid named Eddy. Sometimes he wondered if everyone had an Eddy. The need arose when he was eight, at a time when Eddy was big, tough, and uncontrollable. Joe assured him many times that he could beat Eddy. It didn't matter that Eddy was bigger or older or had a reputation. It was true. Bobby's Eddy was two and a half years older, six inches taller, and fifteen pounds heavier. In fact, he was just plain big and fat, but Joe said it didn't matter. He showed

Bobby what to do and made him practice doing it. At the time Bobby thought that everyone ought to have an older brother in their lives.

In practice he never really hit Joe but they worked out the moves and repeated each again and again until Joe was tired. Being tired didn't mean practice was over–it was too important to get Eddy. Nine years old and life for Bobby was all about getting Eddy. When he was eight, Eddy had hit him when he wasn't looking: knocked him down, kicked him, hurting his arm, and his ribs. For days afterward, he could hardly breathe. He remembered Eddy. Eddy was all he ever seemed to think about.

Bobby practiced beating Eddy with his fingers wrapped around a small iron rod, making his fists hard as steel. He practiced blocking Eddy's first thrown fist, blocking it away from his body, not too far, just enough to make him miss. And then he practiced stepping inside Eddy's punch, throwing all he had at Eddy's face, chin and stomach. It was a move that belonged to Bobby.

It happened just as Joe had said it would. Initially he'd been afraid because Eddy was bigger, older, and more terrifying. He shouldn't have been afraid; he was prepared. Joe said he didn't need to be afraid, just patient. After fighting Eddy he wasn't afraid again. Joe had been right. Older brothers are always right. Everyone knows that.

"Block that first thrown fist and it will be a right," Joe said. "Because Eddy is a righty. Block and step inside and punch just like we practiced."

When the time came Bobby swung, not with his meager arm muscles but with his whole body, with all of his leg muscles. He turned his torso into Eddy, throwing his right fist, iron rod and all. He pulled himself tightly around, driving with his legs right into the very end of

Eddy's chest bone. It had been so, so very sweet. Just like he imagined it would be.

Swinging once, twice, he came up hard and compact. He followed with an upper cut, a smash to the lips and teeth, and a left fist to the exposed temple. Eddy landed on the ground and Bobby kicked him, swinging his hard leather shoes into the exposed ribs again and again. Joe had to pull him off. Eddy couldn't run. He was down, cradling his stomach, his mouth bleeding all over his shirt. Revenge tasted good. That's when he knew he could do anything, anything at all. That's when he knew that Joe would back him no matter what. Joe was his hero, his brother. Bobby was nine.

Eddy's father came to the house that evening. That surprised Bobby and Joe, too. Thank God his father had been home. Most of the time his father was away. His mom wouldn't have known what to do or say. His father had listened to Eddy's father. He looked at Eddy, his face all puffy, his front teeth loosened or broken, hardly able to breathe because of his sore ribs. Father immediately turned to Joe.

"What the hell did you do to this boy?"

Joe had backed away from their father. "No, Papa," he said. "It wasn't me. I didn't do anything to Eddy. It was Bobby, Papa. I just watched. I didn't do nothing except tell him to stop."

Bobby could tell that Joe was proud of him. It was the way he held himself, how he talked, the sideward glance.

Then his father had turned his gaze on Bobby: six inches shorter and fifteen pounds lighter than Eddy; little Bobby who never caused anyone trouble. His father shook his head and looked at Eddy's dad.

"Come on, Frederick. Look at Bobby. How could he ever beat your boy, even on a good day? Eddy's twice his size. And older."

Eddy's dad turned to Eddy. "Who did this to you?" he demanded.

Eddy pointed at Bobby. It was so good. It was so fine. He'd never felt better. It didn't matter what his father did to him after that. He'd beaten Eddy. Just like Joe said. Surprisingly, his father did nothing to him. That was even better. Sometimes Bobby Kern thought about that day, wondering what ever happened to Eddy, Frederick's boy.

Other times he thought about Jane Culver and wondered what ever happened to her. He remembered her lips on his for the first time, her arms wrapped around his head, pulling him to her. He thought about her often: sometimes when he was alone, sometimes when he saw a girl that looked like Jane. It was easy for Bobby to think of her.

He also liked to think about the Spanish gold coin that hung around his neck: cool against his chest in winter, cold in the summer heat. It was heavy, solid, something his father directed him to save for a rainy day. It was hard to imagine when it would rain that hard. But he thought about it sometimes when he had nothing to do

There were times he removed it from his neck. If, for example, he were working with wood or iron. Sometimes it dangled in his way. Then he'd remove it, hanging it on a nail to make working easier. In its absence his whole body felt out of kilter. In those times it was as if an arm, a leg, or even his heart was missing. It became hard to breathe, hard to think, until it was safe again dangling from his neck.

It was late Spring when he returned to Deadman. He'd left Montana three years before on a river boat heading down river. He'd left after he'd killed a man, leaving his body in the chair in the house he'd built at Deadman on Cherry Creek. He'd left because he'd never done that before. He'd never taken a man's life. The stranger meant to kill him, to take his gold coin, and steal his horse. It was Eddy all over again and Bobby wasn't going to let that happen. There would be no more Eddys in his life. Not if he had anything to say about it.

Bobby Kern shot the man while he sat in Bobby's chair, putting a small round hole in his forehead. Funny. It had been a misfire. The hammer had landed on the cartridge and nothing happened. The man started laughing, pulling his pistol to kill Kern and then the shot discharged a millisecond later. The delay might have been caused by a slow burn; he didn't know. But it had fired. Mentally, he could still see the dead man through the fog of burned powder smoke, round hole and all. Robert had taken the gold coin back.

Afterwards he closed the shutters, the windows, and the doors and saddled his horse. He left the dead thief sitting in his chair and rode to the trading post on Alkali Creek to catch the last boat leaving Coulson. He ended up in New Orleans a month later. That was a long time ago. He'd returned in the late spring four or five months ago. Maybe it was June. He wasn't sure. It didn't matter.

On this day he sat on a stump outside of the Coulson Trading Post on Alkali Creek in the warm sun and watched a paddle wheeler tied up to a wharf. People, steamer trunks, and assorted cargo--wooden boxes containing who knew what-- disembarked from it.

"Did you see what that buck gave me?"

Robert John Kern's mind was elsewhere as he leaned back against the hitching rail, watching the Yellowstone river running deep, making the turn, disappearing around the bend. The Yellowstone was a big river with the Spring melt. This late in the year it wasn't as big, not as far across. Soon the cold would be here. At the higher elevations the aspens were already turning yellow. He hardly noticed Escalante speaking to him.

He turned to look at the trader. The man nursed a tin can partially full of corn whisky poured straight from a baked clay jar that he kept behind the counter.

"What?" he asked. "Sorry. What did you say?"

"I said did you see what that buck gave me? Take a look."

Kern stared at a gold Spanish coin sitting as pretty as you please in the calloused palm of Escalante's hand. His heart stopped. He grabbed for the chain around his neck, pulling it out from beneath his shirt, coin and all so he could see it. Making sure. No, it wasn't his.

"You have one, too," Escalante stated.

It seemed like a question to Kern but he did not reply. Instead he stared at Escalante, then at the coin in his hand.

"You fool," he whispered. "Do you know what that is? Spanish gold, that's what. My father gave me this one years ago. In London." Kern paused, thinking. "And now the same thing shows up in Montana Territory. What are the odds of that?"

"Nothin' to nothin'," the trader said, fingering his gold coin.

Kern's mind rushed forward. "Did that Indian have any more? Is that the only one?" he asked.

"Don't know."

"Where did he go?"

"Up Alkali Creek. Left when the paddle wheeler came tootin' in. All that racket scared him."

"Do you know him? Would you recognize him if you saw him again?"

"His name? In Crow his name is He That Rides Boldly. Or somethin' that sounds like that. I've seen him several times, comes in once in a while. Brings fur mostly. Buffalo hide. In the Spring, that's when I see him. He's kind of owlly. Ain't into trust. Don't say much. Likes corn liquor. I gave him some blankets and a gourd full of nature's best. He was happy. So was I."

"You speak that language? Crow?"

The trader looked at Bobby. "A little," he said. "Right handy when it comes to tradin'."

"What do you think that coin weighs?"

Escalante tossed the coin in the air and caught it. Then did it again. "Three or four, maybe five ounces," he answered. Both men stared at each other.

"What'd you give for it?"

"Five blankets. Some tobacco. Some corn liquor."

"You could have filled five freight wagons and still gotten the better deal."

Escalante stared at the coin in the palm of his hand, rubbing it between his fingers. "Lord," he said, "I ain't never seen Spanish gold before."

"Now you have. It's sitting in your hand. It's pure. And you didn't have to work for it." Kern spoke slowly, a plan evolving. "We just have to steal whatever he has. From an Indian—that's not even a crime. I wonder if he has anymore. Do you think he does? If he has, we steal it. Steal what he's got."

Kern sat on the stump thinking, no longer leaning against the cedar hitching post. He said, "It's so odd. I didn't think the Spanish got this far north."

The Mexican smiled, "It is out of their way."

"It doesn't make sense. The Conquistadors never ever got this far north."

138

"Somebody did."

"Yes. Somebody did."

"Come to think of it. I saw one of those Crow youngins. He was wearin' a metal helmet for a hat. Never thought about it at the time. Maybe it was a Cheyenne or Arapaho. No. No. It was one of them Crow. Must have been a month ago."

"A metal helmet?"

"Yeah. One of them old-fashioned ones." Escalante paused, staring at Kern. "Say, you don't suppose . . . ?"

"You are right. I don't suppose. But it is worth looking into. Old Conquistador helmets and Spanish gold don't just grow on apple trees. Nor do they up and fall from the clear blue sky. They came from somewhere. And it sounds like that Crow Indian has the answers. What's his name? He That Rides Boldly?"

Escalante slipped the coin in his pant's pocket. "I'd say it is worth lookin' into myself. But the two of us ain't enough. White folks tend to disappear in Indian Country. Permanent. And they ain't never heard of again. I ain't too excited about that."

Kern was thinking aloud. "You're right," he said. "But at the same time the more men we involve the less we get. We don't know if there's any gold to be had. Not yet."

"You sayin' just the two of us?" Escalante hesitated. "There's all sorts of stupid. And that . . . "

"No. We certainly can't do it alone. Obviously we'll need a tracker. We'll need enough men to get respect. Especially if it comes to a shooting. If we don't get respect, we'll be dead. No question there. We'll need you to do the talking. That's three. How many more you think?"

"I'd say five or six."

"So two more, maybe three?"

"Two more."

"Have anybody in mind?"

Escalante rubbed his chin thoughtfully. "There's that trapper, used to be a trapper, J. C. Casper. He tracks. He's pretty savvy. There's that Brown fellow from over in that Red Lodge country. Got himself a rep with a six shooter. Don't know much about him. Ex-army."

"Can they be trusted?"

"As much as the next man."

"How do we meet them?" Robert John Kern looked at Escalante. "I say we meet them, then decide if we like them. Sound good to you?"

"It does," Escalante said. "Casper is camped down on the river. We could see him now. There's sort of a settlement down there."

"All right. Afterwards we can take a ride up river, take the ferry across and ride over to Red Lodge. We can see what this Brown is about. What his interest might be. You good with that?"

"I'm good with it."

"Let's go slow. A mistake could get us killed."

"I'd say we ain't got all that much time. Winter's comin'. Up on the high ridges the aspens are turnin' yellow."

All this talk, Kern thought, *and I'm still nervous. Go slow*, he told himself again. *Go slow. But Escalante's right. This was going to be a short trip.*

J. C. Casper turned out to be a Southerner, a slow talker who drank his coffee, clearly suspicious of the rather indirect chatter that was being exchanged.

"Show him," Kern said.

Escalante eyed Kern, hesitating, then pulled the coin from his pocket and flipped it to Casper. Casper caught it midair. For a moment Casper examined it, turning it in his fingers, rubbing it on his sleeve, biting it, then examining it again. "Gold," he said tossing it back to Escalante. "Spanish gold. Five ounces of Spanish gold."

"Seen it before?" Kern asked.

Casper nodded. "New Orleans in a card game. I lost. So what's the game here? I haven't caught the drift."

"Escalante was given that coin three hours ago by a Crow Indian. It is the same as mine except I got mine from my father twenty years ago on the Continent. The one I have is exactly the same as the one you just looked at."

"So?"

"Three, four weeks ago Escalante saw a Crow boy wearing a Conquistador helmet. Like those used by those fellows Coronado and Ponce De Leon."

"Coronado?"

"Yes."

"This far north?"

"Yes, we know. It's odd. But we're thinking the appearance of two relics, a helmet and a gold coin is just too convenient. We're thinking there may be more where that came from. You interested?"

"Why me?"

"We need a tracker. Someone good with sign. We're going to be riding into Indian country where white folks disappear. We'd like to be careful. Keep our hair."

"Who else you got?" Casper asked.

Kern responded. "So far the three of us, if you deal yourself in. We were thinking of Brown from up around Red Lodge."

"Ex-army Brown?"

Escalante nodded. "Ex-army," he repeated.

"All right," Casper said. "I'm in." He stood up, brushed the red clay from his cotton trousers and looked toward the river. "I have some men that you can talk to.

141

They might fit your bill. Stuart," he yelled, "you down there? Where the hell are you?"

Turning to Kern and Escalante, Casper said, "Wait here. I'll find this fellow. Back in a minute."

Kern nodded his head and watched Casper's back as he walked toward the river and the campfires and tents of the settlers that were currently residing there. Ten minutes later, maybe less, Casper returned with a young man trailing behind him.

As they approached he could hear Casper speaking to the young man. "Kid, I want you to see somethin' that might interest you. I want you to listen to these two men. Hear what they got to say."

Then to Kern and Escalante, he said, "You'll like this kid. I'm thinkin' we'll be needin' him before the week is over. His name is Stuart. He's good to ride the river with. Handy in a pinch. Mostly, I call him Kid. He answers to it. Tell him your story. We'll see if he's interested. Expect he will be. He ain't got nothin' to do besides fish, eat, sleep, and talk about goin' to Mexico."

Stuart listened without asking any questions, rubbing his hands together as if he were trying to keep them warm. There was no need. It wasn't cold but he rubbed them together anyway. After Escalante finished explaining to the kid the proposed venture, he showed him the coin without handing it to him. He waited for his response.

The kid was staring at the ground still rubbing his hands together. He looked up at Escalante, not reaching to take the coin from him, not saying anything.

"Kid, we're not waitin' for you to get your head around this." Casper stated bluntly, "You in, boy, or am I wastin' my time with you?"

"If you are, I am." The young man nodded, brushing the hair out of his eyes.

Kern noted that for once the kid was not rubbing his hands together. In watching the exchange Kern concluded the kid was far too young. He barely had any face hair. He was probably in his late teens, barely able to be outside without his mother, helpless without someone to tell him to come in out of the rain. He also noted the tied down navy pistol, the loop loosely hanging around the hammer. Whatever he was he was certainly dangerous, a loose cannon rolling around on the deck in a storm. This wasn't good. He also concluded that Casper was impatient, a "push, push, push" sort of man. He didn't like him much either.

The kid asked, "But, how long a trip you figurin', Jake? It's gettin' late. You know I'm thinkin' about ridin' south. Gettin' ourselves ready even now. Be gone by week's end. That's how we figure it."

"Not long, Kid. Short ride. See what we can see. A week, maybe ten days."

The kid nodded slowly. "All right. I'll ride with ya. Then I'm gone."

"Good," Casper said. "Listen, Kid, when I was down there lookin' for you I didn't see Adam. Is Adam hidin' down there somewheres? Was he with you?"

The kid nodded. "Him and me are ridin' south together."

"Go down there and find him would you? Send him over. I want these gents to explain this situation to him. See if he's interested."

"All right, Jake," Stuart said, rising to his feet. "I'll go find him for you."

After Stuart went looking for Adam, Casper turned to the two men sitting away from his campfire. "This next lad you're about to speak with, he's a little off to my way of thinkin', but he's dependable. More importantly, he can shoot the eyes out of a bat. No conscience. No hesitation.

Does what he's told. If you want to pass, I will understand. But he's one hell of an Indian fighter. Better than Brown 'cause he don't ask questions. I'm guessin' you won't be needin' no questions." Casper paused, "What do you think of the kid?"

"All right," Kern said, hesitating and glancing at Escalante, looking for an indication of what he was thinking, getting nothing but a passive stare. "First, let's talk to this Adam."

"Now, Gents, take my suggestion. Don't make your story complicated 'cause this fellow ain't complicated. Keep it simple or he won't be understandin' what you are talkin' about." Casper looked at Escalante as he spoke. "I'd just ask him if he wants to ride into Indian country to see if we could find some gold coin. Like the one you got in your pocket. I'd show it to him. That's what I'd do. So he can fix it in his mind."

Casper paused, looking from Kern to Escalante, "What do you think of the kid?" he asked for the second time.

Escalante nodded his head. "He don't seem too bright hisself. Like he ain't playin' with a full deck, you know what I mean? You had to ask him twice. His mind is on Mexico and drinkin' mescal. I'm not sure we can use him."

Kern found himself agreeing.

"I know," Casper said, "but he does what he's told. I have no trouble with him. I'd like him to come along, if you don't mind." Casper was looking at Escalante, then Kern. "I'd like you to reconsider."

Escalante looked back at Casper. "Well, I suppose," he said. "What do you think, Bob? Do you mind? Have anythin' against that Kid hombre?"

Kern was staring at Casper. "Only if you be responsible for him. I think he's a loose cannon. He's liable to do anything. Somebody has to be watching him always."

"Good," Casper said. A look of relief crossed his otherwise stoic face.

Kern couldn't help but wonder why.

Kern watched as the next man wandered up from the river, taking his time. The closer he got the younger he seemed. He had a boyish face, and a lean, wiry build. Kern guessed he was seventeen, maybe eighteen at the most. *So young. What good would he be?* he thought.

"Jake," the young man said when he arrived, nodding at Casper. "How you doin'?"

"Good, Adam. These fellows got somethin' to show you." Casper looked at Escalante.

Escalante pulled the coin from his pocket and held it in his hand so Adam could see it glinting in the sun.

"That gold, Jake?"

"Sure is, Adam."

"A Crow Indian gave it to me this mornin'," said Escalante.

"Really? Does he have more?"

Casper took over what was a short conversation. "That's what we were wonderin' Adam. We were fixin' to take a look."

"You mean Indian Country?"

"Yes."

"Army won't be likin' that none."

"We weren't fixin' to tell them."

"There could be some shootin'. Army won't like that."

"Yes."

"I'd like to go, too, Jake. I'd like that fine."

"You'll be needin' a horse."

"You got my horse, Jake. I'm meanin' to talk to you 'bout him. I'll be needin' to borrow him. Me and the Kid are fixin' to ride south."

"You ride with us, I'll give him to you. Though don't you be gettin' into any more card games, you hear? I don't want you to be losin' him again."

"Thanks, Jake. No card games. No, sir." Adam stood up looking down at Jake Casper. "When we leavin'?"

"Give me a few minutes. I'll be roundin' up that horse."

"All right, Jake. I'll be waitin' yonder." He nodded at Escalante and left them sitting in the shade of a cottonwood.

Casper glanced at Escalante. "Good enough for you? He's hell on wheels when it comes to shootin'. Just not too bright."

Escalante nodded his assent. "That'll make five," he said.

"Good," Casper said. "When do you want to leave?" he asked Escalante. "I expect the trail is gettin' cold."

"Tomorrow too late? Waitin' make any difference?" Escalante asked.

"Yes," Casper replied. "Tomorrow will make a difference. Every minute makes a difference. The longer we are here the more people talk. We don't want people knowin' our business. Nobody needs to get all stirred up and start to thinkin'. Best be movin' right away if we possibly can. Now would keep the trail we're followin' fresh and we'd be out of mind. Besides it's gettin' chilly. Soon turn cold. I see this as a short trip. It may be too late already."

Kern felt what control he had quickly slipping away. He glanced at Escalante then back at Casper. "Whenever you are ready," he said.

"Sooner the better," Casper answered.

The cavalcade left the Coulson Trading Post riding up Alkali Creek a little after one in the afternoon. Casper led off with Escalante bringing up the rear. A mile up the creek Casper picked up the trail of He That Rides Boldly. He rigidly insisted that everyone ride behind him, that no one bastardize the trail before he had a look at it. The man's eyes studied the ground, reading the message written in the dirt. No one bothered him or interrupted his thoughts.

Behind Jake Casper rode the kid Stuart. Kern was not sure he'd heard his first name or that it mattered. The kid was trailing close to Casper. Too close, in Kern's opinion. The kid clearly saw Casper as his boss, the leader of this expedition. Already there were too many cooks paddling around in the soup. Kern did not want a boss. He did not need directions or to have someone tell him what to do. He told himself that he could leave anytime-- that he didn't have to put up with any bullshit. Now might be a good time, he thought, before he was too deep in the mud of indecision.

He glanced at Adam, wondering about his last name, what he was about. There were just too many unknowns. Removing his hat he wiped his brow and glanced at the glaring sun, thinking there was no room for error and all sorts of possibility for it. Kern noted that Adam paid little attention to Stuart or Casper, that his attention, too, was on the trail. From the beginning he'd been watching both sides, looking, listening, aware, riding straight up in the saddle. Kern appreciated Adam's continual attention to detail. There was more to Adam than met the eye.

For the better part of two hours Kern had become increasingly wary and edgy. The trail deserved more scrutiny. He knew it. Certainly he did not want to get himself killed and he wasn't sure Casper and Stuart had that same concern over his well-being. He was certain they were not giving the present environment as much attention as it deserved. Kern dropped back, letting the distance lengthen between Casper and himself. He rode noting the rising countryside, the stands of pine and aspen, the horse's foot falls, the song of the meadowlark and rancor of the magpie. Nothing seemed out of order but it was. Again he told himself that now was indeed a good time to get himself out. Just leave.

Escalante caught up with Kern, pulling his Appaloosa gelding beside him, a nervous horse that Kern didn't trust. He broke the silence with the very questions that plagued Kern. "What're you thinkin'? Everythin' all right?"

The question sounded like something Kern's mother would ask his father. His father? *Damn that man.* He always showed up in his head at the most inopportune times. Now was one of those times, a time when Kern wasn't sure of himself nor of the people with whom he was riding.

"I don't know," Kern said. "If I understand your question it is whether we helped ourselves taking on these three. I'm not high on trust right now. I don't know who or what I'm trusting."

"Take it easy, compadre. We're kind of stuck with them. Let it play out. As my padre used to say . . . Now is the time to watch the corn grow, not dig up the seeds we planted." Escalante laughed. "My padre, he was always full of frijoles."

"I don't know, Escalante. We're stuck with them that's true enough. We'll wait and see. But don't expect me to wait long for the corn to grow ears worth eating."

Escalante nodded. "I hear ya."

Evening came too soon, lingering, a dim musty red that painted land and sky. In the growing darkness they continued riding upcountry, slowly eating into another three hours until there was no hint of a setting sun and the trail difficult to see. The mountain was closer, rising above them on the south. Snow was high up on the westerly slopes, the last sunlight of the day bathing it in diminishing shades of reds and pinks until there was no more.

Tired and antsy, they stopped. While the others dismounted, Kern sat his horse watching the last light disappear over the Yellowstone. Except for the night birds it was quiet. Maybe too quiet. He forced himself to listen. To his left he was conscious of Casper removing the saddle from his horse, reins dragging on the ground and of Stuart starting a fire. Fire? Kern sprang from his horse, sprinting toward Stuart. In a heartbeat he stamped out the flames, pushing Stuart to the side.

"Idiot! No fire," he whispered, his voice strained. "No fire. Hear me?"

Stuart, surprised, was caught off balance. He came up swinging, swearing at Kern. Kern avoided him by stepping back, causing Stuart's swing to miss.

How stupid can you get? Kern thought. *This kid needs a lot of learning. If he doesn't get everyone killed first.*

"Kid!" Casper said. Stuart stopped mid-stride, trying to recover his balance. "Knock it off. Kern's right. No fire."

"The sonofabitch pushed me," Stuart hissed. "What're we gonna do for coffee? How we gonna eat?"

"Kern wants to have his hair tomorrow sunup, kid. We all do. No fire. No smoke. You'll live without coffee. Drink water. Suck on some jerked meat. We ain't livin' in your granny's kitchen. Be careful. Our lives depend on it."

"But--"

"No buts. Understand me? No fire. No smoke. No coffee. No nothin'. Get it?"

Stuart nodded, staring at Casper, then Kern. Finally, tight lipped, the kid moved off, taking his horse with him. A few minutes later he came back without him. Kern stood feeding his bay a hand full of oats. He looked at Stuart and shook his head again in amazement.

"What's wrong with you?" Stuart challenged.

"If you don't want to be walking," Kern said, "you'd better not picket your horse out there in the trees. You'd be smart to keep him closer to hand." He paused, waiting for some kind of response, then continued. "Suit yourself, kid, but keep your voice down. Even the dead can hear you. Tomorrow when that horse is gone you'll be walking. Mark my words."

"Who the hell do you think you are?" Stuart stared at Kern angrily.

"You know who I am, boy. If I had my way, I'd put a bullet in your head right now. You are hell bent on getting us killed. You're not thinking. Come to think of it, killing you would be a waste of powder and lead."

"What?" Stuart was ready for a fight, striding straight for Kern.

"Stuart!" Casper said ever so quietly, a brittle quality in his voice. "Keep your voice to a whisper. We do not want no Injun hearin' you. And go get your horse before he's stolen. Take no chances with our lives, understand?"

Stuart kept coming.

Casper stepped in front of Stuart, inches barely separating them. "No more bullshit, boy. If the wrong people find us, hear us, even think we're around, we're dead. Understand?" Casper paused. "I'll kill you myself, you get out of line again."

Stuart nodded, glanced at Kern and quickly stomped from camp to fetch his horse.

Casper looked at Kern then, and shaking his head. He said, "You might loosen the loop some. Cut him a little slack. I suspect we'll be needin' him before this is over. I'll keep an eye on him."

Kern nodded wordlessly and turned his attention to his horse. Leaving his own words of warning, he said, "Casper, you better keep more than an eye on that runt or we aren't going to see daylight tomorrow."

"I'll watch him."

"You'd better."

Three days later they ran into an encampment of Crow Indians. He That Rides Boldly had not left a straight trail nor had he attempted to hide it.

CHAPTER FIFTEEN

Four men handed the reins of their horses to Adam. Leaving their hats hanging on their saddle horns, their rifles in their scabbards, they crawled on their bellies to the edge of the ridge. A cold breeze blew down from the mountain rising nine thousand feet behind them, the top hidden in white fluffy clouds. The cries of snow birds, killdeer, and meadow lark were all that could be heard over the roar of wind shifting through pine needles. Peering at the scene below, each was silent in his thoughts. No one seemed to have anything to say.

"He's down there?" the kid asked, a sliver of incredulity tainting his voice. "Now what?"

The question was mostly rhetorical but Casper responded anyway. It was a question that deserved answering for what it didn't ask, what it didn't say, regardless of who asked it. "That's where the trail leads," he said.

Below them, moving down the Creek, stretching around the far low hill, was lodge after lodge after lodge. No one counted. Closer and on the flat below were a few ramshackle structures that made up a no-named community that hadn't existed long. Beyond was a large gathering of Crow, more than Casper had seen in any one place. Kern hadn't ever seen more than thirty in one place, counting women and children, and they'd been moving, a long line of travelers that stretched over a quarter-mile.

Escalante had seen a few more because of his employment as a trader at the Coulson Trading Post. He'd been around. Adam and Stuart were new. Both were inexperienced, young, and just passing through, going to some place that they hadn't thought of yet. Neither had seen twenty birthdays.

"Lord," Stuart said to no one in particular. "That's a passel of redskins. I sure as hell ain't goin' down there. We'd lose our hair and everything. There'd be no comin' back."

Escalante was thinking aloud. "I say we pull back and wait."

"Pull back? Where? How far? For how long?" Stuart asked, rattling off the questions as if they were bullets. "What for? I ain't tacklin' that bunch."

Escalante glanced at him as he lay on his belly, staring at the columns of smoke rising from campfires. "You got a better idea?" he asked. "We're just this close to askin' our boy a simple question. That red bastard with the answer is not a mile from here eatin' buffalo tongue and playin' games." Escalante shook his head, the frustration riding low in his voice. "I say we wait. This celebration can't last. Not enough game around here to keep that many eatin'. Not for long anyway. They'll all be leavin'. I'm guessin' soon. They'll be spreadin' out so they can find fresh meat. They'll have to—no choice."

Casper nodded and looked at the side of Stuart's face. "It's either that or quit. You for quittin', Stuart? Had a belly full? It's been three days."

"I'm in. I said I was. I'm just sayin' I gots a week or two and I'm headin' south. I ain't goin' through another cold spell like the last one. Damn near froze to death. In a few days I'm gone. Gold or no gold."

"A week or two?" Escalante pushed himself back from the edge of the ridge that looked down on the creek bottom. "That's enough time. In three or four days we'll ask the question we want answered." Escalante looked at Stuart, smiling, his eyes and his voice teasing him. "Think you can wait that long?"

"It's a little question," Casper said as he turned his gaze to Escalante. "But we got bigger problems. After this get together is over and we ride down there, which trail we followin'? This is where the trail ends for that Indian we're seekin'. I see five hundred, more, countin' dogs, horses, mules, the young. Add the old women and the old men, those walkin', and the stragglers that follow . . . " Casper stopped talking, hesitated, staring down at the gathering, noting the small figures standing in groups on the flat below the buildings.

"Kid," Casper finally said, "this right here might be the end of it. A week or two is more than enough. Escalante is right. Four days might be too many. You might be headin' south the day after tomorrow. No tellin'."

Stuart could feel the words poking at him and it didn't set well. "Well, come winter," he said, "I ain't settin' round here freezin' my ass when I could be drinkin' mescal in Sonora. Know what I mean? I ain't fixin' to be doin' that. I figure no gold is worth another cold winter in this hell hole."

Kern smiled as he studied the scene before him. He saw the end of his venture, thinking "ah, well, better luck next time." Already he'd written this experience off as 'too much,' 'too soon,' with 'too many.' He would be glad to get loose of this bunch. In the middle of the conversation, he'd bellied up on the other side of Stuart and continued to stare at the scene before them. Escalante and Casper had seen enough and had edged

154

their way back leaving Kern and Stuart side by side and alone.

An agitated Stuart turned his attention to Kern, seeing his smile. A reddish color stood out on his cheeks. No one was making fun of him, not at his expense. And no one was laughing at him. Quitter wasn't a label he cared for and that's what they meant. Was he going to be a quitter?

"What you gigglin' at, Laughin' Boy?" he said to Kern. "You findin' somethin' funny?" There was an edge to his voice that said he didn't plan on taking any more of anything from anyone, that if there was a pecking order, he was about to rearrange it in his favor.

Kern didn't appear to take offense. Truthfully, he was taken aback.

"No, kid," he said. "Nothing funny. Take it easy. Who put the burr under your saddle? I was just thinking about you and Mexico. That's where my brother was going last time I saw him. He thought he'd see Texas, then ride across the border into Mexico. I was just thinking about him drinking mescal in Sonora, his arm wrapped around a senorita. Having a good time."

Kern stared back at Stuart, holding his eyes with his. For a moment he said nothing, just stared. "Kid?" he said slowly, the British accent coloring every word. "You're plainly on the prod. You've been on the prod, looking for trouble since I jumped you a while back. I'll be telling you this once so you damn well better be listening. You ever speak to me that way again . . . I'll kill you. Do you understand?"

Behind them Adam and Escalante had mounted their horses. Casper stood twenty feet behind Kern and Stuart, listening. He said, "We'd better get off this ridge before someone sees us and takes objection, or you two roosters get us killed squabbling."

Kern stared at Stuart. "You hear me, boy?" His voice a whisper. "Your worthless life depends on it."

Stuart nodded and began backing away from the ridge line. Kern followed him, watching him closely. *One couldn't be too careful,* he thought, *not with this young skunk stinking up the place.* At the same time he was wondering where the sudden display anger had come from. He had said nothing to Stuart to warrant any reaction. Now he had.

The others waited while they mounted. Stuart, his face pinched, festering, deliberately looked in another direction as if something on the mountain had his attention, or he had an embarrassing thought he wasn't sharing. Each man was buried in his own thoughts as they retreated from the ridge, backtracking four miles. Kern kept to the rear, making sure that Stuart was in front of him.

In the midst of scrub oak, a stand of quaking aspen, and a few solitary pines, they found an opening to a short canyon. In the middle was a seep spring that bubbled out of the rocks before disappearing into granulated granite thirty feet below. Deciding it was a place to wait, they pulled the saddles from their horses, built no fire, boiled no coffee, roasted no meat. It was the driest of dry camps.

Kern had other thoughts on his mind as he waited for the shadowy darkness that hovered over the kid to work itself to the surface. He hoped it would come without gunfire but he wasn't counting on it. It was coming--of that he was certain. Youth seldom waits. It pesters, pushes, prods, tugs and pulls, and does so relentlessly. Stuart would erupt. The question was when? Kern decided not to wait for there was no controlling Stuart and too much danger in letting Stuart's emotions choose the time and place. So with Stuart standing by the remains of an old cottonwood, Kern drew and threw his heavy, balanced blade at the remains of a dead cottonwood tree, striking it less than a foot from Stuart's head. There was a loud, solid thunk and Stuart jerked around to stare at a throwing knife sunk three and a half inches into the trunk of a dead tree. There was no quiver to the steel.

It had his attention. Before Stuart could react, his thoughts were interrupted by a second thud, this time at his right ear. A second blade was buried deep in the white barkless tree trunk mere inches from his skull. Kern stood in front of him, staring at him. His face displaying a menacing scowl, he waited, a third blade in his right hand. The kid stood very still.

"Boy!" Kern said to him. "I want to know how deep your need to die runs." Stuart's pistol was holstered and tied down, hanging on his right thigh, the hammer thong empty. "I'm willing to bet, boy, that I can throw this blade and stick it in your blockhead before you can draw that pistol of yours and fire." Four sets of eyes were on the kid. They waited.

The kid hesitated. He blinked.

Kern watched youth being served pressed into action by two blades buried in a tree trunk. He hoped that the kid was not feeling lucky. His hope was not disappointed; the kid kept his hands held high around his shirt pocket where a packet containing fixings for a smoke bulged. Kern kept his eyes on Stuart knowing he was angry, young, and chancy but the time for action was gone. Stuart had felt the shadow of death.

In Stuart's hesitation, his resolve, if he had any, wilted. Kern relaxed his grip on the steel of the blade knowing the moment for Stuart to prove who he was had vanished . . . for now. In that instant Kern's place in the pecking order changed. He wasn't aware of what it had been. With the flick of a blade Robert John Kern announced he wasn't to be bothered either.

Half an hour later the Mexican spoke to Kern. "Lord!" he said. "Where did you learn that thing with the knife?"

"My father. He taught me," Kern replied. "My father was into killing. It was his job. He taught my brother and I that a knife is quicker than a pistol. No one expects it."

"That's a right handy skill. Is it quicker? Can a knife beat a pistol?"

"Sometimes," he answered. "Surprise does gives an edge. As I said, no one expects it." While he and the Mexican talked, Kern watched Stuart.

Change was inevitable. Nothing was static. Even after the kid had moved away from the dead tree, the third throwing blade remained light in his fingers. He thought he would have only one chance and he wanted to be ready. But the kid kept his arms high, his hands visible, his face averted. There would be no confrontation that day but Kern remained alert to the possibility. Joe had taught him that.

"It's handy all right," he said to Escalante. "My brother is better with a blade than me. He worked at it harder, longer; knew the tricks."

"There are tricks?"

Kern smiled. "There are tricks," he said. "The biggest trick is just hard work."

Casper checked the Crow encampment three times a day. As Escalante had expected, they didn't have to wait long. The rendevous broke up three days later.

On the fourth day the small cavalcade of five riders rode out of the canyon and followed the creek bottom, retracing their steps back to the ridge. When they arrived, the encampment was gone. All that was left were the fire circles and larger circles of stones that secured the lodge skins, keeping them from flapping in the wind and being carried away. The remaining grass was trampled. Along the mesa rim the ridge grass was cropped short. Drying bones, gnawed and discarded by the dogs, were strewn about. The creek bottom was stripped of dry wood.

The buildings were seemingly all deserted, except for an old, crippled, black dog that wandered up the dusty, dry street and the barflies that hung out at the "Lucky Chance" bar and saloon. The group dismounted in front, looking up and down the street.

"Adam," Jake Casper said, "stay with the horses. Be ready. Whatever you do, don't leave the horses. We might have to get out of here fast." They wrapped the reins around the cedar hitching rail. Kern and Casper handed their reins to Adam.

Adam nodded, pulled a six shooter from his belt and checked the loads. He posted himself on the first step, looking up and down the empty street as the others ventured inside. He kept the reins to his horse in hand as well.

To the man, the leather loops were off the hammers, their pistols loose in their holsters. Casper went in first, carrying his Winchester, his index finger resting on the trigger guard, rifle pointed at the floor. *Only dead men take chances.*

Inside they found a rotund Indian working in the center of the room clearing tables of bottles and empty glasses. He'd been talking to three men who stood watching him, their backs to the bar. A fifth man stood behind the counter, arms folded across his chest. When he saw the four white men, he moved closer to the bar, his hands out of sight.

With Jake Casper in front, Kern moved to his left. "Escalante," Casper said, "ask our friend here the

159

whereabouts of He That Rides Boldly. Kern. Watch the buck behind the bar." Stuart was slightly behind him on his left, his hand resting on the butt of his pistol.

Escalante looked at the fat Indian, two bottles in one hand, glasses in the other, and a wiping rag over his shoulder. He asked the large man if he knew He That Rides Boldly and if he knew where he was. He listened to the response, asking another question for clarification.

"He says that He That Rides Boldly is dead and cannot be named any longer nor brought back from his journey to the lodgings of the dead. He says a white man named Pistol killed him with a knife. Says it was interestin'. He'd never seen a fight like that because the white man was reluctant. He that cannot be named wouldn't back down so Pistol killed him. Threw a knife a good distance, stuck it in the throat. This man thinks it was lucky, a fluke. He says that he that cannot be named was plenty tough: a good warrior, counted plenty coup. Just not that day."

"Did you say by throwing a knife?" Kern asked, leaning forward to hear, keeping his eye on the fellow behind the bar. "Ask him if this fellow, Pistol, had a shotgun."

The fat man did not wait for Escalante to respond, setting the bottles and glasses on the closest table. "I see no shotgun," he said in English. "It is said he kept a big gun for rabbits, birds. I no see. Why you ask these things? What business is it of yours?" The bartender, his belly hanging over his belt, looked at Escalante and wiped his fingers on his buckskin shirt. "Why you here to speak to dead man?" he asked.

Escalante looked at Jake Casper. "He speaks English," he said. "Ask him your questions yourself."

Kern interrupted. "Where is he now? Where is this Pistol?"

The bartender looked at Kern. "I do not know. He has a new wife, a son and two daughters. He has gone away. Maybe he hunts. Maybe he's dead. Probably he's dead. A white man like that does not live long in our country."

"Sounds like my brother. He carried a shotgun. Show him the coin, Escalante." Kern stared at the fat man, saying, "Look at this coin. I want to know if you've seen it before."

Escalante showed the bartender the gold coin.

"Yes," the bartender replied to Kern. "The one who cannot be named had such coins. Are you seeking this?"

Escalante pressed forward. "Do you know where he got them?" he asked him.

The Crow Indian with a big belly, long hair and short, thick legs thought a moment. "No," he replied. "Only he that cannot be named knows this. Why are you asking these questions? What business is it of yours?"

Kern listened to the short answer and then asked, "Does anyone else know where the dead Indian got these coins? Maybe his sons? His daughters? His woman? Did he have these people?"

The bartender nodded. "He that cannot be named had a son and two daughters and a new wife. Now they belong to the Pistol. I not know yellow metal. Why you ask this? What business do you have?"

"First," Escalante asked, "what were they fightin' about? A woman, perhaps? Or did they fight over gold?"

"He that cannot be named not like white man much. He want kill him. White man kill him first."

"This white man? Did he take the dead man's family, his son and daughters, his wife?" Escalante asked. "Why?" he continued. "This does not make sense. Why did he do that? Was he lookin' for the yellow metal? These coins?"

"They his. It decided. If he not to be named won, he hang scalp of white man in lodge. All see it. If the Pistol won he to have lodge, horses, wife, son, and daughters." The bartender laughed, fingering the grip of the dragoon pistol stuck in his belt. "They belong to the Pistol. He won. Big surprise. White man won. He took gold coins, woman, everything." The fat man stopped and spoke in Crow to the men at the bar.

Following the conversation the rotund bartender was amused. As was the man behind the bar. As were the three men standing at the bar staring at Escalante. Casper watched. The bartender laughed again, his belly jiggling. "The Pistol not possible him win," he volunteered. "He dead no matter. If he not named not kill him, his wife kill him. Her brothers, her uncles kill him. Grey Elk not like white. I not like white. The Pistol is dead man, no matter." The bartender stared at Escalante. "You are the trader from Alkali Creek, at the place called Coulson? Yes?"

Escalante nodded. "If she killed him where would she go?" he asked.

"She go to her people. Maybe she take young ones to the lodges of their mother's people or the mother's lodge of one not named. Why you ask? I think you leave. You not belong here. Here gold is not business of white man trader."

Escalante did not pay him any attention. "Now, what?" Escalante asked Jake Casper. "Anythin' else you want to know?"

"Watch out!" Kern yelled.

The bartender had pulled the heavy dragoon from his belt and through squinty, angry eyes brought it to bear on the Mexican. Kern jerked his weapon, firing. Casper fired the round that he'd chambered in his Winchester. The Indian rushed his shot, the lead slug going wide of

Escalante's head. Seconds later, Adam rushed through the door, a pistol in each hand. The bartender was re-cocking the dragoon when the room erupted in gunfire. Casper and Kern dived for cover.

Stuart shot at the three men who had scattered from the bar. Two were slightly behind the bartender. The third ran, dived through a glassless window, busting board and shingle with his shoulders. Two slugs followed him out the hole. But he was lucky that morning and escaped untouched by Casper's singular intentions. The man behind the bar had a Henry rifle and he fired it without aiming, firing through the wood counter, then ramming another cartridge into the chamber. His first shot just missed the Mexican, throwing splinters. The second creased Stuart's stomach, running just under the skin and out his stomach wall, from one side to the other.

The dragoon exploded in a cloud of burnt powder, killing the bartender and wounding Casper as parts of metal tore into his left arm, chest, and scalp. Adam killed the two that had been standing at the bar. Or so he claimed. Later he and Stuart would argue as to who shot who, but in that fleeting second both fired repeatedly at the same targets. Those two went down, joining the bartender in the dust and spilt booze on the sawdust-covered floor. Neither was aware of Kern firing from the floor. Bob Kern never mentioned it. Suddenly the room was silent.

In the acrid smoke Kern jumped up and ran out through the door to see to the horses. Adam's bay was trotting down the street. Kern caught him by the reins, then checked himself to see if he'd been shot. There was no blood. Miraculously, he hadn't suffered so much as a flesh wound. It made him smile. His father had said a target on the ground was smaller, harder to hit. "Make yourself small. It'll keep you living longer."

Standing in the dusty, empty street, the morning sun beating down on his shoulders, he caught his breath. Adrenaline buzzed in his ears. His fingers tingled. His heart thumped heavily feeling like a blacksmith's hammer banging on hot steel, sparks flying with each thump. Kern stared at the front door of the "Lucky Chance Saloon," holding the reins to Adam's horse, and waited.

Inside, Casper got to his feet, blood running down his cheekbone onto his shirt, his chest and arm bleeding. He replaced the spent cartridges in his rifle, counted the bodies, and glanced at the kid bent over his belly. There were four dead, one behind the counter with the Henry in his limp fingers. Casper choked on the smoke and backed out through the front door, rifle in hand. Escalante followed, supporting the kid by the shoulders. Unscathed, Adam came last, a pistol in each hand. He'd already reloaded.

Casper caught his mount by the reins, dust boiling and curses flying around him. The bay turned into him as he tried to get a foot in the stirrup and pull himself into the saddle. Around they went, milling about in the dusty, rock rough street. Kern caught up the horse's reins and held the bay while Casper managed the flopping stirrup and drew himself into the saddle. He took the reins from Kern and turned down the street.

With Adam holding the reins in one hand and a naval colt in the other, Escalante and Kern assisted Stuart onto the saddle. The stomach wound produced prodigious pain in waves, almost more than he could bear. With Stuart bent over the saddle horn trying not to move and barely holding the reins, his horse started forward. He moaned like death had him by the throat, squeezing. Behind him, Adam waited for both Kern and Escalante to mount up; then they followed. Five riders left the "Lucky Chance Saloon" at a lope, riding toward the mountain, galloping past the crippled, black dog who ran down the street dodging the horses' flying hooves. Casper was in the lead in spite of his wounds. Adam brought up the rear, standing in the stirrups, holding Stuart on his mount with his left hand, mindful of the trail before him. Stuart's saddle already was soaked blood red.

Behind them they heard the repeated repercussions of a Henry being fired. No one was hit. No one stopped to return fire. Instead they kept riding, reaching the south ridge above and behind the flats before looking back. Miles later they pulled up and slowed to a trot, allowing their horses to catch their breaths. Kern and Escalante both studied their back trail, seeing no one. No one suggested stopping. The grim riders rode without comment.

CHAPTER SIXTEEN

Belly wounds are painful; worse than a vertebrae lying on a raw nerve pinching until hell won't have it. At least for a while it's that bad. No matter which muscle moves--an arm bending, a leg twitching--it ends in pain to the belly muscles. Some say a movement as small as folding a finger will send pain rippling through the belly. To the sufferer everything seems to be connected. There simply is no getting better quickly from a belly wound. If the pain doesn't diminish, it won't.

The Henry slug had grazed Stuart's stomach muscles, cutting a swath a quarter inch deep as it passed under the skin from one side to the other. The wound bled profusely where the slug entered and exited.

Stuart lay in his blankets hardly able to breathe, cursing his lungs because he couldn't stop breathing, cursing his body because it wouldn't let him. The wound was first cauterized by the hot lead of the bullet and further cauterized when Kern cleaned it. He broke open two cartridges, poured gun powder on the exit and entry wounds, and lit it up. The kid passed out, mercifully leaving this world for another.

Jake Casper was stoic about his wounds. He'd been shot before--wounded and left for dead on the battlefields of Gettysburg and Vicksburg and, seemingly, a thousand burgs in between. Somehow he'd survived. Unmoving, he stared at the sky above, watching a drifting cloud rise above and float through the saddle between the East and West Pryors. During the cloud time Kern worked on Casper's wounds. With his knife cleansed in hot flame, he pulled parts of the exploded dragoon pistol from Casper's chest wall, his arm, and six other places of which Casper wasn't even aware.

After Kern finished cutting, after whiskey had been poured into the open wounds, Casper's attention simply wandered off. He did not gain even a semblance of consciousness for three hours. In his dream he remembered wounds suffered at Gettysburg, at Vicksburg, and a small one at Shiloh. In his mind he saw the Army surgeon, the mole on his nose, the beads of sweat running off his forehead. He remembered the knife cutting, incredible pain, and no whiskey.

Somewhere in the night he awoke sweating profusely. First he became conscious of bright stars strung across a black Montana sky. In spite of the pain, he was thankful he was alive, holding himself very still against the pain. In the quiet he listened to Stuart's groans and asked Escalante to build him a smoke. When he finished smoking the first cigarette he asked for another and a swallow of whiskey. With the taste of whiskey still in his mouth and bitter, tart smoke in his lungs, he grew silent and without another sound simply waited for the morning.

It was two weeks before Stuart could sit in a saddle and endure the herky-jerky rolling gait of his five-year-old gelding. Pulling himself up into the saddle was something he couldn't do, not without assistance. The freshly scarred and torn stomach muscles wouldn't allow such foolhardy misconduct. The powder burns were healing but inside him was another world of pain. The wounds turned purple-red with no sign of infection. Progress? Maybe. But he still wasn't excited about moving. The pain, fresh and newly seared into his memory, was like nothing he had ever experienced or wanted to experience again.

Jake Casper wasn't as high maintenance as Stuart. His wounds were of a different sort, requiring different care. Early on he could move but with difficulty. In a couple of days he could get around. In five he could ride. Whiskey had killed any possible infection so he healed nicely. He'd done it all before.

They hid in a pine-infested draw on the side of a mountain. Options were limited. They were exposed and far too vulnerable. Having escaped undetected was a miracle and Casper knew it. Especially considering how they'd shot up the bar and left so many dead. Kern did not assuage the mood when he pointed out they'd left a witness: someone who knew who they were, what they looked like, the direction of their retreat. Fortunately their trail had been obliterated by a cloudburst, the blessed wind, and the passage of time. It also helped that there were few available men to follow them before their trail grew cold.

Two weeks and three days later Casper delivered them back to the Coulson Trading post. It was a place to heal, a place out of the winter winds. Instead of going to Mexico, Stuart holed up in a back room. He endured the winter, watching Escalante trade beads, blankets, and powder for buffalo skins. In December he saw the Crow kid wearing the tin soldier helmet like those of Cortez and Ponce De Leon. In January Escalante traded for two more gold coins. All four of his confederates came to look. No one was surprised to learn that each coin had passed through the fingers of He That Rides Boldly.

In the evening they sat around the pot bellied stove drinking coffee laced with Escalante's home squeezings, thinking. They'd nod to each other and smack their lips, jawing about He That Rides Boldly and the gold just beyond their reach, of the riches they hadn't found, theirs for the taking. It was easy to imagine the soft metal hanging in the deep corners of their pockets. *If only,* they thought. *If only.* Soon it would be Spring. Soon they'd try again and this time it would be different.

Stuart repeatedly cursed his sore belly, the cold winter, and the fact that he wasn't in a dusty cantina in Sonora drinking mescal, spending Spanish gold, with his arm around a lovely senorita. *Holy hell,* he said over and over again. *If it weren't for bad luck, I'd have no luck at all.* They all agreed, especially when they grew tired of his song.

CHAPTER SEVENTEEN

Spring was a time for planning and preparation, a time full of expectation, of relief from the cold wind and drifting snow. It was the ritual time of gathering. Walking Bull came with Crazy Head, his brothers, his uncle, and nephew to Dry Head Creek. He was met by Grey Elk's people who were wintering on Sage Creek and the bend of the west mountain. Soon, in the month elk dropped their calves, they would cross the Big Horn River below the narrows. There was a certain urgency because they needed to cross the river before the flood waters rose and turned the Horn into a raging torrent of melted snow water. Once on the east side of the river they would travel across Low Mountain and the canyon to the Bull Elk. There, since time out of mind, they spent their summers.

Cherry Blossom, Scolds the Bear, Gazes at Stars, and Chaser of Rabbits had already left Deadman. They traveled with Autumn Flower to meet Walking Bull and her mother. They camped on Dry Head Creek in the place Cherry Blossom's family had camped since before she could remember. They were accompanied by Long Nose, her uncles, and her three brothers. If they had wanted, they could have stayed on Cherry Creek and waited for the group to pass through Deadman on the way to the crossing, but Cherry Blossom wanted to be with her people. She was anxious to see her mother and her brothers. It was a time of great excitement.

As planned they would spend three weeks on Dry Head Creek followed by two weeks on Cherry Creek. Afterwards they would follow the old trail south to the crossing. They would ford the river above the narrows and sometimes below it, sometimes where the Stinking Waters joined those of the Big Horn. Cherry Blossom left Cherry Creek while her father and her man were hunting white tail against the rock towers of the East Pryor. Her father and her husband intended to spend a few days longer hunting, then meet them on Dry Head Creek. That was the plan. That was how it was supposed to work.

On Dry Head Creek, under the watchfulness of Long Nose, Walking Bull, and those men with Crazy Head, the women and girls gathered dry wood for the cook fires. In the morning they worked their way up the creek where it bends and turns south before making its way up into the pine forest of the East Pryor. Once their arms were full of dry wood, Cherry Blossom and the girls walked back to the encampment with firewood to unload and returned for more. Autumn Flower had returned to the gathering of lodges a few minutes before. Scolds the Bear was on the north bench watching the horses with the other boys. By the time Cherry Blossom's little group had reached their lodges to drop their wood the main group was a half mile away working around the bend in the creek. Soon they would have enough wood and return.

Her sister and Old Dog, a man of untold winters, were at the encampment. The old man could not travel far. Moving was very difficult for him; his eyesight dim; his teeth all but gone. In the mornings his joints were sore to the touch; too sore to bend or to stand until the sun warmed them. He was always hungry. Having no teeth, he ate little. He spoke day and night with the demons that surrounded him, muttering nonsensical words as he went about his business. No one knew what that business was. No one asked. It was best just to leave him alone.

Fully expecting to find her sister waiting for her, Cherry Blossom stopped to catch her breath. Her daughters followed behind her chattering about their heavy loads, about being finished with their chores, and what they would do next. The girls were so preoccupied they nearly ran into her. In front of the lodge the old one lay on his back speaking, talking to his imaginary friends in the language no one understood. His voice was neither loud nor soft, his words strung together like a juniper berry necklace, one word unrelated to another. Towering above the old man stood two men. Old Dog looked at no one; his eyes flitted about and seemed to see nothing but the deep blue sky above him. From the cool earth he lay waving his arms in a struggle with unseen ghosts.

Astonished, she stood frozen. Her first thought was run; her second, escape. Her reaction, however, was pure anger. Cherry Blossom turned and found herself and the girls blocked by another white man. The two men, wearing big hats, their eyes and most of their faces hidden beneath wide brims, were armed, their hands full of weapons and rifles. Cherry Blossom had nowhere to go. She was trapped.

"What's he sayin'?" Stuart demanded.

"Nothin'," Escalante answered. "He's not sayin' anythin' at all. His words make no sense. They ain't words. Just gibberish."

"Nothing?" Kern repeated.

"I know he's talkin'. But he's not sayin' anythin'. It's just gibberish."

Stuart turned from Escalante and spied Cherry Blossom, her arms full of dried juniper wood. "Well, what do we have here?" he said.

Escalante turned to see what had Stuart's attention. He saw Kern and Stuart both staring at a young woman accompanied by two little girls, their arms full of firewood. Sticks tumbled from the young woman's arms. Panic registered in the faces of the little girls who also dropped their loads of firewood, the sticks scattering at their feet.

"Ask her," Stuart said. "Ask her. Go ahead. See what she knows."

Escalante turned from the old man. He looked hard at the woman, feeling her eyes measuring him. It was his intention to nail her down with his stare but he found no fear in her, no cowering, no visible reaction to his attempt at intimidation. Escalante thought her easy to look at, enjoying the way she stood, how she held her head, the way her doeskin skirts hung on her body. He couldn't help but admire her, standing in front of the lodge, full of defiance. The two girls hiding behind her skirts were easier to read. He liked frantic fear. It was easier to work with.

"What do you want with the old man?" The woman asked him in Apsaruke. "Why do you mistreat the old one? A man with so many winters he cannot defend himself . . . even from the wind."

"I have no business with him," he said in reply.

"Why did you knock him to the ground? Out of fear? Perhaps you fear an old man that cannot lift a knife or pull a bow string. Because you had no business with him? My husband, he will kill you for this disrespectful thing you do."

"I want to know if you've seen one of these before." The man held a gold coin in his hand.

"You would attack an old man for a piece of worthless yellow metal? You are but an old woman with

173

no teeth. You shame yourself and the woman who bore you."

"Shut up. Mind your mouth. Tell me if you've seen one of these before?"

"Shut up? You tell me to shut up before the lodge of my husband? What have I to fear from an old woman with no teeth? From a shadow of a man who pushes feeble old men to the earth, who counts coup on the aged?" Cherry Blossom stepped back from the approaching man. The girls cowered behind her.

"Tell me," he said again, "have you seen one of these before?"

Cherry Blossom glanced down at the coin in the big man's hand and back into his black eyes. "It is a circle of yellow metal meant to warm the heart of a coward, a woman with--"

"No teeth," he said. "Yes, it is. Have you seen one like this one before?"

"I see white men in my husband's lodge attacking a woman, an old man and two girls. I will see the earth drink your blood."

"What is she saying?" Kern said, a pistol stuck in his waistband, his hand playing with the grip. Then, as an afterthought, he added, "We'd better not hang around here too long. We're going to have more trouble than we can handle. What's she saying, Mex?"

"She's sayin' we're a bunch of toothless old women, so weak we must count coup on old men and small girls. She's sayin' we're dead men. She promised me that her husband will kill us for pushin' the old fellow to the ground, for makin' war on children." Escalante chuckled. "She don't think much of us. She has not talked about the gold coin."

"Lord!" Stuart said. "She said all of that?"

Having interpreted the prior conversation, Escalante turned back to the Crow woman. "We ain't got much time," he said. "We'll leave when we find out what you know about this yellow metal."

"You lie. The truth is not in you."

"No. We'll leave soon as I find out what I want to know." He reassured her.

The Crow woman glanced at the metal. She said nothing.

"Look what I found." Everyone turned to the voice of another white man emerging from her husband's lodge. The new man glanced at Cherry Blossom, then at his companions.

The three men looked at what the man held in his hand.

"All right," Stuart said. "We found it."

"We got the right place," Kern announced. "Escalante, we need to know where these coins came from. There has to be more. Probably a lot more. Four in one place. Ask her."

The big man turned to her, speaking slowly. "I want to know where those coins came from. I want to know where you got them. I will make war on these two little girls, on you, and on the old man if you don't tell me what I want to know." He closed in on her using his size to scare her.

Cherry Blossom recognized it was hopeless. She wished for Long Nose and Crazy Head's return. She hoped they would soon realize she was gone, that she and the girls had not returned to gather more wood. She said, "He that is not to be mentioned had them." Immediately she regretted saying anything, wondering where her sister was, if she was dead or injured.

"Who is he that is not to be mentioned?" Escalante repeated her words.

"He who is not to be mentioned is dead. He cannot be mentioned."

"Is it He That Rides Boldly?"

Cherry Blossom nodded, waiting, surprised that the Mexican knew her deceased husband.

The big man glanced at Gazes at Stars as she hid behind the woman's skirts. "Have you seen one of these, child? Where did it come from?"

Without looking Cherry Blossom put her hand on Gazes at Stars' head to reassure her, pushing her behind her skirts. She noticed that the four white men were on all sides of her, closing in, making escape impossible.

"You frighten her," she said. "You intend to take our lives. So kill us. Cowards. Make your war on children and old men. It is such a brave thing you do. Kill us. Our death will be easy. Yours will not."

"I want to know where these coins come from."

She did not respond, holding onto her daughters with both hands as a sage hen protects her chicks from the hawk.

"Are you the woman of He That Rides Boldly?" Escalante asked.

"He is dead," she replied. "He has no need of a woman."

"Woman, you're tryin' not to answer my questions," he said and struck her across the face, knocking her to the ground. The girls began to cry, tears streaming down their faces. Cherry Blossom said nothing, wiping blood from her lips, glaring at the man who'd struck her.

Escalante knelt in front of her. "I want all of these coins," he said. "Where are they?"

"There are no more," she said, again regretting having answered him.

"Where did He That Rides Boldly get them?"

"I do not know," she answered, dabbing at her mouth. "No one does. Now leave. You do not belong here."

Escalante nodded, staring at her. She stiffened, expecting to be struck again. Without turning his head he said, "She says she don't know where he got the coins. I don't know if she knows or not. She really ain't talkin'. She refuses to answer my questions."

CHAPTER EIGHTEEN

"We got choices here," Kern said. "We better be quick in deciding."

"What choices?" Stuart asked.

Kern thought before speaking. "Well," he said, "we can take the four coins we have and call it good." He paused as if lost in thought. "Or we can take the coins and take these people and hope to find the rest, or at least some more. Maybe this woman and those kids know where he hid the rest. Where he got them. Maybe they don't. We'll have his woman, his kids. He's dead so I don't know how much good they are. We do have four coins. Certainly not as much as we hoped we'd find." Kern turned and looked at the other three men. "If more gold exists, it has to be close. That's my feeling."

"Yeah," Escalante said, "and the woman knows where, if anyone does."

"She says she don't. Ain't that right, Mex?" Casper replied.

Escalante nodded.

"You gonna believe an Indian?" Stuart enjoined. "We don't know whether she's lyin' or not. Most likely she's lyin'."

Silence reigned for a moment. Kern looked at his hands. Escalante looked at the woman on the ground.

"The two youngsters," Casper said, "they probably belong to He That Rides Boldly. Ask her."

Escalante turned to the woman and said to her in Apsaruke. "These girls belong to He That Rides Boldly? They his?"

Cherry Blossom did not answer him.

Escalante turned to the two girls. "Shut your whimperin'," he said. "Your father, he is He That Rides Boldly?"

Chaser of Rabbits shook her head. "Pistol," she said simply.

"No. They're his," Escalante said aloud. "This Pistol won them. He's their new father. I'm guessin' that the woman's probably his, too. She ain't sayin'. This is where we found the coins. This is the place."

"Bein' young don't make them stupid," Stuart said. "They slept in the same tipi with their old man all their lives. They ain't deaf. They know. I'd be surprised if they don't. We just need to start whittling away. Lop off a finger, an ear, a nose. They'll talk plenty. The woman will talk if she sees us whittlin' on her youngin. She'll talk. If they know; those girls will talk. I would."

"They can't tell what they don't know," Kern said.

Stuart glanced at him. "We can find out. I say we do a little whittlin'. We'll know for sure quick. I'll do it. I don't mind cuttin' on an injun kid where gold's in the offerin'."

"Yes, well, I'm sure you would," Casper said. "We certainly can't stay here. So we have to decide. And now." Casper hesitated. "There is somethin' to be said for cuttin' our losses and gettin' the hell out of here."

"I like easy money. I like gold," Stuart said.

"And you'd like more."

"Sure, I'd like more. Don't you?"

Casper looked at him. "I ain't for cuttin' up no kid. I ain't for cuttin' up no woman. I ain't havin' no part of that."

"No one's askin' you. I'll do the cuttin'. It needs to be done. We need to know. Can't just leave a fortune in gold sittin' on the table 'cause of you bein' squeamish."

Kern looked at Stuart. "No," he said to him. "I won't allow it. There will be no torture of women and youngsters. It's not right and I won't have it."

Stuart glared at him.

Escalante rubbed his chin. "We don't have to decide it now," he said. "We can think it over. Take the women, the two girls, the gold we have, and decide the rest later. But we need to get out of here. I mean now. We don't go now, we'll be the ones whittled on."

He took his eyes from the Crow woman and glanced at the other three men in time to hear Casper shout, "Hell's fire!" followed by the percussion blast of a rifle fired. Escalante jerked around to discover four riders bearing down on him at a full gallop. A bullet whined past his head. Firing erupted beside him.

The Crow woman came to her knees scrambling. "Run!" she screamed at the two girls. "Run! Run!" A horse went down kicking and squealing, its shoulders barely missing Escalante. Dust billowed up. Another horse hit him broadside, sending him sprawling, and knocking the air from his lungs. He rolled, came to his feet cursing, pistol in hand looking for something to shoot. Something knocked him up along the side of his head, sending him sprawling. Gunfire continued then suddenly stopped. In the swirling dust he got his feet under him, wobbled, nearly falling, pistol still in his hand.

He heard Kern say, "I think I got one of them. Anybody hurt?" Escalante wondered if he was shot and what had hit him, dismayed that he hadn't gotten off a single shot. There was nothing to shoot and he was looking.

Barely twenty feet away the saddleless horse was kicking and squealing, trying to get up, his front right foreleg bent awkwardly. Escalante shot him. No one said anything. He wondered where its rider had disappeared to and looked about expecting to be attacked. From the east side of the encampment he heard firing.

"Adam?" Casper said, ejecting the spent cartridge from his pistol. Kern and Stuart started to run toward the sound. It stopped abruptly. A minute later Adam rode into the encampment at a gallop leading four horses and four pack animals.

"That settles it. Let's get the hell out of here," Kern said. "Where's that woman? We'll need her. Where'd she go?"

There was a sudden scramble for saddle horses. Casper ran from lodge to lodge looking inside. Kern swung into the saddle without touching a stirrup, finding the loose stirrups with both boots and spurring his horse forward. Around the six lodges he rode at a fast trot. By the time he reached the last lodge all four of his companions had joined him.

Stuart swore at his horse.

"There," Kern yelled, pointing down the creek where they could see a child disappearing into the brush. "See them? Where are those other bastards?" He looked about for signs of the four riders that had just attacked them. It was time to be alert–particularly with three armed hostiles on horses and one on foot. The woman and the two girls had disappeared into the brush along the creek. Casper, Stuart, and Escalante immediately pursued them.

Kern glanced at Adam. "You all right? We heard shooting."

"I'm fine," Adam said. Both men nudged their horses forward, Adam trailing, the pack animals following behind him. "I was overrun by three riders on horseback.

Came out of nowhere. Thought I saw a woman running up over the ridge."

"Did you shoot anybody?"

"Don't know. It happened fast. They were shootin'. I was shootin'. I came near gettin' myself killed. Damn near lost the pack animals. I got to you as quick as I could. I don't know what happened to those men or the woman. They disappeared."

"We'd better catch up," Kern said. "See what Casper has found."

"Why?"

"They know where the gold is. At least some of it."

"Oh," Adam said.

They spurred their horses into a trot, pulling the pack animals behind, looking for trouble. Expecting it. A couple hundred yards down the creek they located their companions with the woman and the two girls. Additionally, there was a boy of about ten years. He stood quietly in the group of captives.

"Where did you get the extra?" Kern asked.

"He was with the woman when we found them."

"That's not her," Adam said.

"What?"

"That's not the woman I saw runnin' over the rise." He looked at Kern. "That's not the woman I saw."

"Well, we better be movin'," Casper said, "and now."

Quickly they put the smaller girl and the woman on the pack animal that carried the least weight, shifting part of its load to the other two animals. The remaining girl and boy were tied on the backs of two mules. The loads were no longer balanced but there was no time. They resolved to re-balance the loads later. For additional security they tied the children to the backs of the mules and bound the woman's hands behind her with leather straps.

As soon as they could, they started down the creek at a trot, leading the pack animals with their additional burdens. Casper led. Stuart and Casper each led a pack animal with a child on its back. Escalante led the horse with the woman and child.

Kern brought up the rear. He was anxious. Often he looked back to see if they were being followed, consciously pushing as hard as he could to make up distance. They kept in a tight group moving quickly, not bothering to cover their trail. Speed was more important. Later they'd start covering it. For now, distance was what they wanted.

An hour later Escalante dropped back with Kern. "See anythin'?" he asked.

"No, but they'll be comin'."

"Oh, they'll be comin'. You know what the problem is," Escalante said. "These people don't give a damn about gold. They care about eatin', about horses, and stayin' warm. They care about countin' coup to see how brave they are. That's it. They don't much care for real wealth. Money and gold have no value. Gold and silver mean nothin'."

Kern nodded thinking about what Escalante had said. "You know, Mex, I'm thinking we aren't going to be getting more. I'm thinking one of those Spaniards got to being chased. He ran and ran and finally died in some canyon somewhere and this Indian fellow finds him and he happens to have some gold coin. The gold we have is all we are ever going to see. I'm thinking the well's dried up. We would be better off to just get the hell out of here. Leave everything and get while we can."

Stuart turned in the saddle and looked back at Kern. "No," he said. "I need to grind these girls. What have we got to lose? We came this far. Let's finish it."

183

Escalante looked at Stuart and then at Kern and nodded in agreement. "I agree," he said. "Let's get out of here. Get somewhere safe. Question the woman. Kern, you think we are bein' followed," Escalante continued. "So do I. Look at that woman. If by some chance we didn't already kill him, her man will come lookin' for her. Count on it. I'm bettin' she's related to a whole bunch of folks that feel the same way about her. Her man will not be comin' alone. Let's push it. Get while we can. If nothing else, we can trade her for something we want."

CHAPTER NINETEEN

Autumn Flower saw the white men moving quickly and silently into the encampment. But they didn't see her. She'd hidden herself intending to get help, to warn the others, but her sister had followed after her too fast. She didn't have time to sound the alarm. She wanted to. She'd witnessed the attack on the white men by Crazy Head and Long Nose, and Crazy Head's two uncles. She saw the big Mexican trader shoot the horse of Long Nose with his pistol. She stayed hidden, afraid of being caught, or captured, or killed. Half an hour later, after the sun had barely moved across the sky, she left her place of hiding and found Long Nose. He'd been shot through the leg and couldn't walk. Crazy Head was with him. He'd suffered an arm wound. The uncles had gone for help and to protect the women and the children; they couldn't be left alone. It was too dangerous.

Long Nose looked at the young woman as she tried to make him comfortable. "Get your father," he said to her. "Go. You must hurry. I will be all right. You must get Grey Elk and the white man, Pistol."

Autumn Flower stood up looking at Long Nose.

"Go," he said again. "You must hurry."

Autumn Flower began running. She ran across the prairie grass, her moccasin-covered feet barely touching the sod. She ran with tears in her eyes. She ran with Cherry Blossom's image in her heart, with the cries of

Gazes at Stars in her ears, and feeling the large, round eyes of Chaser of Rabbits following her as she fled. Autumn Flower ran.

Behind her the hands of her sister were tightly bound, the little girls tied to the pack animals, their hands also tied behind their backs. She was sure the men had found Scolds the Bear. He would try to stop them. They'd kill him. They'd try. Autumn Flower ran.

She followed the old trail to Deadman, her feet hurting, her lungs bursting. She did not notice the killdeer's song, the sharp cry of the snow bird, the melody of the meadow lark, nor the ceaseless sound of the wind brushing through the leaves of grass. Somewhere in front of her, her sister's man, Pistol, was with her father. She imagined they were eating beans and bread; they were laughing about something, about nothing. She reached the first rise. Autumn Flower ran.

She stumbled, fell, got up and ran, placing one foot in front of the other, pushing herself. She thought of her oldest sister taken from her sick bed, taken while her father hunted, while her husband and her uncles were down the creek not two hundred yards away watching her mother and her aunts and her sister Cherry Blossom gather firewood. They protected them and kept them safe. But her oldest sister had not been safe. Nothing was safe, ever.

For days, months, and years her father had searched for her sister, never finding her, always looking. Autumn Flower stopped, bent over herself, grabbing her knees, looking forward across the grassy plain, waiting for her lungs to grab the thin mountain air. Deadman was so far away. Then Autumn Flower ran. She ran before she even caught her breath. She ran thinking again of her oldest sister, wondering where she might be, if she were even alive. She ran hard, fearing that she might lose another.

She reached the red hill and the grey rock ravine that followed the trail to the ridge overlooking Deadman and Cherry Creek. Her grandfather's bones were lodged in the heart of the oldest of the cottonwood trees above the lodge of Pistol. She did not stop again. She did not hesitate. She had one more mile to go. Autumn Flower ran, her feet numb and bloody, her throat raw and bleeding. She ran without feeling, pushing herself beyond endurance, beyond her limits, beyond what she ever imagined she could do. She ran, carrying on trembling lips the horrible news.

She reached the north ridge, saw smoke drifting above the chimney of the log house, saw her father's horse standing in the corral with the dun of Pistol. Nausea washed over her. She nearly fainted but steeled herself, refusing to give in. From the ridge she attempted to cry out, to shout, but could not. Taking a step, she stumbled, then catching her balance, ran, ran as fast as her feet could carry her, tears running down her cheeks, her lips pink with her own blood.

Down the red hill she fled, across the red hard pack clay of the front yard and through the open door. Crossing the threshold she ran, stumbled, and fell, striking her head on the corner of a table, rolling on the floor. She tried to cry out. She felt warm red blood running into her eyes as she struggled to rise. She heard her own voice screech from her tortured throat.

Autumn Flower did not feel herself being lifted from the wooden planks of the floor and laid on the table, her head gently laid on a folded blanket. She barely felt the wet towel wiping the blood from her lips and from her forehead. She did remember Pistol standing over her speaking softly as he would to a child, his soothing voice calling to her. She felt his hand behind her head, lifting it to pour cool water into her open mouth. She remembered her father holding her hand, rubbing feeling back into her fingers, his worried eyes looming large over her.

She coughed. She tried to speak but the words were stuck in her throat. She heard her father tell her to slow down, to breathe. But she had to hurry; she had to tell them the terrible news. Then the words came rushing over her lips. They came pell-mell, a torrent falling into the quiet room.

She heard Pistol tell her father to stay with her, that he'd get the horses. His face disappeared. She heard his footfalls fading. In the craziness of the moment she wanted to call him back, to tell him again how it was. How Cherry Blossom had stood up to the big Mexican, how she protected the girls, but he was gone. In silence she lay on the hard, unyielding table top, felt her lungs expanding, the air rushing over her lips. She felt her heart beating in her chest. Her arms and her hands lay numb at her sides. She felt again the cool wet rag wash over her face, heard the cooing voice of her father administering to her. Carefully he removed what remained of her moccasins and gently he washed her bleeding feet. She felt the damp rag on her toes, felt herself drifting, drifting, drifting.

Later--how much later she did not know--her eyes opened. She heard Pistol telling her father to take the shotgun; that they should wait for Autumn Flower to recover enough to ride; that whatever had happened had happened; that they'd catch up to trouble soon enough. Pistol talked about riding ahead. He suggested that her father look after her. Grey Elk said it would be better if he rode ahead and picked up the trail. Pistol should stay and look after his daughter and he could catch up later. So the argument went. She coughed.

Suddenly the faces of the two men appeared above her. Pistol lifted her head to give her another drink but

Autumn Flower struggled to sit up. Her father protested but she sat up anyway. She took the drink and blinked her eyes as she tried to focus. She felt cold. She felt herself trembling as they steadied her, gripping her arms to keep her from falling off the table.

"We must go," she said.

The two men stared at her.

"We must go," she pleaded again.

"When you can sit up," her father said.

"I am sitting up. We must go."

Pistol and Grey Elk studied her. Neither said a word.

"I am sitting up," she repeated. "We have to go." She started to cry. Her father hugged her to him, holding her tightly. She sobbed against him, her body trembling uncontrollably. "Father, Father," she cried. "We must go. We must go now. They have them."

She heard Pistol ask her father if his horse rode double. Her father said no. "The dun will. Give her some more water. See if you can get her to eat something, then bring her outside. Maybe she can suck on some jerky. She needs to get her strength back." Pistol left the room, going outdoors, leaving her with her father.

"Father, we must go now. I will be all right. I can sit on a horse."

"Drink first," he said to her. "Drink, then I will get you some jerky to suck on. We will go then. Drink slow. Do not make yourself sick."

With her father's hand at her back, she sipped the cool water, forcing herself to relax. She tried to clear her head of the storm that raged inside, sipping again. With some effort she concentrated on holding herself still, trying not to tremble and shake. It didn't work.

Her father offered her a small piece of jerky. "Keep it in your mouth," he said. "Just suck it." Autumn Flower did as she was told, keeping the sliver of dried meat on her raw tongue, wet from spring water.

A few minutes later he lifted her from the table. She didn't remember the sun being so bright. She had to close her eyes against it. In her father's arms she felt safe, light as a goose feather floating on the wind. He lifted her and Pistol took her, setting her upon a blanket, holding her in his lap, her head against his chest, his arm around her. The horses were moving.

Pistol's chest was hard. He smelled of sweat, smoke, of beans and bread, of sage and wind drifting through pine. She heard him speaking to her father and she heard her father's voice as he replied. Then she was drifting, fast asleep in Pistol's arms.

They made Dry Head Creek in less than an hour, turned east and rode into the evening. They found the encampment half an hour later. It was empty except for Old Dog who sat silently in front of his lodge, rocking back and forth, mumbling words of anger, despair, rage, and grief. No one else was present. At their approach the old man stood on unsteady legs. The riders did not dismount. The old man looked at their faces. Amazingly, he was coherent.

"Is the one in your arms alive?" Old Dog asked Pistol.

"She is," replied Pistol. "She sleeps. Her feet are swollen. She ran all the way from here to Cherry Creek to give us warning."

"Leave her with me," Old Dog said. "She will slow you down. You must ride fast to catch the thieves who have stolen our hearts."

Pistol looked at Grey Elk. "I do not mean to dishonor the old man, but she will have no protection. Old Dog is too old to fight. What do you wish to do?"

"I am not dishonored," Old Dog said. "I am old. I can no longer lift the shield and spear. The ones you seek left before the sun was high. They will ride into the night. I have seen it. You must hurry if you are to catch them. And when you do you must leave no one alive. You must kill them all."

The girl stirred in Pistol's arms. He felt the warmth of her breath through his shirt. He thought of Cherry Blossom, impatient to be riding, but he also did not want to have this girl of sixteen winters harmed because he was in a hurry. It was better to take her with them even though she would slow them down. He waited for her father to decide.

"Father," the girl spoke, "I must go with you. I will not slow you down. I must, Father. I must go with you."

"Can you ride, Daughter? Should you not stay and hide with Old Dog in the trees and in rocks until I return?"

"Grey Elk," the old man interrupted, "I am too old to run and hide. Your daughter would do well to ride with her father. Do not concern yourself with me."

Pistol said, "Let's get another horse for her to ride."

Grey Elk decided.

CHAPTER TWENTY

"How long?" Pistol asked, sitting on the dun horse, his hat sitting on the back of his head, revealing a white forehead, narrow eyes, and bushy eyebrows. His chin sported a three-day growth of whiskers. Autumn Flower, her feet swollen, sat silently on the back of Walking Bull's war pony where she had ridden for hours. It surprised Pistol that she was still on the horse's back. Certainly she had grit. It made him feel a little embarrassed at being dead tired and wishing for blankets, a bed, and quiet.

Grey Elk squatted, studying the trail left by a number of animals. "Less than half a day," he replied. "They are heading east toward the gap in the big mountain."

It was several hours before dawn. No one had slept.

"How many you think?"

"Five riding heavy. Three, maybe four riding light. I believe we follow five men and maybe three or four mules. I think the mules carry my grandchildren and my daughter. They are not traveling fast. They must be thinking that no one is after them, that no one dares."

"Why do you think that?"

"They make no effort to hide their trail."

Pistol took a tobacco paper from his shirt pocket and rolled a cigarette. He lit it and took a long draw before he offered it to Grey Elk. The offer was accepted. While Grey Elk smoked, Pistol checked the loads in his Henry and on the SAA Colt Model 73, making sure there were no empty chambers. Grey Elk carried Pistol's shotgun. He wore a pistol stuck in his belt and a bow and quiver of arrows around his chest.

"What do you think?" Pistol asked, feeling the cool morning breeze on his shoulders, the damp spreading through his bones and muscles. Somewhere it had rained. He could smell it. It was a good morning for the business at hand. He only wished he weren't so tired. He glanced at the girl, then at her father. Today, he thought, someone was going to die and it wasn't going to be him.

Grey Elk looked at Pistol then swung up on his war pony. "We should ride fast," he said. "Get in front. Then we wait. The sun will be in their eyes, the wind in our faces. We let them come to us. We kill them. We have surprise in our favor. They will expect us to come from behind."

Pistol nodded. "I agree," he said. "Kill as many as we can before they know they're dead. We'll have to be careful. Then we kill the rest."

The girl remained silent.

Grey Elk nodded, adjusted the shotgun across the horse, cradled it in his left arm, his right holding the reins. "They'll be waiting for us if we're not careful. Maybe even if we are."

Pistol waited as Grey Elk finished adjusting himself on his horse, thinking about the ten gauge. "I'd shoot that from the ground if I were you. The kick will knock you off your horse."

Grey Elk nodded in agreement. "Let us go," he said and reined his mount around, looking at his youngest. "You good to ride, Daughter?" he asked.

She nodded.

"Can you ride even more?"

Autumn Flower nudged the war pony forward in answer to his question, then followed the two men at a trot.

These boys are pretty cavalier, Pistol thought. *They don't bother hiding their trail. No one's that good. No one lives forever.*

The hunters moved quickly, doing anything and everything they could to make time stand still, wishing they could fly on the wings of an eagle. Both men rode thinking of two small girls and a boy, hands tied, frightened and alone, perhaps beaten, even tortured. They hoped the captives had hope, that they knew Pistol and Grey Elk were coming for them. It was a time of hope. They hoped Autumn Flower could stay on the back of her horse. They hoped they'd reach her sister in time; before she was killed, before the children were dead.

By the morning of the second day they had maneuvered themselves in front of the pursued, cutting in front of them by a roundabout route. It was possible for them because they were traveling faster; they were not dragging four pack mules and watching three kids and a woman. Their only distraction was a sore footed sixteen-year-old girl. Thankfully, she was holding her own.

All three were bone tired, and hungry, their stomachs rubbing raw against their backbones. Even with their bodies pushed past reasonable endurance, they did not stop to think of food or drink or sleep. They could not stop if they wanted to get there in time.

The warm morning sun on their backs was some solace. There was no breeze. Absently, Pistol listened to the song of the meadow lark, the magpie, and the shrill call of the snow bird, and waited, silently. Neither man said anything about the nasty business ahead.

All three sat their horses, concealed in the brush among the cottonwood trees above the creek bottom. They waited. From the north side Pistol caught glimpses of three, then, four men riding through the tall pine timber at the edge of an old forest. It was slow riding among fallen trees. They heard the sound of someone swearing. The sound of a child crying out in pain drifted upwards.

A scattering of cottonwood and aspen trees grew along the north side of Deer Creek. The hunted walked their horses along the edge of a pine forest toward an elongated meadow that stretched eastward several hundred yards on the south side of the creek. A breeze picked up, rattling new cottonwood leaves.

Pistol wondered about the fifth rider; so far he'd only seen four. He sat imagining the wind drifting through pine needles, creating a roar in their ears, perhaps making them complacent to the dangers around them. *Soon*, he thought. *Soon enough they'll know.*

Pistol studied the long meadow that the horsemen must cross from one edge of the forest into the other. "Grey Elk," Pistol said, "let's wait until the first three are in the open." Pistol pointed to where he anticipated they would emerge. "I'll take the third man out. I'll try and put two rounds in him. You take the first. We'll both take the second. If we're lucky that will leave two." He paused, looking at his father-in-law. "No quarter, no prisoners, no mercy. Today they all die."

Grey Elk nodded in agreement. "As soon as it starts they will know we are coming. We must give them little time."

"Yes," Pistol said turning in the saddle to Autumn Flower. "And you who cannot walk, will stay here." Pistol smiled as he looked at Autumn Flower. "It will be helpful if you would stay with the horses and wait. It will be good if we know you are safe, out of harm's way."

Autumn Flower smiled at Pistol and nodded.

195

He turned to her father. "Wait until I open fire on the third man out. Right now they are strung out. There's a distance between each man. That will give us time. Hopefully it will be enough."

Pistol again turned to the girl. "As soon as we free them, we will send the girls, your sister, and Scolds the Bear to you. Keep them here so no one gets shot sneaking around trying to be helpful."

"Yes, I will do this," Autumn Flower replied.

The three riders continued to wait. Minutes dragged. Their eyes followed the first rider as he came out of the pines in the clearing. He rode a black horse, wore a dark blue shirt, a red bandana around his neck, shotgun chaps on his legs, and a silver grey hat. Above him a chicken hawk circled in wide lazy circles. Just as they had planned, the sun was bright in his eyes. They watched as the rider pulled the hat brim lower, hiding his face.

The rider stopped, looked back, and spoke to someone. Minutes later a second rider joined him. Both men studied the meadow in front of them. The second rider led a pack mule with Scolds the Bear perched on top of the packs. The boy appeared to be tied down, his hands behind him. A sack covered his head.

Pistol looked again, blinking his eyes to focus. On second thought it could be one of the girls. It was hard to tell given the distance. Dropping the identity of the child from his mind, Pistol ceased worrying about who it was. It didn't matter. Wordlessly, he glanced at Grey Elk. Grey Elk nodded in agreement to the unspoken thought, dismounted, and moved quietly away on foot. He crossed Deer Creek, carrying the shotgun in one hand, the bow in the other. A buffalo quiver containing seven arrows hung strapped across his back as he disappeared in the brush.

Except for the song of a meadow lark it was quiet. A breeze picked up and rattled the cottonwood leaves.

Glancing at the girl, Pistol dismounted, preparing to steady the upcoming shot.

"If you can," he said aloud, "get down and hold that horse and your father's, too. They are liable to jump when I start shooting." He watched the diminutive girl slide from the horse's back, watched her grab the hackamore, speaking low to the war pony. He noted her trembling knees, the set of her jaw; then Pistol turned to the business at hand.

Moments later the third man, riding an Appaloosa, came out into the clearing. The horse danced, tossing its head as it moved steadily away from the cover of pine trees. The rider's dirty, faded, yellow shirt and bat winged chaps blended with the old brown grass in the clearing. The horse did not. A pack mule tied to the latigo straps of his saddle followed him. One of the children was perched high upon the packs, hands bound behind, a sack over his or her head.

Rifle ready, Pistol grew impatient. The mule carrying the child walked between Pistol and his intended target. Pistol swore. Seconds later the rider's horse stepped in front of the mule and Pistol fired, ejected the empty round, chambered another, and fired again. The rider appeared to be falling from the saddle. Or so Pistol hoped.

Pistol looked for rider number two, noting that the mule and riderless Appaloosa had bolted and were running full out across the meadow, bellies to the ground. He could hear the high-pitched scream of a girl echoing off the ridge behind him. Rider number two had vanished from sight, hidden by the foliage of the creek bottom.

The child's scream had cut Pistol so deeply he could barely breathe. Without thinking he jumped onto the dun and rode to the spot where he had last seen Grey Elk. He wondered what had happened with the first rider. Guilt clutched at his throat. He wished he'd taken rider number two instead of three.

A shotgun blast boomed, reverberating against the side of the mountain. A moment later Pistol found the first rider lying at the foot of a cottonwood, an arrow in his chest, his throat cut. One of his legs was in the creek the other out. It amused Pistol that he still had his hair. About twenty yards farther he located the second rider's saddle horse and pack mule. They were twisted together, caught between trees, hung up on the lead rope. The pack animal had gone in one direction and the grey saddle horse another. Both were standing between and around a tree trunk and some skunk brush, fighting the rope. The pack had slid from the mule's back. Staring at the situation, Pistol heard the muffled grunting of the child tied to the slipping packs. Jumping off the dun, Pistol ran to the mule, gentling him with his voice, his hand on his rump. Using his knife, he cut the lead rope and pulled at the cloth sack that covered the head of its captive.

It was Scolds the Bear. Quickly Pistol cut the bindings loose from the boy's feet and hands, lifting the ten-year-old out of the packs and setting him on the ground beside the mule. "You all right?" he asked.

The boy shook his head no.

"Anything broken?"

Again the boy shook his head no.

Pistol knelt beside the youth, ignoring his tears, his somber, frightened face. "You are very brave," he said. "Autumn Flower has your grandfather's horse across the creek under a cottonwood tree. It's the only cottonwood. Go there. Take this horse, this mule. Wait with her. Your grandfather will be along soon. Go there now." Pistol had the boy by the shoulders. "I need to help your grandfather. Do as I tell you. When I find your sisters and your mother, I will send them to you."

Without looking to see if he'd been obeyed, Pistol walked toward the dun. He caught up the reins and swung into the saddle. He knew one of the hunted was dead--the first rider. The third, wearing the yellow shirt, was somewhere out in the meadow. Maybe dead. Maybe not. The second? He didn't know about him, either. Pistol decided to concentrate on rider number two.

Pistol walked the dun another hundred yards, keeping close to the trees along the creek bottom. Keeping an eye trained on the area where the first rider had emerged from the timber, he hoped that Grey Elk had been successful in killing the second. Inadvertently, he found the second rider, almost stepping on him. Cut in half by a shotgun, he was very much dead. Dismounting, Pistol bashed in his head with the stock of his rifle thinking that made him really dead.

Kneeling in the tall grass of the meadow beside the corpse, Pistol forced himself to think. Two of the five were dead. Maybe three, if he could shoot worth a damn. That left two men, two girls, Cherry Blossom, and Grey Elk unaccounted for. He had not seen the last two riders emerge from the trees. Now, with all the shooting, they wouldn't. He was sure of that.

Cold anger washed through him. His woman and his daughters would remember this bullshit the rest of their lives. And they didn't need to, shouldn't have to. He glanced in the direction of the pine forest, then back up the creek, wondering about Grey Elk. Where was he? There was no time. Pistol caught up the dun. This time he did not mount. Instead he walked beside the horse, using him as a shield against whatever evil lived in the forest or lurked in the tall grass. Ten minutes later horse and man stepped under the shaded pine canopy.

The breeze picked up again, pushing itself through the pine needles, magnifying itself into a dull roar. No birds sang. No rock dogs barked. No chipmunks chirped. They were there but silent, holding their breath. And so was he. "In this situation look for anything that moves," his father had said. "Anything at all, and kill it. Do not think. Just shoot. Maybe you'll come out alive."

"Maybe." Pistol came to a stop. He studied the trees, the ground. He listened. He waited and waited and waited and listened some more. Leaving the dun standing ground hitched, its reins dangling, Pistol took to the trees, keeping close to the brush. From somewhere in front of him he heard a child's whimper, followed by a shush.

Pausing, he listened, straining to hear. There was nothing. Impatient, he moved slowly forward, a Colt 73 revolver in hand. It wasn't as though he wasn't prepared. He was and yet he wasn't. The fourth man, big, a Mexican looking fellow, came out of the trees in front of him, walking right at him, not twenty feet away, firing away. He must have been hiding behind a tree trunk watching, waiting for the right moment. Apparently, that moment was now. The man in the grey shirt was working hammer and trigger. His first shot was hurried. It missed. The second caught the flesh of Pistol's left shoulder and hurt like hell.

Somehow, in the roar of gunfire, Pistol got himself going, shooting one shot after the other, aiming at the buttons on the man's shirt. He thought he missed for the man kept coming even after his pistol was empty, the hammer landing on spent cartridges. Abruptly he came to a stop, stood up on his tiptoes, hesitating, dropping his weapon then falling face forward, his head bouncing off the ground. Finally, the big man lay still on the bed of pine needles. Pistol had only one round remaining. *That's three*, he thought. *For sure, three.*

Instinctively, Pistol sought cover to catch his breath, his back against the trunk of a pine. He listened, breaking the pistol down, ejecting the spent cartridges, reloading each chamber with a fresh round. He'd shot five times. Now he had six again. He wondered if it would be enough. That last man just wouldn't stop. Hard to kill. Behind him, barely audible, he could hear a child's whimper. Pistol found himself thanking God and all that was holy for that sound. At least there was a chance. She was alive. Someone was alive. He wondered who it was. Gazes at Stars? Chases After Rabbits? It didn't matter. They were both his. And some son of a bitch had them. Rage washed over him inflaming his face, his chest.

"Hey, Buckwheat," he yelled, "you got my woman. You got my kids. I'm coming for you. One way or the other, you're a dead man. You aren't walking out of here alive. Running, maybe. But you sure as hell aren't walking."

The forest was silent. Waiting.

Then came the voice. "Joe? That you? What are you doing?"

For the second time in Pistol's life his heart stopped beating. The first time: that was when he'd felt Cherry Blossom's lips on the skin of his neck, something he'd never felt before; a time when his fortune was so good he could taste it. Nothing else had mattered and nothing felt so good. Even the death of his brother no longer mattered. That was the first time. And now his heart had stopped a second time: at the sound of a voice, a voice he had thought to be lost in the cold earth of Cherry Creek at Deadman, a voice from across oceans of water, across dry deserts of Texas and Northern Mexico, across a long winding trail through Utah Territory and Wyoming. Years and miles away. And here it was again, from his very youth. The voice of his brother.

"You got my girls, Bob. You got my woman." That was all he could think to say. The unsaid things were a blank to his mind.

"Yours? The girls? They're a little dark, Joe. Haven't got your eyes. Your skin. Your hair. You sure? Now, this woman. I can see that. She's a looker, brother, even tied up and mad. She's a looker."

"She's mine, Bob. So are the girls. You better not hurt them, Bob. I'm not going to be forgiving."

"I haven't hurt her, big brother. The Mex popped her a bit. That's about it. Can't believe it. I'm an uncle? A damn brother-in-law." Bob hesitated. "Now you stay back, Joe. Stay where you are 'til we sort this out."

"There's nothing to sort out, Bob. You're holding my woman."

Then Pistol heard a long, loud groan, almost a bark, followed by the blast of a pistol. He came to his feet running toward the sound, a girl's scream assaulting his ears, tearing at him. He could hear the soft voice of Cherry Blossom speaking to the child.

Then he heard Bobby's strained voice. "My God, I've been run through. That kid yours, too? You teach him the lance? Jesus, Joe. Why'd you go and do that?" The words were followed by silence and then a string of cussing.

Pistol found his brother behind a fallen log and a standing tree trunk. Bob was on his knees, his hands wrapped around the shaft of a lance protruding from his abdomen. Blood leaked about his fingers dripping onto a bed of pine needles. A pistol lay on the ground at his side. The lance had skewered him, entering his back, forced out his belly, stained red and bloody. Twenty feet away stood Scolds the Bear. Pistol motioned him closer. He told him to untie his sister and his mother.

"Good Lord, you speak that kid's language?" Bob's voice was strained and weakening. He gasped for breath.

"I do. Why are you here, Bobby? I thought you were dead. I was told you were dead. What are you doing?" Pistol stared at his brother.

"Looking for easy money, Joe. Easy money. Listen, Joe, I'm not long for this world. Love to mother." Bob collapsed, holding the protruding end of the spear. He did not utter another sound.

Pistol stared at his brother's body for a moment then quickly walked over to Cherry Blossom, knelt down and helped Scolds the Bear remove the sack from her head. He waited for Scolds the Bear to untie her hands, wiping the tears that flowed from her eyes. As the boy worked the knots, he kissed her forehead, her lips. Once her hands were freed, he helped her to her feet, hugging her to him, not wanting to let her go . . . not ever. Abruptly he realized where he was and cursed himself. *Got to be careful. Bobby made four; there is still another.*

Gazes at Stars cried, sobbing when he reached her. Once he untied her, she threw her arms around his neck, her tears wetting his skin, her small body clinging to him tightly. He hugged the little girl who'd brought him dandelions and bluebells for his hat, and a slippery frog for him to look at and admire. He didn't want to let her go either.

Four accounted for, but there was one more. *Be careful,* he told himself.

"Be still," he said to his daughter. "There is one still alive. One that I don't know to be dead. Be still so I can listen."

With Gazes at Stars in his arms, he looked at Cherry Blossom, and Scolds the Bear. "Stay here," he said to his woman. "Take this little one. I must make sure there is no one else. Be very quiet." He looked at Cherry Blossom

203

and handed her his pistol, pulling the hammer back, a live round in the chamber. "I'll be back," he said. He noted that Bobby had been right in his observation. Cherry Blossom was as mad as she could be, madder than he'd ever seen her.

At his brother's body he retrieved Bobby's Colt, checked the loads, and replaced the single spent cartridge. At the body of the big Mexican he retrieved another pistol, reloaded it, and shoved it in his waistbelt. He waited, listening. He heard the wind, the meadow lark, and some black birds. He saw a robin, some nesting material in its beak. Normal things.

The dun was where he'd left him. At the edge of the forest he met Grey Elk. Both agreed there were four dead. Neither knew anything of the fifth man except that he existed. But where?

"Do you have Chaser of Rabbits?" Grey Elk asked.

"She's with Autumn Flower. Grey Elk, you get those two. I'll get the others. We'll meet here. Then we'll deal with the missing man. I think they'll be safer together with one of us watching."

"I agree," Grey Elk said.

From the north ridge, Adam Scofield held his horse's nose and waited. He watched the girl approach the broad-shouldered man. First she walked, then ran through the tall grass. Because of the terrain and the dense foliage, it was difficult to see very much. He saw the man with a child in his arms, her arms wrapped around his neck. He saw the Indian woman standing beside him. He watched her wipe tears from her eyes and saw the boy with her, holding her hand, her arm around the white man. He saw a younger woman with her. They looked a lot alike. *Beautiful women,* he thought.

He watched the white man kneel in the grass, taking the second girl in his arms. Now two girls were clinging to him. They were together, standing at the edge of the forest primeval, hidden by trees and undergrowth. The wind had picked up, roaring through the pine needles, fluttering the leaves of a stand of quaking aspen and cottonwood. A meadow lark broke into song.

A few yards away Robert John Kern lay dead, impaled by a spear shaft. Casper was dead, shot through the chest. Stuart had an arrow in his chest. Dead. He wasn't sure about the Mex. Adam knew the Indian was after him next. Moments ago he'd seen him disappear into the undergrowth that surrounded the creek bottom. That man was a hunter.

Time to go, Adam thought. Quickly he mounted the bay horse, nudging him forward. Moving in the direction he'd come, retreating into the pines, he moved on.

Time to get lost. Nothing for me here. Better be quick about it. That damn woman . . . she'd been right. Her man wasn't leaving anyone alive. What had the Mexican said she said? "My husband has no enemies. They are all dead. And you will be, too."

CHAPTER TWENTY-ONE

Sheriff Al Billings left Red Lodge on Tuesday morning, July 13, 1883. A killing is what he'd heard. A station master had shot and killed a passenger named Steeples. No one told him why. He'd ridden all morning. The first day he'd gotten as far as the upper Sage Creek and he camped at Indian Spring. The next day he crossed Dry Head Creek and headed for the Deadman substation.

Odd, he thought. *No lodges on Dry Head Creek? A lot of tracks, though. Several well-used circles of stone. Maybe there had been ten lodges. Where did they go?* The number gave him pause. After he'd come out on top above the creek, he saw his first Indians. They were headed south with him. That wasn't good. South was off the reservation. Why south?

Billings watched them and swore to himself. He should have brought a posse. Ever since the stage company put the road through from Hardin to Crooked Creek there'd been nothing but trouble. Sometimes progress just made things worse. None of it was good.

He wasn't sure Deadman was on the reservation. It was hard to tell. Probably not. Sort of a checkerboard. *Maybe the Army should take care of this problem.* But if it wasn't reservation it was his jurisdiction, particularly if someone had been killed. That was his business.

When he and the bay topped the ridge above Deadman, he swore he saw over two hundred lodges.

This was not good. *Where the hell was the Army?* This was an uprising. He wanted to turn back but he couldn't. He'd been seen.

He imagined the short count would be about twelve hundred Crow, if he counted women, kids, and dogs. Lodges were to hell and gone up and down Cherry Creek. Rising in his stirrups, Billings glanced north in the direction that he'd come. There were at least five stragglers following him across the flat. Probably more. The hair stood up on the back of his neck. It was clear to him that this sure as hell was no ordinary killing. Coming down off the hill, he met more riders than he could easily count. They were everywhere. For a moment he thought he was dead. But he wasn't. Somehow he made it to the creek bottom and to the door of the way-station and dismounted. Taking his time, surprised he was yet alive, he looked around deliberately avoiding eye contact with anyone.

Someone took his horse and he couldn't help but think that was the last time he was going to see that horse, not to mention his saddle, bridle, rifle, saddlebags, and his extra knife. Billings opened the door and let himself inside. There was a marked difference in the temperature. Maybe fifteen degrees. The floor was wet under boot. He heard the heavy labored breathing of someone not yet dead; then he saw him. It was ugly. Shirt torn to shreds, ripped. *Shotgun*, he thought. *Had to be.* The man was fairly torn up.

Across the room he saw a white man, probably the station master. Good man, he'd heard. He was engaged in an earnest conversation with several others. It wasn't English they were speaking. He understood not a word. They were all Crow as far as he could tell. Excepting the man he thought was the station master. He'd heard he was a squaw man. Who'd told him that? He tried to think. It sure as hell didn't matter here.

"Pistol?" he said aloud.

Startled, the white man turned in his chair looking toward the sound of the Sheriff's voice. "Yes. That's me."

"I'm Billings. I'm the Sheriff."

Pistol looked at him. Still sitting in his chair, he smiled. "Sheriff," he said, "how are you? Didn't expect you. Not this soon."

"Fine. I'm fine. Least I think I'm fine. Hard as hell to tell with all of this commotion. What's going on? I was told there was a killing." The Sheriff turned his attention to Steeple. "That fellow doesn't look so good."

"Yes. There was. Sorry to say. That feller sitting there in the chair is trying to die. He shot and killed my woman. I shot him."

The Sheriff walked across the room, glancing at the tall Indian who stood beside Pistol. Both men were watching him. He could feel their eyes following him. *Where's the army?* he thought. *I sure as hell need the army. These boys are not looking friendly.*

"I see he's shot. And it looks like he's dying or trying to but why is he in the chair? Ain't that a bit much?"

Pistol answered him slowly. "He's dying. Sure as hell. He's dying."

"What was he doing when you shot him?"

"Getting on the stage. Least that's what he had in mind. Billy jumped out of the way so as not to get himself shot. I got him. Gut shot. Right where I was aiming. The son of a bitch."

"I see that. This woman . . . ?"

"My wife."

"And, I gather, someone's daughter?"

"Grey Elk's. They'll be attending the funeral this afternoon. You are just in time."

208

"I see." Billings saw that this was no time to point out that the present deceased was a mere Indian woman. He did not, recognizing that it would be stupid to do so. It was also no time to point out that revenge wasn't a defense of one's life.

Grey Elk? Might as well be his kin that was killed or Black Kettle or Crazy Horse. Except Crazy Horse was dead. He'd sure stirred himself up some trouble.

"Well, Pistol, I sure as hell wish you hadn't shot this poor bastard. Why are you keeping him alive? Can't you cut him down from that chair?"

"No. I'm making him suffer as much as I can."

"Pistol, for crying out loud. I have a helluva problem here. You sure ain't helping it any. Not one bit."

"Sheriff, what would you do to a man who shot your wife because of a rabbit bone? Besides," Pistol said, a wry smile on his face, "he was going for his short gun. He gave me the opportunity to make things right. I would have, anyway, but he gave me reason and I took it."

Al Billings stared at Pistol. *What would he do? He'd shoot the SOB, that's what he'd do. Didn't make it right, though. Didn't make it wrong, either. But she was an Indian. Sure as hell, she was an Indian.*

Al Billings shook his head. "Pistol, get me my horse."

"What for? You just got here."

Billings shrugged his shoulders, glanced at the big white man, then at the Indian girl sitting in the corner watching him. "And I'm just leaving," he said quietly.

"Suit yourself." Pistol spoke to a Crow lad standing in the door. The boy disappeared.

"Pistol, I've heard good things about you. This ain't one of them. But I ain't sticking around to get my hair lifted on the off chance that I might keep it."

Pistol nodded in understanding. "Well, Sheriff, if it means anything, by the time you reach Red Lodge this one here . . . " Pistol pointed at the big man bent over himself, "he'll be so deep in the ground his own mother couldn't find him with a witching stick." Pistol paused. "Another thing, if you come back to get me for any reason I couldn't save your life if I got up real early in the morning and wanted to. My woman was Grey Elk's daughter. This SOB killed her. He has to die. Understand? The second he pulled the trigger he was dead."

Al Billings nodded, pulling on the brim of his hat in frustration. He understood all too well. This killing, the second one, was a righteous killing. Sometimes a death was demanded. Sometimes it wasn't. There was a difference. He wondered what it was? The Sheriff of Carbon County turned and walked out the front door, found his bay horse and mounted, noting that the rifle scabbard was real empty. He didn't ask about it. A man could always get another Winchester. Can't always get hair. As an afterthought, he imagined his saddlebags were probably cleaned out, too.

Instead of running off at the mouth, he rode back the way he came and never looked back. No one followed him past the north ridge overlooking Deadman. He didn't stop to wonder why or question his good fortune. Once up on the flat he passed two groups of Crow Indians going south. He didn't stop to say hello, just looked straight ahead and pretended they didn't exist. It wasn't his damn business where they were going and he sure as hell wasn't going to question them on the direction their horses were walking.

CHAPTER TWENTY-TWO

They had been together for a long time. First, there was Grant at Vicksburg when Stringham was a Lieutenant, J.G., a shave tail, and William Oliver, a corporal. Grant assigned both he and his sergeant major to Phil Sheridan. What an experience! They tore the hell out of everything, leaving nothing of use. Burn, burn, burn. Ride hard, ride fast. After Phil Sheridan, he had been assigned to General Crook in the Arizona Campaign. When he learned his assignment, he immediately asked for and received William Oliver as his sergeant major.

"Do not reinvent," his father said. "If you get a good one. Keep him. It will make all the difference."

It certainly had made the difference. How does one defeat such an illusive enemy? One that you couldn't see? One who knew where all the water holes were and you didn't? William Oliver did it by hiring the best scouts, Chiricahua Apache. And not just one. Three.

"Know the enemy better than the enemy knows himself." Who said that? He tried to remember. Guessed he was getting too old, too tired. Probably his father.

As soon as they had been transferred to Fort Smith, Montana, his sergeant major had been on a crusade of sorts. First: learn the language, learn the language, learn the language. Second: Learn the people, what makes them tick, why they do what they do. And lastly, don't be stupid. The last was the most difficult. The Crow had been there a long time; the captain and his sergeant major--ten minutes. Guns do not win every fight. In fact they win very few. Folks with brains win battles and ultimately wars: not the toughest, the meanest, or the most willing.

Captain Earnest Stringham sat in his chair, thinking and staring across the parade grounds. Today on his morning ride he noted eight empty lodge circles. Five the day before. Lodges gone. What could it be? *Probably nothing*, he told himself. *Nothing at all. Just some Crow traveling south. But where were they going? Hunting party, maybe? Looking for elk, a stray buffalo? In July? So what if they were? When had they left? Why had they left? Where had they gone? All these damn questions.*

There were still plenty of Crow. It wasn't like there were no Crow at Fort Smith. But he'd received several annoying reports about the people moving from Lodge Grass and from St. Xavier's. It wasn't a big movement, a few more every day--every hour actually. *Since when? Three, four days?* In addition, he'd received a report from the Hardin Stage and Transportation Company that one of their passengers was killed at Deadman, a way-station on Cherry Creek. Some white man killed by another. Not his problem. So he dismissed it.

Just the same, something was attracting attention and it was all over the reservation. But where were they going? That was such a big country. Was it still the Crow Trail? It was just an old trail. "Very old," the scouts said, "since the beginning of time, before the Crow people." Where? Where?

Well, he thought, *I'd better do something before whatever it was that has everyone's attention gets completely out of hand.* He needed information. Then he remembered the old man, the scout. But he was a drunk really, a worthless man. The

Captain thought about him. Maybe he was worthless, maybe not. Stringham sent for the scout. The Army didn't use the man. Never had. But the other scouts were all gone on patrols: He Who Counts Many Coups, gone. Black Leg, gone. That left the old drunk. The Sergeant Major just called him Scout. Stringham didn't know the man's name.

When the Sergeant Major arrived that morning, he had asked him about the man. "The old guy that can hardly walk. You know who I mean? That drunk lives south of here behind that red ridge, down on the creek."

The Sergeant Major had nodded.

"Well?"

"Scout."

That's what Stringham thought the Sergeant Major had said. "Scout?" he repeated. The Sergeant Major corrected him.

"No, Stout. Stout Buffalo. An old name for a very old man."

"Stout? Stout Buffalo?"

"Yes, sir."

"Pardon me. I thought you had said 'Scout.'"

"He was that," the Sergeant Major said. "Very good, I understand. But no good for the Army."

"Why not?"

"He's old. Doesn't get around very well and he doesn't like us much, sir."

"Do you think he'll know what's going on? Where these people are going?"

"Oh, he'll know, sir. You can count on it. The question isn't whether he knows. It's whether he'll tell you."

The old man smelled awful. Alcohol, smoke, and urine. Quite a potent combination, especially for the nose.

And he wouldn't stand up. Not for the Captain. There was some recognition, however, for the Sergeant Major. He'd talk to him. The old man laughed but the Captain didn't know why. So the Captain addressed his questions to the Sergeant Major. "Ask him if he has any idea why these people just packed up and left? Where are they going?"

The Sergeant Major spoke with the old man. The response: a chuckle, a belly laugh, an awful smelling belch. Before the Sergeant Major could respond, the old man had grabbed his arm and pulled himself upright, leaning against the younger man, steadying himself. The Sergeant Major did not move. The old man looked at the Captain, stared at him a long time, like an old wolf eying a grey rabbit bounding before him, inches from his nose, a mouth full of fur.

The old man spoke. The Sergeant Major listened. In turn the Sergeant Major translated for the captain.

"He says Grey Elk's people."

"Grey Elk? Who is that?"

"Sir?" The Sergeant Major stopped mid sentence, said something to the old man. He did not pat him on the arm. He looked at him when he spoke, but did not speak down to him. There was almost a reverence, the younger man for the old. The old man spoke again. The Sergeant Major translated.

"Grey Elk, sir. You asked who he is. The old man said this is the man that told the chiefs you have at the Crow Agency that they could go down there. That they could talk to our people."

"I didn't know there was such a man among the Crow."

"I heard there was someone, sir, but this is the first I knew his name."

"Ask him why they are going south. Ask him where they are going. See if he knows."

The Sergeant Major turned to the old man, spoke to him. The old man listened, smiled as if tolerating the young man's misuse of words. The conversation lasted a few minutes.

"Sir, pardon me. Stout Buffalo was teaching me to say what I wanted to say the proper way. He said that some fool killed Grey Elk's daughter. Shot her. Grey Elk's people are going there to watch the man die . . . before they tear his heart out of his chest and feed it to the camp dogs. He said they probably wouldn't do that but they would think of it."

"Did he say to watch him die? Is he still alive? This man who shot Grey Elk's daughter, is he still alive?"

The Sergeant Major turned to the old man whose fingers were wrapped around his forearm like the talons of an eagle. He seemed taller, growing as the Sergeant Major spoke to him in the language of the Crow, then waiting for the old man to reply.

The old man nodded, released his grip on the Sergeant Major's arm. He didn't immediately answer. Instead he stared through old grey eyes at the Captain, then in broken English as if the saying of it was to be relished, said, "The tall woman killer. Not dead. Soon dead. His death much celebration. People happy. Heart to dogs to be fed. Shot in stomach. Death long. Suffering much. Much dance. Bad death. Very bad death. People happy."

The Captain turned to the Sergeant Major. "Does he know who shot this man?"

The old man answered immediately. "Husband of Crow Woman." Then the old man reverted to speaking Crow. The Sergeant Major listened without interruption.

"He is called something like 'Knife Thrower, Hunter for Old Dog' I didn't understand exactly what he said. Apparently this man is white and he killed someone of strength with a two barreled shotgun. He said something about feeding the old people fresh meat. Something like that. Apparently, he is someone they hold in high regard who doesn't like fighting but when he does fight, warriors of note die quickly in his presence. Something like that."

The Captain leaned back in his chair. A white man who had a Crow woman for a wife. The woman happened to be Grey Elk's daughter. She was killed by a white man. And this 'Knife Thrower' shoots him in the belly.

"Sergeant Major," he said, "at your earliest convenience have the patrols return immediately. Have the lieutenants report to me as soon as they are able. We're going to have to move on this quickly if we are going to avoid trouble. I smell trouble."

"Sir. There will be no avoiding trouble. The old man, sir? I should return him to his lodge."

"You, Sergeant Major? Why?"

"Sir, he's seen more wars, fought in more battles then you or me. He's counted more coup than we have men in this garrison. He deserves the respect, sir. He is who he is . . . a warrior."

"Of course, Sergeant Major. See to it. With my compliments. See me as soon as you return."

"Sir."

When the Sergeant Major returned forty-five minutes later, Stringham was still at his desk, seemingly staring out the window. He returned the Sergeant Major's salute without moving from the oak chair.

"An old bastard huh, Bill?" He dispensed with the protocol. They never used it when alone. There was no time for it. The Sergeant Major had hauled the Captain's hide out of danger too many times. If there was a fire fight, the Captain wanted the Sergeant Major at his side. No one doubted it. Everyone knew it.

There was a time at Vicksburg when First Lieutenant Stringham had ridden back to get his sergeant, disobeying orders, orders made directly to him. He made the mistake of asking for permission. The colonel said no. He went anyway. Having found his sergeant, the first lieutenant threw his unconscious and bleeding body over the saddle of the colonel's horse and walked him out of harm's way. He'd borrowed the horse. It just happened to be the closest and he was in a hurry.

"You disobeyed my direct order," the colonel had said. "My direct order," he fumed, ready to shoot someone. Disobedience was not something he tolerated or ignored. And don't get him started on horse stealing. The colonel was certainly someone to be reckoned with.

"Yes, sir," he answered.

"I'll bust you to a private. In fact, I'm busting you to a private."

"Thank you, sir."

"Thank you? You thank me? I've just busted you to a private and you thank me? What the hell's wrong with you, Lieutenant?"

"Sir, I cannot fight without this man. With him, dying still isn't all right but I can deal with it. Without him, I can't lead men into battle and know we are coming out. Can't explain it, sir. He's saved my life too many times. I cannot go forward without him. It's just the way it is. Sorry, sir. Sorry to disappoint you but I can only fight this war knowing he's my sergeant. It doesn't make any difference whether I am a private, a corporal, or a first lieutenant."

Colonel Samuels was his name. He'd stared at him in disbelief. He said, "I'll be damned." And "I hope you don't do this often." Then he made him the acting captain immediately under him, made Oliver, unconscious though he was, his sergeant major. Stringham had just stood there, not knowing what to do.

The colonel, seeing his distress, came to his aid. He said, "Captain, at your earliest convenience, get your sergeant major to a medic. As soon as you have seen to his aid get yourself back here. I'll need you right away. We have a war to fight . . . and hopefully win."

The colonel never lost after that, never retreated, never lost advantage, not with the captain there, not with the sergeant major at the captain's side. Casualties dropped. They constantly advanced. Men wanted to fight for Samuels. Grant noticed Colonel Samuels. Sheridan noticed the captain and his sergeant major.

"Old?" The Sergeant Major replied. "Ernie, he knows them all. Black Kettle, Crazy Horse, Sitting Bull. They were together at one time, Curly and him. Friends. He knew his father. He's not Crow. He's Sioux. Ogalala. Married a Crow woman. Never left. He's old all right. He was too old for Greasy Grass. He watched it though. Saw our man fall on the ridge above the Little Big Horn. Said he was a brave man Told me about it. I figure he was in his late sixties by his description. Could have been his early seventies. He's been there."

"What do you think about our current problem?"

"Hard to put a finger on it, Ernie. We don't know enough. I don't think you should mount the entire garrison and charge over there. That could turn a simple fist fight into a full-blown cannon and Gatlin war. The kind that General Custer ran into without the cannon or the Gatlin."

"I agree. What we have is an Indian woman killed by a white man in the Red man's back yard. That can't set well. It will be dicey at best. No one will be happy. It seems that the entire reservation is moving south for a funeral, a lynching, and a celebration. I feel as if I am sitting on an open powder keg smoking a four-cent cigar."

The Sergeant Major nodded. "What do you want to do?"

"I've decided to send Barrett and ten troops . . . just to look. I want you to go, too. Bill, don't let this get out of hand. Get that shave tail back here alive with all ten troopers. Understand? The getting back is just as important as getting there."

"I understand. Be good experience for Barrett. Maybe he'll grow up along the way."

"Maybe. Bill, I don't want to lose good men to further his education. No letters to mothers. No letters to widows. None."

The Sergeant Major smiled. "Okay," he said. "When?"

"Now, Bill. Make it happen yesterday if you can."

"I'll make it happen, Captain." The Sergeant Major stood. "See you in a few days."

"Oh, Sergeant Major. Remind the Lieutenant from time to time, if you will, that this is history. We're just passing through it. Don't let him get lost on the pages. He doesn't need to be a footnote. Better to be no note at all."

CHAPTER TWENTY-THREE

The patrol left the confines of Fort Smith forty-five minutes after the official order was given by Captain Stringham. The ten troopers knew this was no ordinary patrol out to the creek and back. No, it was certain that this wasn't that sort of patrol because the Sergeant Major rode with them.

Sergeant Major Oliver had gathered them about him ten minutes before the Lieutenant had arrived, after speaking with the Captain. This patrol required everyone to be alert. There would be shooting. Some of them may not be coming back, their bodies slung over their saddles or not at all. They were to ride in pairs, not single file. The left directed to search the left continually, the right, the right. They were to look for anything that was moving, anything that may be a Crow warrior, any sign of an ambush.

"Immediately notify him," he said. The order of 'immediately' was repeated three times. Did they understand? Their continued living would depend on being alert all of the time. Listen for his orders. And if they had side arms, bring them.

Abruptly, he'd turned and walked away. Out of his hearing the Corporal had said, "Sergeant Major is riding with us. I do not remember him ever saying, 'If you have side arms bring them.' Gentlemen, this is not a drill. So if you got 'em, get 'em."

As a matter of U.S. Army policy, sidearms were issued to officers. These were enlisted men. But the Sergeant Major had long ago made it clear that they'd better have one or two themselves . . . and know how to use them. For close fighting there was nothing better, he said. If you want to stay alive . . . that is what he said. And he always meant what he said. Nothing was ever just for practice with the Sergeant Major.

They rode fully mounted. The Sergeant Major had checked each mount himself. So had the Corporal. Two were replaced at the Sergeant Major's orders. Something had not been quite right. The Lieutenant rode out front followed by the Sergeant Major, then the first four. Between them were the ammunition mule and the four mules that carried ten days of provisions. Then the last four. One trooper for the ammunition mule, one for the four mules carrying provisions.

Ten days meant twenty to the Sergeant Major and the ammunition mule carried enough cartridges for a minor war. As the Corporal had said, "This was no drill." Normally the pack mules and the ammunition mule would be in the rear. Not this time. The Sergeant Major thought they were too important for "normally." Everyone was a guard. Everyone was assigned to watch the "damn" mules.

The Captain's orders to the Lieutenant were simple. "You are to reconnoiter and report. Do not engage. I repeat, do not engage. Do you understand, Lieutenant?"

Ironically they were similar to the orders given by General Terry to Lt. General George Armstrong Custer six years before, a few days prior to June 25, 1876. The Captain had said something else that was not part of the recorded orders. He'd looked the Lieutenant right in the eye, without blinking, without smiling.

"Bennett, I'm sending Oliver with you. If there is any doubt in your mind, let me remove it. Compared to him, you're a babe. He's more experienced than you. He's been in more scrapes than you. He's killed more men in battle than you. And each time he's walked away--alive. He simply knows more than you. You listen to him. If you and he have a difference of opinion, take his. Understand? You take his. That's an order, Lieutenant."

It was not far from Fort Smith to Deadman on Cherry Creek. Maybe a slow day's ride, but they started late and this was a big country. Big enough to get lost in. Getting lost was something the Sergeant Major didn't tolerate. "If you don't know where you are going--don't go there." They arrived at Dry Head Creek two miles south of the buffalo jump in the late evening and made dry camp. There were no fires. Guards were posted immediately, to be relieved every three hours.

Five and a half miles away the tall, heavyset, white man, Steeple, was still alive, though just barely. He stared at the young Crow woman sitting in the chair across from him. From time to time she poured water on his head, giving him none for his parched lips and his thick, swollen tongue. Shaking his head, he wondered why she was not dead. She should be. He'd shot her, shot her in the chest over a rabbit bone. He knew he had, yet there she was, tormenting him. *How much longer*, he thought? *There.* He saw her move. She was coming again. A hand struck him hard across the face. He could hardly feel it. The blow cleared his senses . . . somewhat.

Battles are won and lost in the morning. Troop 23, U.S. Third Calvary sat their mounts overlooking the substation at Deadman. It was morning, a little after eight by the Sergeant Major's time piece. The troopers sat in a line of ten, the ammunition mule in the middle just behind the line, the pack mules on either side. Lieutenant Barrett was in front with the Sergeant Major. The Sergeant Major sat in the saddle easily, as if he were at a Sunday picnic watching laughing youngsters jump in a pond full of ducks and geese. The Lieutenant, on the other hand, sat ramrod straight. It was the Sergeant Major they watched, every man jack of them. They saw him study the lodges up and down Cherry Creek. They watched him calmly pull a Colt SAA .45. Army issue, roll the cylinder across a sleeve, then push the revolver behind his service belt. Every man did the same without being told. The flap on his second service revolver was unsnapped, the revolver loosened. He had two. Three of the troopers, having only one pistol, started wishing they had two.

Barrett could see the smoke from the campfires rising slowly above more than one hundred lodges. There was another hundred he couldn't see. To his left and right were groups of Crow warriors, sitting their war ponies watching him, waiting. In front of the substation were thirty-five or maybe forty more, also watching, waiting. Across the bridge were even more.

"Sergeant Major? Have the men pull their carbines."

"Sir. If I might suggest, we leave them in the boot."

"Sergeant Major! I gave an order."

"Yes, sir. It is only a suggestion. From what I can see it looks like a twenty or thirty to one ratio in fighting men. If they wanted us dead, we'd already be. They haven't wanted that. We're alive. Let's ride down this hill confident in who we are and see what's going on, without a senseless show of force-- force, if I might say so, sir, we don't have. We'll all live longer."

The Lieutenant hesitated.

"Did you say forward, sir?" The Sergeant Major nudged his horse forward. Behind him they all moved as one. As did the Lieutenant. Down the long hill, following the wagon road in part, but in a straight line. Warriors filed in behind them as well as to their right and left. The Sergeant Major spoke. "Sir, might I suggest that upon reaching the front of the substation, we dismount the troops and form a half circle around the entry. You and I may then go inside with our backside covered. What do you say, sir? What are your orders?"

The Lieutenant nodded. His mouth was dry, his palms sweaty, his heart beating rapidly in his chest. He wondered if he'd ever see the pine forests of Maine again.

The Sergeant Major gave the order to the Corporal loud enough for all to hear. *So far so good*, he thought. This was much more serious then either he or the Captain had imagined. These Crow were decked out for war, riding war ponies, painted, carrying repeater rifles probably better and quicker than their carbines. There were easily two hundred of them.

The patrol reached the doorway. The Lieutenant dismounted, giving the reins to Private Jenson and moving toward the door.

The Sergeant Major nodded to the Corporal and dismounted as well. Everyone followed suit. "Corporal," he said, "side arm flaps loose. Have the men pull their carbines, put a round in the chamber."

Then he smiled, removing his leather gloves. "Corporal, watch that ammunition mule. If he looks like he's going to get away, shoot him and be quick about it. Questions?"

"None, sir."

"Ever eat mule meat?"

"No, sir."

"Did once. With the Captain and General George Crook at a place called White Mountain. Apache were trying to spook our ammunition mule. Had to shoot him to keep him from getting away. So we ate him. Not bad if you're hungry."

"Yes, sir," the Corporal said, a smile on his face. He liked this sergeant major. Nothing ever seemed to phase him. He was always in control, never upset, always mindful of the men watching him. If they were to live through this, it would be because of that man. The lieutenant, on the other hand, couldn't find the barracks with a map and a Chiricahua Apache to guide him.

"Gentlemen, flaps loose on your side arms," the Corporal said aloud. He knew they already were. "Pull your carbines. Put a round in the chamber. Be at ease. Keep your fingers off the triggers."

It was cool inside. The Sergeant Major found the Lieutenant standing in the middle of the room, facing armed men on three sides. *Gutsy bastard*, he thought and admired him for it. To their left sat the perspiring body of a large man bound to a kitchen chair. His belly was extended, a mass of blood and infection where a shotgun blast had torn into his right side mangling his intestines. He heard the Lieutenant swear. He could understand why. This was no picnic on the Potomac. There were no fair haired lasses carrying picnic boxes and peeling grapes for their handsome, fair-haired officers.

"Do any of you speak English?" The Lieutenant asked. There were no other Anglos in the room. To the right a man with a large nose spoke. A young woman sitting in a chair on their right rose, moving quickly past a low counter between two armed Indians, disappearing from sight.

The Sergeant Major counted sixteen armed men. They didn't look happy.

225

There was a conversation in the Crow language. The men who spoke were looking directly at the Lieutenant. So were their weapons.

"Sir, they are asking what you want," the Sergeant Major said. "They want to know what business you have here."

"What I want? That man is suffering. He's dying. I want him cut away from that chair. Given medical attention. I want the man that did this arrested and put in irons. That's what I want."

"Yes, sir. You also have sixteen men carrying carbines pointed at your chest and mine. They do not want what you want. They have some strong feelings about this, sir. At this point what you want is not likely to happen. Is there something else that you wish to discuss with these people . . . that you wish me to tell them? If I might say, sir, it is best to talk about something that may be negotiable. I doubt that this man being given comfort is something they will allow."

"Sergeant Major, we're talking right and wrong here."

"Yes sir, we are. May I suggest their right and wrong is different from your right and wrong? We must be careful in our demands. It is senseless to demand what we aren't going to get. If I were you, I'd find out what's going on. The why of this situation. Identify what we're are up against, and who the men are we're up against. West Point surely taught you to respect a superior force, sir. This is that time."

"Jesus, Sergeant Major."

"Yes, sir." The Sergeant Major watched the young lieutenant process what he'd told him, thinking this was the first turning point.

"All right, Sergeant Major, find out who's in charge, find out what we are dealing with."

"As you wish, sir," William Oliver turned to the room of combatants. He spoke first to the man with the big nose because he had spoken first, sending the young woman from the room. Several others spoke when he asked questions.

"Sir, they say no one is in charge. This is about Grey Elk though. His name comes up a lot. This one," he pointed at the man tied to chair, "killed a Crow Indian woman. Something about a rabbit bone. They wish him to suffer for what he did to an innocent woman. What makes it a little more dicey, sir, is that she was Grey Elk's second daughter. He was quite fond of her. Interesting enough, sir, she was married to or maybe just living with a white man. No one seemed to know. The white man shot this fellow here. That's the story, sir."

The Lieutenant was silent, staring at the suffering white man, then at the Sergeant Major. "What do you suggest, Sergeant Major?" The dying man groaned, breathing long, the air catching in his throat. "If I had my way, I'd order you to cut this man down, find the man that shot him, and put him in irons. I'd order these people to immediately disburse, and go back to the reservation."

The Sergeant Major wasn't looking at the Lieutenant. He was watching the room as the Lieutenant spoke. It changed perceptibly. Rifle barrels were no longer pointed at the floor. Someone had put his cigarette down. It lay smoking on the counter. Another had pulled back the hammer on an old Russian revolver. Ten seconds had elapsed. Someone understood some or a lot of English.

The Lieutenant was angry. "Sergeant Major . . . "

"Sergeant Major, sir--" Private Jenson hurried into the room. "Sergeant Major, sir, we have trouble. The Corporal asks that you come at once."

"Private, I am in the room. I am clearly the officer in charge here. Not the Sergeant Major."

"Yes, sir. Begging your pardon, sir. We have a situation, sir. The Sergeant Major should have a look at it, sir."

"All right, Private, all right." He glanced at Steeple roped to his chair and exited the room. The Lieutenant walked through the doorway followed by the Sergeant Major and the private. Outside he stepped past the nine troopers, their horses and the pack mules, and walked out into the brilliant morning sun.

From left to right, thirty feet from where he stood were well over two hundred armed men. Many carried rifles. Some were armed with revolvers, others bows and arrows, notched. In front and in the center of the group stood a stately man, a Crow Indian, simply dressed. He weighed 180 pounds. He stood perhaps five-eleven in height. There was no fear in him, no emotion at all. He carried no weapons of any variety. The man spoke to the Lieutenant, largely because he was out front. But the Lieutenant could only listen to the rhythmic language. When he finished speaking, the Lieutenant was forced to turn to the Sergeant Major.

"What did he say?" he asked. "Was it important?"

"Sir, whatever Grey Elk says or, for that matter thinks, is important. He said that he came to watch the white man die. He wants to know what you are doing here. And he reminds you that the room behind you is full of his people. 'On all sides,' he said."

Grey Elk spoke again only this time directly to the Sergeant Major. The Sergeant Major nodded as he understood his words. He replied. The two talked without interruption until the Lieutenant broke into the conversation asking, "What is he saying?" But the Sergeant Major waited until Grey Elk had stopped speaking to respond to the Lieutenant. After making a short reply the Sergeant Major turned to the Lieutenant.

"You have a decision to make, sir. Grey Elk has come to watch the big white man die. The man killed his daughter because he found a piece of a rabbit bone in his beans. He wants to know if you wish to join the coward in death." The Sergeant Major waited for the Lieutenant's reply.

"Is that all? Is that all he said?"

"No, sir, it is not."

"What else did he say?"

"Sir, he wants to know why the Fathers in Washington would allow a grey rabbit to stand beside a wolf. He asked if I was on the Greasy Grass in the month the elk and buffalo drop their calves, when the soldiers fell into the camp of Sitting Bull and Crazy Horse. I told him I was there with Reno under Captain Stringham. He paid me respect for what was done there. He noted the bravery that was exhibited. I thanked him for the compliment. His son scouted for George Custer. Apparently he was there with Stout Buffalo. He mentioned his name twice. Stout Buffalo happens to be married to his sister. He wants you to get out of his way, sir. I doubt if he is going to ask again."

"Why, Sergeant Major, is everything I want to do, that I need to do, wrong? Not to mention impossible?"

"Sometimes, Lieutenant, retreating is winning."

"Tell that to my instructors at West Point."

"May I point out, sir, they are not here. You are. I'd rather have you."

"Why is that, Sergeant Major? I find I know shit and I'm a breath away from getting everyone killed," he whispered.

"Sir, those who think they know, never learn. They die. Those who don't know and need to know, learn. Maybe they live. Captain Stringham has a philosophy that I have made my own. He reminds himself at times such

229

as these that we are passing through history and must try not to get lost on the pages. If I might add, sir, it is better to read about the Indian wars when you are an old man than be mentioned as a casualty on Cherry Creek at a stage coach substation."

"You are not writing the report, Sergeant Major."

"No, sir, you are. Live to write it."

"What do you recommend, Sergeant Major?"

"Sir, I recommend that we get out of their way. That we let them watch the bastard die. Justice is being served, sir. He shot and killed a young woman because of a rabbit bone in his beans. It really doesn't matter whether he's white, red, or green."

The Lieutenant sighed, nodding as he listened to the Sergeant Major. "All right. Give the order, Sergeant Major. Move the men from the front door. And watch that ammunition mule. I want to talk to the white man that shot him."

"As you wish, sir."

"Sergeant Major, Grey Elk's son? Did he live?"

"No, sir."

"A footnote?"

"Not even that, sir. In Benteen's report he was listed as a Crow scout." The Lieutenant turned his gaze to the men who surrounded his small detachment. He nodded to Grey Elk and stepped back.

The Sergeant Major gave the orders.

The Sergeant Major had suggested they move the detachment to the corrals. It was easier to defend and the ammunition mule could be kept securely in the barn away from prying eyes, loose lips, and thieves. The Lieutenant had readily agreed, mentioning again that he wanted to speak to Pistol.

"With your permission, sir. I will get him for you."
The Sergeant Major stood looking at him.

"You can do this?"

"As easily as anyone," the Sergeant Major replied.

There was something about the Sergeant Major that the Lieutenant couldn't help liking and other things that he absolutely abhorred. He tried to isolate the negative characteristics to no avail. The Lieutenant simply had far too much on his mind and his emotions were not under control. Not like he imagined they would be. In this frey he wanted to say nothing, decide nothing, do nothing, except take his troopers and leave. Right now. "Please bring him to me," he heard himself say.

"As you wish," the Sergeant Major replied.

The Lieutenant watched the Sergeant Major's back as he walked toward the corner of the substation, disappearing around the corner. He was gone the better part of an hour. The time didn't bother the Lieutenant for he was thinking of the man tied to the chair, unable to move, surely dying. He remembered the smell in the room: the smell of a gut shot man, his intestines shredded, leaking, rotting, slowly killing him. No water for his parched lips. The Lieutenant stared at the crowd of Crow warriors sitting upon their mounts on the north rim and shook his head.

The Lieutenant remembered West Point and the old man, grey beard neatly trimmed, his legs slightly bowed from riding an army mount. He limped from wounds acquired at Vicksburg, Gettysburg and a hundred other places. No one was ever sure of his rank but everyone saluted him any time they could. He had asked about him. Who was he? What was his name? "It was Mr. Carlyle, sir." The man never raised his voice. Even the commandant smartly saluted the old man. There was a certain reverence that the Lieutenant couldn't understand and no one explained.

In the hot sunlight of the Deadman substation he remembered the words he'd heard within the safety of four walls in a classroom in New York State, a classroom on the Potomac. So far away. "You young men," the speaker said, "will come to a point in your careers, in your lives, where everything you do will seem wrong, where you have to make decisions that no matter what you do will be wrong. Wrong to leave a man on the field of battle, right not to. You'll have to sacrifice all you believe in for all you believe in. May God be with you," he said. "May God be with you." He seemed so tall; he spoke so softly. "Just make the decision and move on. Get on with it. Get over it. Do not spend another minute rehashing."

The Sergeant Major returned the same way he'd left, shoulders straight, eyes straight ahead, seeing everything. "Said he'd be here in a few minutes, sir," he said. His voice was well modulated: not discouraged, not excited. It was just his normal speaking voice, as though telling a joke in the barracks a million miles from trouble.

"When?" the Lieutenant asked.

"In a few minutes," the Sergeant Major repeated. "With your permission, I'll see how the men are holding up, sir."

"Good."

A few minutes turned into twenty-five before he saw someone coming around the edge of the substation wall. It was a man wearing a high crowned hat, who was maybe five foot ten inches tall, and, he estimated, weighed one hundred eighty pounds. On either side of him were two young people. On his left was a boy, maybe fourteen or fifteen, gangly and lean. On the man's right was a girl who looked to be nine or ten. Neither appeared to be frightened. It certainly wasn't the show of force that the

232

lieutenant had expected. It was as if the man didn't care at all about the Lieutenant, his rank, his flag, or what he was doing there. There was a confidence in the way he approached that was hard to miss.

"Lieutenant," Pistol said, extending his hand in greeting.

The Lieutenant took his hand, shook it wondering why he didn't just arrest him, place in irons right then and there. He could bring him to the Captain, write a report, and forget it. "You are the man called Pistol?"

The man nodded. The girl held his hand, looking at the Lieutenant with innocent eyes. Her eyes were red from crying. He could see the streaks on her face, the red in her eyes. He guessed she'd lost her mother.

"What can I do for you?" Pistol asked.

"Who are these children?" the Lieutenant asked.

"They are mine." Pistol offered no further information.

"What's going on here?" he asked. The question seemed inane even to him.

"A funeral, if you were here yesterday. An execution for the fellow that killed my wife. He's dying slow. Hard to tell when that will be over. Soon, I expect."

"An execution? Who's in charge of that? Who passed sentence on this man for killing an Indian woman?"

"I did because he shot and killed my wife. This boy and girl did. He deprived them of a mother. She was twenty-four years old, Lieutenant-- twenty-four winters. Grey Elk did. The son of a bitch stole his daughter from him, his unborn grandchildren, and a thousand good times. Three hundred of his friends did because it is wrong to take the life of an innocent woman. The God of Israel did when he declared 'an eye for an eye, a tooth for a tooth . . . a life for a life.'"

233

There followed a silence such as the Lieutenant had never experienced.

Abruptly Pistol said something to the two that were with him. Without any hurry the three turned and walked away.

"What? What did he say?" He turned to the Sergeant Major. "What did he say?" For an instant he wanted to have Pistol shot and killed, right there and right now. Because he could. Because that man didn't care about his uniform, who he was, his importance.

The Lieutenant's thoughts were interrupted by the Sergeant Major's answer. "He was speaking to his son and daughter, sir. He told the boy and the girl that it was time to go. That there was nothing else that needed to be said."

The Lieutenant turned around and glanced at the retreating man, a girl wearing a doeskinned dress decorated with constellations, and a boy in leggings and a plain, doeskinned shirt. He wondered what he was supposed to do. What was the right thing to do? In the hot Deadman sunlight he decided to do nothing. If it was about a report, he had enough information for that. Pistol was right. There was nothing else that needed to be said. The Captain could start a war if he wanted. To hell with right and wrong.

"Sergeant Major?"

"Sir?"

"Mount the troops. Let's get the hell out of here before I start another Indian war."

"As you wish, Lieutenant."

CHAPTER TWENTY-FOUR

He stank. Gut wounds can be like that. Only the movement of his chest remained, a steady breathing, a rattling in the throat. Sometimes it would stop. Everyone would turn to see if he was dead but it would start again. Disappointed, the watching men would return to their chatter: conversations about a girl they knew or wanted to know, of a hunt on the north slope of the Pryor, of a raid against the Lakota that went well, of returning with many horses and much to brag about.

The girl, Autumn Flower, the sister of Cherry Blossom, had left her chair of torment the day before. Now the torment was for the living, the waiting upon the body that refused to die. It was the eighth day, the last day of his life; the day life slowly ebbed away and sank into the wet floor below the chair to which he had been tied.

Grey Elk came to his son-in-law in the substation. They sat together in the cool shadows, drank the spring water, smoked, and said little. Pistol watched the rise and fall of Steeple's chest, listened to the shallow breathing. *This was good*, Grey Elk thought. *A weak death. A death reserved for one who killed a young woman of twenty-four winters over a small piece of rabbit bone.*

In the afternoon Pistol gave Grey Elk what remained of the dying man. It was done with a wave of the hand, a word. There was no life left. Pistol was tired and wanted the dead man out of his home so he could clean the floor, make some more beans, bake some bread, and think of a butterfly whose wings would not bring her back from her journey. He wanted to gather his son and daughters about him and hide in the shadows. He wanted to care for the stage horses and forget the huge hole in his heart and the anger that kept him awake nights.

The ropes tied by Hank and Billy were cut. The body fell to the floor in a heap. There was a groan of pain, air whistling from tormented lungs. A rope was tied to Steeple's feet and he was dragged from the substation, dark red blood smearing the floor. Long Nose took the rope's end and, using Pistol's horse, dragged the big man's body through the camp, bouncing it over rocks and through sagebrush. This was done over and over again so that the people could beat him with sticks, throw rocks at him, count coup on his head with war clubs. There could be no honor in this death as there was no honor in his life.

After the fires burned down to embers, after the dancing, his dead, broken body was dragged to the edge of the canyon and dropped over the rim. It fell two hundred feet before it hit the sheer canyon wall, rolled, disappeared and dropped another hundred-fifty feet. Bouncing twice, it lodged in an old scrub juniper tree that was half dead, half alive, and three feet from the next seven hundred foot drop that would have taken it to the canyon floor and the river.

In the early morning only the raven and magpie knew of him. Of his twisted, limp, and lifeless body they did not tell. On the flat above the canyon walls the grass bent by his passing had risen and turned their flat blades toward the sun. Later they drank the cold rain from a thunderstorm and no trail remained to follow. Ted Steeple had disappeared.

CHAPTER TWENTY-FIVE

Deadman in August is hot and dry. It was the time of the locusts. The cottonwood ached with the sound of them. Thousands of locusts sound like a symphony of out of tune fiddles reaching a crescendo then backing off to a mere whisper. Again and again they sing out, each time louder still. They sing until August melts into September and the cottonwoods dream of sleep, of the time of yellow leaves, and brown buffalo grass.

Autumn Flower came to Deadman on the yellow horse her father had stolen for her. He'd taken it from the ranch situated where the Horn narrows and plunges into the big canyon. The little mountain horse had an IBAR burned into its left hip. It was a gelding whose hooves were pounded into iron by red rock; red rock of the east mesa of Low Mountain, where it drops off from the spires of Medicine Mountain. The rancher from whom the horse had been stolen lived in a far place called Abilene and sometimes in another place called New York. He never missed it. He didn't even know that it was stolen. That is the way of a rancher with too many horses, so many he cannot count them, and living so far away it did not matter.

She crested the north ridge overlooking Deadman at ten o'clock in the morning. As was her custom she waited for a minute, studying the substation before nudging the yellow horse forward with her heels and riding to the doorstep of the substation. She dismounted. Her hair was short like her sister's, like her mother's. She was a waif of a girl wearing a buckskin dress, plain and unadorned by bead work.

Across Cherry Creek and up on the south rim, the stage had crested and stopped, getting ready to wind its way down the roadway to the wood plank bridge and the substation. She watched it, heard Hank talking to the lead horses as he prepared to ride the brake into Deadman. Autumn Flower dropped the reins of the yellow horse at the doorway, looked again at the stage sitting up on the south ridge, then went inside through the heavy pine door. She'd done this many times with her father and Long Nose, Scolds the Bear, and her two nieces. Inside she found Pistol standing in front of the black stove, stirring beans in a black pot.

He looked up. "Kiddo, what are you doin' here?" His hands were busy with wild onions, rabbit meat, venison, prairie dog meat, a bit of left over blow snake, and chili peppers.

"The rolling wagon, the one for white people, is at the top of the South Hill," she said, addressing him in the language of her mother.

"I'll be damned," Pistol said. "Hank's early. I'll need to harness three sets of two. Here, Kiddo. Take this spoon and stir these beans. Keep them from burning. In five minutes take the bread from the oven."

"Five minutes? What is this?" she asked, looking at him as he wiped his hands and fingers on the rag her sister used to clean the bread knife before she died.

"Yes, five minutes. Five minutes is the time it takes you to walk that pony of yours to the top of the red ridge. After that amount of time take the bread out of the oven. This is understood?"

She nodded as he walked out the back door of the substation. She heard him swear at something, talking to himself angrily, then laugh as he walked, his voice fading away.

The ladle was buried in the bean pot, hidden except for the wooden handle hooked on the edge of the pot. Curiosity struck her. She pulled the little bucket up to the surface, then to her nose. She sniffed it, stuck her finger in the porridge, and tasted it. Flat. To the broth she added salt until she liked what she tasted. She added pepper because she liked pepper. She poured the chopped up venison, snake, and dog meat in and added the chopped wild onions and some ground up sage leaves. She stirred the pot and added more chili peppers.

Long ago her sister had shown her these things. "Good to eat" food was ruled by tongue taste and smell, tested until the stomach liked the thought of it. That's what her sister said. For a moment she stopped stirring and looked at the bread. It needed more time. That, too, was a matter of smell. A few minutes later, after the beans had joined the onions, the deer meat, and the snake meat, she took the bread from the oven. It smelled good. She placed it on the counter to cool. Its fragrance touched the air of the substation. *Soon,* she thought, *it will be needed.*

There were no passengers on that day in August. Just Hank Stumble and Billy Caldwell. Both nodded at her when they came inside. She smiled at them as she dished up beans in wooden bowls, handed them hot bread with the yellow grease white men called butter. Both men sat down and started eating, looking up when Pistol opened the door and walked inside.

"Hell of a porridge ya got here, Pistol," Hank said. "Beans ain't half bad. And I'd fight a gang of magpies for a crust of this pan bread."

239

Pistol took off his gloves and glanced at Hank. "Yeah, Hank," he said. "Got a new cook."

"She's easy to look at, that one."

Autumn Flower dipped her finger into the porridge, not realizing they were talking about her.

"Come on, Hank. You're a married man," Caldwell said, laughing. "How do you expect to get away with saying that?"

"I am that. But bein' married don't make me blind. What's her name, Pistol?"

"Ask her." Pistol replied.

All three turned to look at Autumn Flower. Hank, with warm buttered bread almost to his mouth, stopped to say, "Hey, sis, what's your name? What do folks call you?"

Autumn Flower said nothing. She didn't even look their way. When she didn't answer, Pistol spoke to her in the language of her mother. She nodded as he spoke, then looked at Hank, bean broth dripping from her fingers, a smile on her lips.

"Kiddo," she said.

Both Hank and Billy started laughing. "Kiddo, huh?" Hank said. "Wonder where the hell you got that name."

Hank and Billy had more beans and warm bread before they left the table to return to their work.

After they took their bantering outside of the substation, after the coach had turned and Hank started the pull up the north ridge, she asked Pistol what they said and why they had laughed.

Pistol smiled at her. "They like your beans, Kiddo. And your bread and they hope you'll stick around. Otherwise they might starve to death or die of some sort of stomach poison."

"This is a good thing for them to say?"

"Yes, it is," Pistol said to her. "They are good people. Which brings me back to you. Why are you here? Not that you are not welcome in my lodge as in your father's lodge, for always."

"I came to see Cherry Blossom, the place where she last lay. I came to collect her bones and hide them from the sly coyote and brother wolf."

Pistol nodded and smiled. "Brother wolf, huh? Well, Autumn Flower, you know where she is."

Autumn Flower smiled shyly. "Yes," she said. "I do. I am to tell you that Scolds the Bear will be here in a day or so with his sisters. They want you to go with them to the Bull Elk to be with Grey Elk, Walking Bull, and Crazy Head. I said I would tell you."

Pistol smiled and replied without hesitation. "I think I will go with them. Wouldn't miss it."

In the evening, when it was late and it didn't look like she'd be riding back to Dry Head Creek, Pistol helped her put her pony in the holding corral. They gave the gelding some Timothy hay and a bait of oats courtesy of the Hardin Stage and Transportation Company. The north flat was lonely at night, unsafe for a young woman to be traveling alone, even if she was the youngest daughter of Grey Elk. Pistol fixed her a bed of blankets and buffalo skin in the room used by her sister to cook beans and apple pie. She watched in silence.

Later, after Pistol retired, she went outside and watched the moon sink in the west, dropping into the saddle between the east and west Pryor. Behind her its last light fell into the mouth of the Big Canyon into which the Big Horn river had flowed for all time. She felt the deeper shadows of a now moonless night surround her, the mountain coolness creeping down Cherry Creek to the big river. She listened to the hoot owls and the coyotes hunting. She was tired. It had been a good day.

Inside, she walked through the dining room of the substation where she had long ago taunted the white man Steeple. Using her finger she tasted the cold beans, still liking them. It reminded her of Cherry Blossom, her smile, the way she looked at her. For a moment she recalled a time when she was ten and her sister was fourteen, the two of them rolling in the blankets and buffalo hides, laughing together in the lodge of their father. From the spring box she took some water and drank it, then made her way through the kitchen, passing the bedding that Pistol had so carefully prepared for her to sleep on.

She made her way to Pistol's bedroom, pushed the door partially open and listened to the deep sleep breathing that rumbled in his throat and nose—sounds her sister had listened to, in fear and in love. In the partial silence, she slipped inside, removed her dress, and climbed into bed, lying beside him.

Two things happened that night on Cherry Creek of some note. Pistol ended his forced celibacy and put to an end any argument of whether or not he slept with an Indian woman. In the passage of time, Autumn Flower bore him four sons: good men, tall and true, hunters of deer, elk and buffalo, like their grandfather. And, according to Grey Elk, they were men like their father and they were his grandsons and he loved them.

The End

About the Author

G. R. Howe was born and raised in Northern Wyoming. He graduated from Brigham Young University with a degree in Political Science. He received his law degree from John Marshall Law School in Chicago and became licensed to practice law in 1976. He pursued a career in law for thirty years in Ventura California. He returned to Wyoming to ranch and write western novels. He has written a collection of short stories of his hometown, Kane, a small town erased by flooding by the Yellowtail Dam Reclamation project in 1965, entitled *Short Stories Out of Kane. Crow Woman on Deadman* is the third of several western novels he has written.

Visit his website *Empty Saddles and Rusty Spurs* at www.emptysaddles.com